I0682028

Shadow Hunter

Shadow Hunter

Craig Godfrey

Copyright © 2015 Craig Godfrey

All rights reserved. No part of this publication may be
reproduced, stored in a retrieval system, or transmitted
by any means, electronic or mechanical, without written
permission from the author.

Published in Australia by
Craig Godfrey
17 Hunter Street
Hobart, Tasmania

ISBN 978-0-9805678-2-3

WRITER'S NOTE:
Shadow Hunter is a work of fiction. The rich history of
Tasmania is the background for murder and mahem.
Protagonist, Caspian Hunter, is an entirely fictional character
as are all of the pantheon of characters that inhabit this
novel. However, if any characters seem familiar, they may
well be as the Tasmania of the 21ˢᵗ century has as many
villians and rogues as the Tasmania of the 19ᵗʰ century. The
only difference being that today most have all their teeth.
Happy reading. Craig Godfrey.

Cover design by Sebastian Godfrey and Warren Boyles

For
Brierlie and Simon

Prologue

MY NAME IS CASPIAN HUNTER. I AM TWENTY-SEVEN. In the twenty-second year of the reign of Her Majesty, Queen Victoria, I sailed from my home in Birmingham to Van Diemen's Land to take up the position of second-in-command of the newly formed police detective agency in the fledgling colony. Little could I suspect how my life would change from the moment I sailed up the mighty River Derwent towards Hobart Town. An abandoned ship drifting at sea was but the beginning of a mystery that would lead me after villains the likes of which even Old London Town had not seen. I kept a diary of my first weeks. This is my story. The story of the beginning of an illustrious career as a crime fighter.

Hobart Town 1855

Day One – Friday

5am – Becalmed in Storm Bay – Southern Tasmania 1855.

I WILL FOREVER REMEMBER THAT EARLY FRIDAY morning in midsummer when I first set eyes on the three-masted *Ocean Maiden*. She loomed from the fog like a spectral vision; her sails set but sagging in the breathless sphere, as she drifted aimlessly upon millpond waters, while all about us a fine mist settled.

'It's a real pea-souper,' I heard a Londoner remark. And he was dead right. There was not the slightest breeze and only the monotonous clangour of the fog bell interrupted our tranquillity.

'There's no one at her helm!' a voice echoed across the calm.

'Ahoy there!'

Nothing.

'Where is everybody?' I heard the bosun ask our captain, Captain Durward Slade, who had delivered us from London to the mouth of Hobart Town's River Derwent without mishap thus far. The bosun's voice carried across the stillness like a town crier's.

'Don't know Seabert,' the captain on the quarterdeck said, stroking his spade-shaped beard while halos of yellow light swirled about the lanterns behind him. 'Strange affair if'n I ever seen one.'

By now all the crew and passengers on the *Georgette* were lined along the starboard bow, their eyes as curious as mine, while our ship drew alongside the mystery ship, our starboard to her port side.

'Mr Ransford,' the captain called to his third mate.

'Sir.'

'Take a crew in the jolly boat and board her if you please. Secure her to the *Ranger* with grapples. Seabert, furl our remaining sails.'

'Aye cap'n.'

'If'n we weren't so close to 'obart Town I'd be seeing this as a curse, Mr Hunter,' the ship's cook muttered to me as he leant on the gunwale. He was a usually happy fellow who made extraordinarily good bread at sea. I returned a smile but he seemed preoccupied with the unfolding conundrum.

Minutes later the third mate was promptly back on the main deck of the *Ocean Maiden* 'Nothing cap'n,' he called back, 'there doesn't appear to be a soul aboard her sir. No one at all.'

All about him the jolly boat crew were securing the vessel to our passenger ship.

'Mr Hunter,' Captain Slade hailed me from the quarter-deck.

'Yes Mr Slade ... ah ... Captain.'

'A word if you please.'

Captain Slade met me at the bottom of the gangway from the quarterdeck.

'Well Mr Hunter, your voyage from Birmingham is almost at an end and already we have a mystery for you.'

'It appears so captain,' I said.

'Aye.' He cast another glance over at the deserted ship. The carved wooden figurehead was of a bare-breasted maiden. Captain Slade shook his head.

'You know sea lore dictates a maiden's breasts are supposed to shame stormy seas into a calm. God only knows what happened here.'

'Are you a superstitious man Captain Slade?' I asked, knowing most seafaring men were.

'No,' he formed a perfect circle with his lips. 'No Mr Hunter.'

But I sensed he was not exactly speaking honestly.

'Don't sail on Thursdays, Fridays, the first Monday in April or the second Monday in August. Always set sail on Sundays. Goodness me Mr Hunter ... you know I've heard men say you mustn't whistle into the wind or you'll whistle up a storm. Flowers, bells and clergy are all bad omens to have on board, as they all represent funerals. No women on board. Never change the name of a ship. Cutting of hair, beards and fingernails are all bad omens sir. Superstitious? Me? I think not.'

We looked on in silence a short moment.

'Hmm,' the captain began again. 'So, as you are to be an investi-gator of criminal activity in this 'ere fledgling colony, you may like to commence duty this very morning and board this *Ocean Maiden* and form your opinion and suspicions.'

'With pleasure.' And it was with a measure of trepidation that I transferred to the stricken vessel via the bosun's chair; a form of transport I would rather avoid.

'Meanwhile Mr Garyson,' the captain ordered his second-in-command. 'Prepare a skeleton crew to sail 'er up to Sullivan's Cove the moment our pilot joins us from Bruny Island.'

Whether it was the fog and the early morning chill or another malevolent force I will never know, but below decks on the ghost ship, for that's what the crew had already named her, all was eerily maleficent. The third mate, Mr Norvin Ransford, struck flint to tinder and lit two gimballed lamps on the stern cabin's walls. The pursuing yellow light was welcome but did little to settle my nerves, especially when he left me alone in the captain's cabin to search the rest of the ship. I took a notebook and pencil from my coat pocket and, as I had been taught back in Birmingham, I started making meticulous notes.

Captain's cabin. Table set for seven. Meal served on table with cutlery neatly placed next to the plates. Food untouched. Wheel of Gouda cheese on the table. Wax freshly cut. Wine in glasses. All untouched.

I smelt the meal. It was clearly mutton and although fat had solidified about the meat and on the gravy it was without doubt only served the evening before.

Whatever happened to these people happened early evening at mealtime.

To one side of the stern cabin a small sewing table was cluttered with knitting and sewing equipment. A child's dress was in the process of manufacture. There were child's toys on the cabin floor.

Carved animals from what I suspect is part of a Noah's Ark set. Wax headed doll on the lower bunk. I sized up the child's dress. Must be young girl 7-8 maybe. Captain's daughter?

I held the doll to my nose but smelt nothing untoward, such as evidence of a sickness. As I returned the doll to where I found it I noticed an iron cashbox half-exposed on the cabin floor beneath the bunk. I pulled it free. The key was in the lock. I wrote:

Found the captain's bullion chest. Empty except for some copper coins. Five pennies, two halfpennies and three farthings.

Mr Ransford's voice from the dark passageway startled me. 'Mr Hunter.'

I jumped.

'Sorry sar, I didn't mean to frighten yer.'

'Please,' I said. 'We have been travelling together some time, call me Caspian, Norvin.'

'Aye. Caspian.' He looked pleased with himself. 'The captain said I'm to report everything to you.'

'Yes. Any sign of anybody?'

'No si ... Caspian. Not a ruddy thing. Damned crazy it is. I've been at sea twenty-eight years and I never seen nuthin' like this. Damned sinister I gotta tell ya.'

'All cabins empty?'

'Aye. And the forecastle is like the men left 'er. Sea chests untouched. Oilskins in place and their pipes in a rack ... never a seaman would leave a ship without 'is pipe and baccy, that's for certain.'

'But the ship's jolly boat is missing.'

'Aye.'

I cast an eye back across the table talking to myself more than Norvin. 'There's wine on the table, unspilt.'

I noticed a questioning expression come over the third mate's face.

'If there had been a freak wave the wine and meals would have been disturbed ... everything would be in disarray, is that not correct?' I said.

'Aye, and we 'aven't had a storm for more'n a week.'

'Correct. How about the water barrels?'

'Full si ... Caspian ... and the store's pretty full as well. Plenty salted pork and pickled mutton, cheese, flour. Plenty everything.'

'Cargo?'

'Well Edmund Smith found the manifest and log in the first mate's cabin, I 'ad a quick gander and it appears the cargo is barrels of Indian rum mostly, with some brandy, salted meat, household ironmongery, tea, tobacco, preserved fruit and barrels of grain alcohol whatever that be.'

'Has it been checked?'

'I 'aven't tallied it yet, but it looks all there. Although ...' and his voice trailed off.

'Although what Norvin?'

'Well there seems to be a few barrels broke like. It was 'ard to tell in the dark. But it looked to me like they wasn't tethered proper and fell orf the pile.'

'Spillage?'

'Poured down into the bilge I guess.'

Valuable cargo untouched. I wrote, mumbling to myself.

'So that rules out piracy. Any barrels tapped?'

'If ya be thinkin' the crew got drunk I'd say it's all intact. Why? Are you thinkin' the crew killed the cap'n and his family, chucked 'em in the sea like?'

'Now I didn't say that Norvin. Can't have you starting rumours already.'

'Aye. The crew don't need my 'elp Caspian. They'll come to their own conclusions soon enough. Ignorant superstitious bastards ... even if I do say so meself.'

I heard the patter of a seaman's bare feet down the companionway.

'Mr Hunter, sir.' It was the *Georgette's* carpenter.

'Yes.'

'I inspected the hull as you asked, she's fully seaworthy. No damage ... not a hole in 'er anywhere. Sound as a sixpenny whore she is.'

'Thank you ... ah ...'

'Bancroft sir,' he answered and his eyes lit up like lanterns. 'Master carpenter Bancroft.'

Day Two – Saturday

I MET HENRY FOX YOUNG, THE GOVERNOR OF VAN Diemen's Land – about to be renamed Tasmania – at the building site of the new Government House on the Queen's Domain in Hobart Town. Its chosen position, facing north-east, was perfect, overlooking the blue expanse of the great River Derwent – the best part of a mile wide at this point if I was to hazard a guess at its width.

'Beautiful isn't it?' The voice at my side was deep, authoritative.

'Your Excellency,' I said with a start. 'I didn't hear your approach.'

The fifty-three-year-old governor looked every bit his age and more. I suppose the full-length beard and balding pate didn't inspire a vision of youth. He was taller than me by several inches and handsomely attired in a charcoal grey, full-length, double-breasted frock coat. He tucked his top hat under his arm and offered me his hand.

'Mr Caspian Hunter, we meet at last.'

I took his hand and we exchanged a firm greeting.

'Can you believe,' he said standing erect and pushing his chest out across the river, 'that the first settlement here in Van Diemen's Land or I *should* say, Tasmania, now we are to be self-governed and the transportation of felons has been ceased, was in a swamp over there.' And he indicated an inlet further up river and on the opposite side.

'So I heard sir.'

'Yes,' he scrutinised me momentarily before looking back up the river, 'founded by a certain dullard named John Bowen, a lieutenant in the Royal Navy. Thank heavens for my predecessor Governor Collins for settling yonder eh.' And he nodded sagely to the port town over the Domain behind us. I could only agree.

I liked the man instantly as he appeared to have a candid nature and I guessed that after governing South Australia for six years before moving to this island colony his stuffy English protocol had relaxed somewhat.

Then I froze.

Two giant dogs bounded towards us barking. Huge Irish wolfhounds, but they were barking with joy at seeing their beloved master I would soon realise – and much to my relief.

'Ah! Mark … Antony,' the governor welcomed these great slobbery beasts with childish glee. 'You've come looking for me. Isn't that nice?' His Excellency noted my withdrawal. 'Not afraid of dogs are you Caspian?'

'Ah, no. No sir,' I lied, stepping further away from the four-legged monsters displaying their bone-crushing teeth.

'I'm pleased to hear that. They won't harm you. Gentle giants they are.' And he proceeded to pull the largest one towards me by a studded leather collar.

'This is Mark,' he said. And the dog jumped up and licked the man's face. Yes. He actually licked the governor's face.

'And that one is Antony.' As he introduced us the other dog squatted and evacuated its bowels, an act His Excellency chose to ignore.

'So,' the governor said turning back to view the construction site. 'The man at least had a creek named after him.' I clearly looked nonplussed for he added, 'Bowen, that is. Lieutenant John Bowen had a creek named after him.'

We exchanged smiles and His Excellency's attention was drawn back to the building site. I followed the governor's roving eye and together we watched stonemasons laying foundations. 'So Caspian, what do you think?'

'Excellent sir,' I said in all honesty. 'I've heard talk in town already that this building will be as grand as any in England.'

'And that it will … that it will indeed. And the community desperately needs it too; you should see the ramshackle condition of the governor's residence that Macquarie built in '17. Come.'

And the man strutted across the clayey turf in his polished black shoes to the rear of a builder's cart where an architectural plan of the building lay unfolded, its corners weighted with small stones against the stiffening breeze blowing up from the nearby cove. The drawings were grand indeed.

'Seventy-three rooms Caspian, seventy-three!' he marvelled with the sparkling eye of an excited schoolboy. 'Besides the main hall there will be a dining room, ante-drawing room, French room, ball room and even a conservatory. The living quarters upstairs will be done in

Jacobean and Elizabethan styles. Lots of panelled wood. What do you think Caspian?'

'I think it's wonderful sir. Wonderful indeed.' But I couldn't help wondering who was paying for all this since England was tightening her purse strings within the colonies. And especially since the *Cessation of Transportation Act* was finalised two years earlier. This meant the days of cheap convict labour was nearing an end. The governor seemed to read my mind.

'Caspian.'

'Sir.'

'Walk with me.' And he led off at a leisurely pace, hands held at his back, towards a nearby quarry. Mark and Antony dutifully followed.

'Is your accommodation satisfactory?' the governor asked.

'Yes sir, most comfortable.'

The government had provided me with board and food at the privately-owned Red Rose Cottage, until I found something more permanent. Red Rose was a respectable private hotel in Liverpool Street operated by a rather fastidious landlady – a spinster – Rosemary Atwater, who mothered me the moment I stepped over her threshold.

At the quarry, stonemasons worked a chain gang of less fortunate convicted felons wearing restraining irons around their ankles. We watched a moment and the governor explained how the men called extracting the stone from the quarry, 'winning'. The rock surface would be probed until a crack was found where the stone was then split with crowbars and prised loose.

'Arduous gruelling work,' the governor told me. 'If a rock can't be loosened then the men must hammer several holes in a line along the rock, fill the holes with water to wash out the dust and then pointed bars are placed into the holes and hammered until the stone is freed.'

'Crime certainly doesn't pay sir,' was all I could think to say. Governor Fox Young grunted in agreement.

'Over there are the 'bankers,' His Excellency nodded to a dozen stonemasons dressing the sandstone into neat blocks. The 'bankers' being the wooden benches the men stood at with chisels, mallets and mason squares. Other teams of men in pairs, with sturdy stretchers, carted the finished stone block by block to the building site.

Governor Fox stood a moment at the edge of the ever-deepening quarry, his fingers laced behind his back, as he watched the labourers with some empathy.

'You've not met Fabian Winter as yet?'

'No sir I haven't. I only arrived last evening.'

'Of course, and besides the man's on the north of the island.'

Fabian Winter was my new superior. Between us we were to head a team of four constables – some ex-prisoners I would discover – in a new government department. We were to act as detective policemen investigating the more serious crimes occurring in Hobart Town. With the cessation of transportation came uncertainty within the economy. Poverty was widespread and poverty nurtured crime. The governor reminded me our primary object was to prevent serious crime, but how I was to do so, I wasn't quite certain.

'You are to detect and effect punishment of offenders if a crime is committed,' the governor said. 'The protection of life and property and the reduction of crime will alone prove whether or not those efforts by your team have been successful.'

I had the distinct feeling he had rehearsed that line. 'I have every intention of doing my utmost Your Excellency.'

'Wonderful, Caspian, wonderful. Now Mr Winter is due to return from Launceston late tomorrow afternoon I believe. So you can have tonight and Sunday to settle down, see the sights of Hobart Town, familiarise yourself with one of Her Majesty's most remote colonies.'

'Thank you sir.'

'And I'll have my secretary Samuel Wheaton meet you at your Campbell Street office Monday. Mr Winter should be there late morning I would imagine. He is a creature of the night I fear. Then we can get this detective service into action, what?'

We walked around the quarry and into cleared bushland where various English trees grew side by side with Australian gum trees and where vegetable gardens were laid out neatly. An overseer watched over half a dozen prisoners who dug, hoed and raked.

'This is smartly becoming a magnificent Botanical Garden. You mark my words young man. This garden was started over thirty years ago so I'm told and I'm thinking it's already the best in the colonies.'

We strolled by rows and rows of herbs of all varieties, a lettuce garden the size of a village square, and a paddock of healthy beans.

'I do love my beans, Caspian, boiled with butter.' The governor's eyes shone with the thought.

Half a dozen well fed ducks staggered between us quacking noisily and heading to a large pond, close to where a substantial cereal crop was growing. I was thinking to myself how ideal this life must be for them when His Excellency broke my train of thought.

'Ah Martin,' he greeted a rather tired looking gardener in his late forties. The man was tall, striking to look at, sturdily built with a thick crop of hair and, although he had thick mutton-chop whiskers, he had a sad face with startled eyes. I should explain here they were startled, not startling.

'Your Excellency,' the man doffed his straw hat, clearly surprised that the great man himself had called his Christian name.

'Caspian, meet Mr Martin Cash, he is the overseer for the prisoners here in the garden.'

'Sir,' Martin nodded respectfully to me.

'Mr Cash,' I returned the salute.

'Martin here was given his ticket of leave this year,' the governor said to me. 'The garden is looking wonderful Martin,' the governor commended.

'Why thankee sir, I 'ad a bit of bother with downy mildew and some fungi but seem to 'ave got on top of it with me copper sulphate and slaked lime brew sir.'

'Yes, and I notice the leeks are up early. Wonderful.'

We walked on passing a paddock of potatoes and the governor smacked his lips.

'Potato and leek soup ... hmm ... or cock-a-leekie as my Scottish cook, Mrs McMee, calls it. And she puts prunes in hers. Ever had it with prunes Caspian?'

'No sir, I cannot say I have.'

'He was a right villain, that Mr Cash,' His Excellency confided in me when we were out of earshot. 'He was a bushranger you know.'

'Ah, now I seem to recall the name.'

'Yes. They called him the gentleman bushranger. The women loved him apparently. But he's lost the spark out of his fire nowadays.'

Governor Fox Young pinched his lips and sniffed several breaths of air through his nose, which clearly gave him pleasure. 'Eucalyptus, delightful isn't it?'

'It's certainly a pleasure after four months at sea sir, that is for certain.'
'Well now,' Governor Fox Young turned to face me. 'Speaking of
the sea what do you make of this *Ocean Maiden* puzzle?'

I was at first lost for words. After all the investigation was fresh
and I had hardly time to form an opinion. 'I don't know sir, I really
don't have a clue to go on.'

The governor raised an eyebrow. 'You were one of the first to
board her, were you not?'

'Well, not really. Mr Ransford, the third mate on the *Georgette*
was the first to board her, with a few other crewmen. Then I followed
shortly forthwith.'

'So what do you think happened. Pirates? Sealers in Bass Strait
maybe?'

'Impossible ... sir.'

'Impossible? How is that?'

'The valuable cargo was intact and the crew's valuables were
where they left them. And besides, the ship could not sail itself down
the coast of this island.'

'People just don't disappear at sea without trace, Caspian.'

'I beg to differ sir, but this is not an isolated case.'

'Pray tell.'

'Some years ago, 1840 if my memory serves me correctly, a French
merchant ship of over 200 tons, called the *Rosalie*, was found deserted
under similar conditions in the Atlantic. I remember the report said
she had a valuable cargo intact ...'

'Valuable? What may I ask?'

'The report didn't say sir. She was en route from Hamburg to
Havana and she was discovered with sails fully set and holding her
course despite the fact there was no one at the helm.'

His Excellency's curiosity was aroused.

'Like the *Ocean Maiden*, the *Rosalie* was seaworthy. There were
no leaks. A half-starved canary swung in a cage in the stern cabin and
hungry chickens wandered the decks. Like the *Ocean Maiden* the
water barrels were full and there was plenty of food on board and
here's the strange thing ...'

'What may I ask?'

'The cargo, money and valuables were all intact.'

At this point I wanted to tell His Excellency about the empty cashbox on the *Ocean Maiden* but restrained myself, as I needed to discuss this with my new superior first. Besides a handful of cash was never going to be motive for an entire crew murdered, if indeed that's what happened to them.

'What is the cargo on the *Ocean Maiden* anyway?'

'We have the manifest and the log sir. The cargo is rum mostly, and nine barrels of grain alcohol and household merchandise amongst other things,' I said.

'Grain alcohol eh? Well Hobart Town can certainly do with its cargo.' He thought a moment. 'She was a merchantman from Southampton, my secretary informed me this morning, with a Norwegian captain, Brynjar ... Brynjar something ...'

'Brynjar Evjen Your Excellency.'

'Yes, that was it. So what was the outcome?' he finally asked, 'for the people aboard the *Rosalie* that is.'

'There was no trace ever found of the crew or passengers.'

'Captivating story Caspian, engrossing to say the least. It's like something Daniel Defoe would write in a novel or that recent story about the white whale ...'

'Moby Dick.'

'Yes that's him.'

'There have been at least two others I've heard of Your Excellency.'

'Oh.'

'Yes. The *Hermania*, a Dutch schooner and I read in *The Gentleman's Magazine* of a more recent incident off the coast of Canada. Both ships found deserted. No trace of passengers or crew has ever been found. Both vessels similarly situated as with food, water and the like. Total mystery sir ...'

A two-wheeled trap and horse came at a trot onto the building site attracting anxious activity from the site overseer.

'Ah,' the governor said. 'Mr William Kay the architect for my new home has arrived. You'll have to excuse me.'

The governor offered me his hand once again. 'Thank you for your time Mr Hunter,' he said as we walked briskly back towards the building site. 'I wanted to speak with you personally about this matter. However, now I'd appreciate it if you would keep me informed with regular reports, through my secretary Mr Wheaton ... Argh!

Caspian!' the governor almost shouted. I jumped.

'Too late.' He nodded to the grass at my feet. 'You appear to have stepped in shit, Caspian … welcome to Tasmania.'

I followed the riverside back south to the cove a mile distant, taking care to avoid the stench of what I was told was Wapping. Tanneries, accompanied by a miasma of rotting blood and bone, stood next to the town slaughterhouse where I had no choice but to negotiate alleyways and a filthy rivulet to make it to the cove. There I sat swinging my legs over the edge of the wharf watching the busy harbour go about its business, and wondered how on earth I was expected to solve such an impossible mystery as that of the *Ocean Maiden*.

I espied the 'ghost ship' docked by a stone wharf at the eastern end of the horseshoe bay called Sullivan's Cove. I was told later this was originally a small island, called Hunter Island, which was only approachable via an isthmus at low tide. Now a causeway had been built leading to a deep-water landing place called Old Wharf. New Wharf took pride of place at the western perimeter where, from my vantage point, I watched dockworkers struggling to raise barrels of whale oil from the hold of a whaler – the tide being at its lowest ebb.

Captain Slade's third mate of the *Georgette*, Norvin Ransford, had docked *Ocean Maiden* at Old Wharf and reported his find to the harbourmaster. My guess was that the ship would become Slade's property if the owners weren't found, as the law of the sea usually favours the finder of an abandoned vessel.

I looked across at the ghost ship and was pleased to note the red coat of a soldier stationed to keep looters away. And peering about me discreetly, I noticed most residents of this distant outpost appeared as bad, if not worse, than London's Thames-side rascals. Hobart Town, you must understand, was founded by scoundrels and villains. England's thieving, forging, fibbing, embezzling, pilfering and corrupted rogues, too numerous to incarcerate back home, were transported across the oceans to build a new country called Australia to ensure that the French or the Dutch or the Portuguese could not steal the land from the natives before the English. My peaceful thoughts were interrupted by a dark shadow between the warmth of the afternoon sun and myself.

'Ya got smoke matey?'

I looked up into the shadow of the silhouetted figure of a Van Diemen native. The man was tall, more than six foot, muscular, clear of all excess fat except for a pot belly. He had tightly cropped curly black hair and he was the colour of a chimney sweep's apprentice. He was dressed like Lord Nelson in rags; a cast-off military dress jacket complete with shiny brass buttons, tattered britches and bare feet. He raised his shabby bicorn hat, with gold ribbons and feather plume, in greeting, exhibiting a broad friendly smile showing off yellow but healthy teeth.

'Baccy matey?' he asked again and showed me an empty clay pipe.

'Oh,' I said. 'Do I have any tobacco?' I reiterated. He nodded his head vigorously in anticipation. 'No, I don't use tobacco.'

'Ah, bugger,' he grunted disappointed, 'Nebena use tobacco.'

It was then, as my eyes adjusted to the light, that I noticed he wore a crescent-shaped brass gorget about his neck that was inscribed 'Chief Nebena'. He caught me admiring the plaque.

'Him good,' he said stabbing the gorget with his finger. 'Him my father father.'

I assumed he was saying it was his grandfather's originally. I took sixpence from my purse and handed it to him and he looked mighty pleased. He bowed deeply, replaced his hat and took his leave. As I watched him walk towards a dock I heard the cracking of canvas across the harbour. A new arrival sailed into the cove, the men busy aloft furling the sails to the orders of the shrill bosun's pipe.

Nebena noticed also. He immediately climbed into a small fishing boat and proceeded to be rowed out to the ship by two native women who, I found out later, were his wives. I was also told he paid homage to all new arrivals, although he had missed the arrival of the *Georgette*. He climbed aboard to welcome the newcomers to *his* land then, I was told, he asked for brandy or rum to drink the captain's health before going to the galley to 'borrow' supplies from the pantry. So confident, so affable and harmless a character was he, that he was tolerated, humoured and indeed given gifts.

'Five shillin' squire!' Once again my reverie was impeded by a high voice.

'Pardon?' I twisted about to stare up into the face of a young girl, maybe fourteen.

'Ya want company? Five shillin' at me lodgin' or two bob in the alley.'

'How old are you?' I asked, flabbergasted at her cheek.

''ow old do ya want me to be?'

'You're a bit young to be whoring,' I scolded, and fished about in my purse. 'Here.' And I flipped her a sixpence that she caught mid-flight. 'Go and have a bath,' I said.

'What ya sayin'? Ya sayin' ya want me if'n I 'ave a baff?'

'No I am not. Now be off with you.'

'Firkin' fatty!' she yelled. 'Nancy boy!' And she hightailed away before I could give chase.

'Welcome to Hobart Town,' I told myself.

Fatty! I chewed over the thought. I've been wrestling with my weight all my days, but *fatty* – insolent little tyke. The walk from the Queen's Domain had given me a thirst but not wishing to imbibe at the water-front inns – which I noted were as rowdy and of as ill-repute as any I had seen back in England – I turned away from the bustling docks and headed north into Elizabeth Street, which, I was to learn, was the town's high street.

To my left a military guard, shading from the summer sun in a sentry box, watched me with a distrustful eye, like I had designs outside the law. It was then I realised I was passing by Government House, the same residence of disrepair Governor Fox Young had told me about.

I stopped a moment, attracting the red-coated guard's attention. He stood slovenly to attention with his Brown Bess musket and fixed bayonet to convey some authority. Ignoring him I gazed upon the building. It was only thirty-eight years old, but already showed signs of decrepitude. Built to two storeys and surrounded by tall trees, native and English, I imagined it quite grand in 1817 when it was first completed. But poor materials and a lack of expert craftsmanship had taken its toll.

I passed several inns and taverns in Elizabeth Street enjoying the sights and sounds – but not the smells – of the young township before eventually stepping into the Leg Bail Inn on the corner of Liverpool Street. This inn didn't appear as smoky as the others; I find tobacco smoke impedes my sinuses.

The Leg Bail Inn was no more than a stone-walled cottage inside; but comfortable with its worn flagstones and whitewashed stone walls – although stained yellow from tobacco smoke. The low ceiling beams were black and the boards tarred, reminiscent of life aboard the *Georgette*. It was only mid afternoon but the warm weather encouraged a brisk trade and I was appreciative of a better class of clientele than those I saw at the wharf establishments.

The innkeeper was Eve Bellows, a homely soul in her fifties who had lost her husband to Davey Jones she told me. She was a monstrously breasted woman of abundant girth with one tooth missing in the lower jaw and a tuft of hair growing from a mole on her chin that was awkwardly captivating.

I managed a seat next to another imbiber at a high-backed bench next to the huge fireplace that thankfully wasn't lit, when a comely red-headed wench noticed me staring at the cold fireplace.

'If'n ya wantin' vittles the kitchen fire out back's smoulderin',' she said and slopped a quart of hard cider on the table before me. It appeared she had more significant talents than wenching in taverns. Her name, she told me, was Kitty Wiggles.

'If'n there's anythin' else ya desire good sir, anythin' at all, give Kitty a whistle.' And she wet her lips. The two of us squeezed on the bench seat sat in silence a moment and watched Kitty's stern sail back to the bar.

'I wouldn't mind givin' 'er a whistle,' the drinker on my right gave a lascivious grin over his tankard. 'She be a right vixen thart one lad.'

He had intense small blue eyes with pronounced eyebrows leaning in, tapering to the top of his nose and he wore his greasy hair Napoleon Bonaparte style, flat and trimmed over the forehead and curled at the back. His effeminate red lips were wet with cider and with a constant smirk, lusting after Kitty. 'Aye lad, I'd like to show 'er a good time an' all.' And he rasped a laugh through missing teeth before licking spilt cider off his filthy mitten.

The afternoon passed pleasantly enough. Drinkers came and went but I found the atmosphere in the Leg Bail Inn most congenial. By six hours past midday I was feeling as cheerful as the fiddler passing his hat about the taproom to play ditties. I had the remnants of a kangaroo stew on the table before me, I had consumed far more cider than I intended and I had the likes of Kitty Wiggle sitting on my lap. 'Life doesn't get much better than this,' I remember thinking as she took my hand, led me upstairs and relieved me of a half sovereign and the cobwebs of a celibate four months at sea.

Sometime after nine o'clock, I believe, I felt my way up the front path of Red Rose Cottage. And the gatekeeper waited!

The elderly spinster and proprietor of my guest house, Miss Rose Atwater, was less than convivial as I stood unsteadily on her doorstep breathing the fumes of an afternoon and evening well spent – at least that is what I thought at the time.

'Mr Hunter,' she started, her bouffant hair draped in a scarf in preparation for her night's sleep. 'I will have you know this is a home of temperance. I will not, sir, tolerate the temptations of the evils of this town to permeate under my roof. Do you understand Mr Hunter?'

I managed a nod. I really wanted to reach out and pat her hair. How did it stand so? My room was the first down the hall on the right and my hooded eyes tried to focus beyond the angry woman to my door.

'Your evening meal is now cold and in the meat safe and all the lamps extinguished.'

'I've already eaten … mishus Heatwater,' I slurred.

She was too vexed to answer. Huffing angrily she allowed me past the portcullis, locked the front door and retired for the night, taking the key with her.

Day Three – Sunday

I AWOKE TO THE SOUND OF CHURCH BELLS. IT SEEMED they were all around me. My first observations of Hobart Town were that it was well catered for on both sides of the fence. Plenty for the redeemer and in abundance for the sinner. Churches, taverns, churches, inns, churches, hotels, churches, taprooms, churches, and whores ... I lay in bed a moment wondering if whores went to church. The bells grew in crescendo. It was too much.

It was nine o'clock Sunday morning for Christ's sake!

I splashed water on my face and the other extremities from the bedside basin set, and dressed. Whilst delightful aromas of a delicious home cooked breakfast greeted me when I opened my door, I had no desire to come face to face with Miss Atwater, not this morning, not after my shameful entrance last night. And I crept silently out the door unobserved.

'Ah! To be free,' I sighed, and skipped over the cobbles, wet from a refreshing dawn shower. But the sky was clearing and it was showing all the signs of a beautiful day. Hobart Town, I had been assured back in Birmingham, was the second city of the Australian colonies – second after Sydney. However the discovery of gold in the state of Victoria had caused an economic decline in the penal colony with many families leaving for the opportunity of riches in Melbourne and the goldfields. In consequence the Imperial Government in London increasingly withdrew financial support for the penal institutions here in Van Diemen's Land. Wages had dropped I was informed. Prices of produce had slumped. And now the settlement was burdened with massive expenses from projects like the construction of the new Town Hall and Government House; a burden barely sustainable by the moderately sized population of twenty thousand people.

Whilst I mulled these facts over in my mind, brought on by the sight of the good citizens of the township walking to church in their Sunday best, I turned left into Murray Street to be confronted by a pleasant salty breeze off the harbour. The more gentle womenfolk, I observed, protected their milky-white skin under the shade of parasols, whilst their gentlemen and escorts strode the pavement in tailed frock coats, top hats and whalebone walking sticks. We all had to sidestep the horse shit on the roads, of which there was plenty.

My exploration took me over Melville Street and downhill towards Liverpool Street where I noted a gathering of moderately respectable people patronising a coffee-house adjoining a cider mill and brewery called Dickens Cider.

'Just on ya lonesome are ya good sir?'

I nodded to the headwaiter who introduced himself by his Christian name Clyde. He was a jolly soul, in his fifties and waiting on diners all his life I would hazard a guess. His round face was capped with a high forehead free of hair but with a generous growth bursting left and right from his skull covering his ears down to his shoulders. His tired sunken dark eyes were framed with red blotchy skin and a bulbous purple nose. His unclipped moustache finished at the corners of his mouth where his chin was spared a beard except for a tuft of unruly hair in the centre directly below his bottom lip. He led me through the packed dining room filled with mouth-watering aromas and an air of good fellowship, across a sanded floor to a corner table with high-backed wooden chairs.

'The devilled kidneys are the best sir, if 'n ya don't mind me sayin', the bacon nice 'n fatty 'n streaky and the preserved tongue the cook made only yesterdee.'

Within minutes I was surrounded by pewter plates with a quarter-loaf of bread, butter, kidneys, hot fatty bacon, and a china pot of good strong coffee.

'New to the colony are ya sir?' Clyde maintained his joviality amongst the stress and put two boiled eggs in front of me, picking unwanted nesting straw from their shells.

'Arrived Friday Clyde,' I answered, my stomach growling for sustenance, responding to the fare before me. 'On the *Georgette*.'

'The *Georgette!*'

'Yes, you've heard of her?'

'Aye. You was on board then … when they found 'er … the *Ocean Maiden?*'

I nodded, lightly tapping the top off an egg and salivating at the runny yolk.

'Thart's the devils work if'n I ever 'eard of it,' he muttered and crossed himself as he hurried away.

Day Four – Monday

IARRIVED EARLY AT MY PLACE OF WORK. EARLIER THAN requested this first day, to familiarise myself with my new surroundings, only to discover the office address was in the Campbell Street prisoner's barracks. I stood before massive double gates of wood and iron, painted green and surrounded by fifteen-foot high brick walls. Square stone pillars either side of the gates supported an ornate cast iron arch that in turn supported a large oil lamp at its centre. An iron door within the right side gate boasted a large brass knocker, which I recognised from my Ancient Greek studies back at school in Birmingham, as that of Dionysus, the god of wine, ritual and madness. I was contemplating whether the figure was either congruous or unbefitting for a prison when the door unceremoniously creaked open and a lone guard stepped through onto the street. He brandished his Brown Bess musket with a fixed bayonet, which he was only too keen to point in my direction.

'Wha' are loiterin' 'ere for?' he grumbled, straightening his tall leather shako after knocking it on the door lintel. 'Bugger off before I skewer ya.'

If there was one thing I learnt immediately it was that the man lacked social skills.

'Excuse me!' I answered indignantly. 'My name is Mr Hunter and I'm here looking for a Mr Winter.'

He dusted a cobweb, also from the doorway, off his smart blue guard's uniform. 'Fabian Winter?'

'Yes. My services have been engaged by the newly formed police detective agency and I'm to commence employment here this day.'

'Oh! Employment is it? Mr Winter ... o' course ... why didn't ya say so in the first place? 'ere, this way. ... Hunter ya say?' And he ushered me through the doorway walking, I now observed, with a limp caused by a wart on the sole of his foot he was keen to tell me.

Immediately inside the main gate I was greeted by a small

courtyard, surrounded by two storey prison offices constructed of sandstone quarried nearby.

'Wait 'ere,' the guard said and hobbled off through another iron gate leading into the prison grounds proper.

Moments later I was escorted to a tiny room at the end of the prison storehouse right near the main entrance. It was clearly a recent assembly, exclusively for the use of the new police department where my superior, Fabian Winter, was already in attendance. He sat on the corner of a clerk's desk puffing furiously on a stubborn clay pipe.

'Ah, so you must be Caspian,' he seemed friendly enough. His hand shot out as he jumped to his feet, 'Mr Caspian Hunter recently o' Birming'am.'

We shook hands and I noted with some satisfaction that the man had a firm grip; having been taught by my father how important first impressions of a man's character are – a handshake being evidence of this. I stared into his eyes. They were hazel. He was handsome in a rugged sort of way, thin faced and taller than me – only just – and carried less weight, I could tell too readily. He wore man about the street clothes with Scottish tartan patterned trousers, nothing indulgent I should add, and I knew from earlier enquiries the man was thirty-five years old. Below his nose he had a pencil thin moustache of the fashion favoured by the rakes of London and exuded confidence like an advance agent for a circus.

'Ya can let go now,' he said. Face straight.

'Sorry?'

'Me 'and. Ya can let go of it now.'

'Oh yes, sorry. Force of habit I'm afraid,' I said. 'My father ...'

'What sorta parents would call their son Caspian I wonder?' he cut in.

Now that was audacious. Plain rude even. I was somewhat taken aback. However, first impressions and all that. So I answered without hesitation, 'I have only ever met one Fabian before, Fabian. And he was a schoolteacher in Birmingham who had an unhealthy fondness for young boys.' There. That was telling him.

'Bravo! Did you 'ear that Snake?' I wasn't aware that one of the other constables had entered the room and stood directly behind me.

'What's that sir?' The man was being polite, surely.

Fabian pushed his chest out and crossed his arms. 'Our new second-in-command from Birming'am 'ere, Caspian 'unter, just told me he only knew one other Fabian and the man liked little boys. Charming huh?'

'Yes sir, charming.' My first observation of Snake was that he was a nail-biter with most of his fingernails chewed down to the quick, but although this might appear to indicate an anxious disposition I yet felt him a person to take the initiative in a scrap.

'Snake,' Fabian said. 'Meet Caspian. Caspian, meet Snake.'

We shook hands. His was a firm shake but so far I had a higher opinion of Mr Winter's. I also noted the man made a poor attempt at hiding a tattoo on his right hand between thumb and forefinger. A tattoo of a mermaid entwined with chain, which I recognised but couldn't quite identify where I had seen it before. Snake was a sturdy specimen; tall – at least six foot – early thirties, with healthy white teeth and waxed back hair with a part in the middle. He offered a charming smile, friendly enough and on first impressions I considered he would be the type of soldier I would like next to me on the battlefield.

'Hang ya coat there,' Fabian indicated an unoccupied peg on the wall behind the door. 'Oh by the way, Mr Wheaton, the governor's secretary, sends 'is condolences. 'e can't make it this mornin' but said 'e will make your acquaintance later in the week.'

'Thank you.'

'There are four constables,' Fabian went on. 'As I'm certain ya know, Caspian. Snake 'ere is the overseer for the other three who'll ya meet shortly.' Fabian sucked hard on his pipe, pulled a disgusted face and finally placed the instrument of foul odour onto the desk.

'Now follow me,' he ordered. 'I'll show ya 'round.'

We stepped out into the main prison yard, a large rectangular area, maybe a hundred and fifty yards in length, with several prison buildings inside the perimeter.

'This 'ere is where any felons we appre'end will end up and mark me words, it's not an 'appy place.'

'I should think not.'

He scrutinised me a moment. 'Quite,' he muttered. Fabian first pointed to a neat brick two-storey building directly opposite. 'That is the Superintendent's residence,' he said. The building had a large garden in front of it surrounded by a brick wall with a path to the front door lined with rose bushes. It looked so out of character within the prison grounds.

''e's a stuffy old bastard called Simeon Mead, 'is wife died a year back and 'e feels the world owes 'im so keep out of 'is way. 'e lives there alone with his nineteen-year-old daughter Elizabeth.' Fabian studied me once more. 'Ya not married are ya? I mean I didn't read that in ya report.'

'No.'

'Engaged?'

'No.'

'Hmm. Wait 'til you see Elizabeth Mead. She's a real 'oney,' and Fabian let out a sort of snorting giggle. 'Mead, honey. I didn't think of that before.' I rewarded him with a smile. 'Yes well. But seriously Caspian, she's prepossessing, bewitchingly charming.' Suddenly Fabian shot me a conspiratorial and cheeky grin as he lowered his voice, 'She's welcome to rest her slippers under my bunk any minute of the clock.'

I cast an eye over the stylish residence with its enclosed balcony on the first floor and an open balcony on the ground level and fantasised seeing some gorgeous siren strolling the veranda twirling a parasol over a slender shoulder. Fabian must have recognised my dreaming, for he took my arm and led me away.

'The buildings to the left beyond that wall are the treadmill and flourmill,' he continued with the tour, 'with sleeping wards behind them. The big building further on is more sleeping wards and the yellow brick three storey next to it is solitary.'

'How many does the prison house?' I asked.

'Twelve 'undred. And the bloody place is full my friend,' he looked to the sky as a flock of white cockatoos screeched overhead. 'Noisy bastards,' he shook his head, then turned back to face me. 'Ever since they stopped transportin' prisoners from England, over two years now, this 'ere prison is for civilian villains as well.'

We strolled out into the middle of the yard. 'Right down the very end there,' and he pointed south, 'you 'ave the cookhouse, officers' kitchen, bakery, storerooms and the big building – ya can just see its roof – is the mess 'all. Behind that is the shit 'ouse and a bit ripe too when a southerly's blowin' in orf the river.' He hacked a laugh and spat phlegm. 'Firkin' pipe, I'll have to stop smokin', that's for certain.'

A rattling of chains and collective footsteps drew my attention to a work gang of twenty prisoners with two guards marching around the corner from the opposite end where I believe the chapel stood, next to more cells with exercise yards. We watched in silence as the chain gang passed on their way to the mess hall, some pushing wooden wheelbarrows of tools. They were all attired in their 'slops' so I'm told they're called; the standard prisoner uniform of yellow and grey woollen jacket and trousers with leather cap and boots. Each coat is marked with the symbol of the British system; a broad arrow and the letters 'B' and 'O' that I knew stood for British Ordinance. All were shackled by the ankles, with leg irons attached to a leather belt around the waist to aid the men in walking. The sad looking souls belonged to the British Empire now, and it was difficult to face them, all snarling silently at us with hatred.

'Work gang for the mess 'all,' Fabian said after the last man had passed. ''ad some wind damage recently and the roof leaks.' Suddenly Fabian sounded cheerful. 'Say, you'll get to see a hangin' 'ere tomorra.'

'A hanging?'

'Aye. A women what's more.' I must have looked perplexed because he eagerly continued. 'Rosa Blossom 'er name is. She's one o' my cases actually. Confessed in the end. Now she'll swing. Pity 'cos she's a great looker.'

'What did she do?'

'Poisoned 'er 'usband. She's not too clever. She bought a penny's worth of arsenic from the apothecary only weeks before she topped 'im. Put the powder in 'is food over several meals. Then when 'e was bedridden with chest pains and burning throat she fed 'im more of the powder in bed tellin' 'im it was medicine.' A dark thought crossed Fabian's mind and he added, 'poor bastard.'

'So how was she eventually caught?'

'Well 'e was real sick like and 'e vomited regular into a jar in bed and she emptied the vomit onto straw in the backyard but one of 'er pigs ate the vomit and it was found dead the next morning. So was the 'usband. I was suspicious straight away. Neighbours told me of loud arguments they'd been 'avin' and then 'e used to belt 'er from time to time and another neighbour testified that Rosa told 'er she would poison her 'usband if he ever 'it her again.'

'And?'

''e hit her didn't 'e? Doctor Montgomery, our prison surgeon, did an autopsy and found traces of arsenic in the victim's bowel. And the pigs.'

'He did an autopsy on the pig as well?'

'Certainly. Say now. What's your theory on the *Ocean Maiden*?'

'Well I ...'

'I mean it was one 'ell of a coincidence your being on the ship what discovered the *Ocean Maiden*, wasn't it now?'

I was about to answer when Snake slipped up quietly behind me for the second time in half an hour. 'Sir. Excuse me Mr Hunter ... Fabian.'

'Yes Snake.'

'We've a murder. Down Wappin'. Some cove's 'ad 'is throat cut.'

'Wapping huh? Why's it always Wapping?'

'I take it Wapping here is like Wapping in London?' I asked.

'Aye. Although 'ere it ain't named official like. Full of lowlifes, whores and the damned destitute,' Fabian cursed as we marched back towards the office. 'Grab your coat Caspian.'

'Firkin' 'orrid place is Wapping,' Fabian said as he, Snake and myself walked directly down Campbell Street towards the cove. 'Ya got these 'ere stone, wood and brick buildin's but then ya got the rabbit warrens what run off betwixt 'em that lead to alleyways with small shanties, workshops, smithies.'

'Everyone battlin' to scratch a livin',' Snake added.

We stepped out from the corner of Campbell Street into Macquarie Street when without warning twenty or more head of cattle came at us at a pace.

'Careful sir,' Snake snatched my arm and pulled me back as a large bull charged by. 'Firkin' stampede!' Two men followed on horses cracking whips and I could only hope they had control over the animals.

'Them cows wouldn't be in such a hurry if'n they knew where they was goin',' Fabian chuckled.

'Oh, and where is that?' I asked, pushing myself harder against the wall to avoid them.

'Slaughter 'ouse. Can't ya smell it?'

'Oh yes,' I remembered. 'Now you mention it ...'

'Well it ain't just the slaughter'ouse, it's the tannery next to it mostly. Two 'undred tons o' rotten flesh, bones and blood get dumped in that rivulet each year. Firkin' stink. If 'n we're lucky it gets washed out into the river. But ya need a good flood lad, to really clear it.'

'It looks like low floodable country.'

'You bet. Only last year we 'ad the worst flood ever. Wapping was entirely submerged, two foot or more. Ya see up rivulet there's a number o' wooden buildings that perilously over 'ang the creek. Then we get 'eavy rain or snow meltin' and the structures collapse into the rivulet. Casks, kegs, beams, logs, bedsteads all get washed down the rivulet and get jammed under that firkin' bridge.' And he pointed to a stone bridge up ahead.

'It forms an impassable barrier ya see,' Snake said matter-of-factly. 'Then the water spreads over the streets in a deluge. Last year boatmen 'ad to rescue whole families. Shockin' it was.'

'Ya know somethin' else Caspian,' Fabian watched the cattle round a corner to the slaughterhouse. 'There's thirteen inns 'round 'ere, thirteen! And they 'ave a sayin' 'round here. If it's good enough to get wet on the outside, then it's good enough to get wet on the inside.'

'Aye,' Snake nodded enthusiastically and stepped into the alleyway we required. 'Coves 'ere are a hardy lot.'

The body lay sprawled on its back across the floor exactly where the woman found it. A man in his early twenties.

''ave you touched the body?' Fabian asked the landlady.

'Nay,' the toothless woman answered angrily, defensive. 'Don't ya go accusin' me of stealin' nuthin' ya hear?'

'I didn't accuse you of anything ma'am. I merely said did ya disturb anything in this room?'

'I already tell ya.'

'Then leave us.'

The woman cast a vitriolic leer at the three of us and left with a huff. 'You can bet your boots, Caspian, that hag has rifled the man's pockets.' Fabian leant over the corpse. 'Snake.'

'Sir.'

'Take notes if ya please.'

'Caspian, do ya worst man.' I must have looked perturbed. 'Your analysis if ya please.'

'Ah. Right.' I squatted next to the body, careful not to kneel in any blood that pooled about the dead body. The man had clearly died of a nasty cut to the throat. I started to dictate as Snake jotted notes into his small black leather-covered book with a pencil that I noticed was also chewed.

'Blood pool heavy. Visible mucous membrane not particularly pale, the neck wound runs transversely from the middle of one neck muscle to the other ...'

"Old it sir,' Snake was struggling to dictate. 'Trans ... wha'?'

'Transversely.'

"ow d'ya spell that then?'

'T.r.a.n.s.v.e.r.s.e.l.y,' I articulated. Snake put pencil to paper, his tongue protruding from the corner of his mouth in intense concentration.

'Death not due to fatal haemorrhage,' I continued, 'but a result of suffocation from the wound into the larynx and the lower respiratory passages.'

'Phew!' Fabian whistled.

'In other words he choked on his own blood,' I suggested.

'Well why didn't ya just so so?' Snake grumbled scrawling away with little chance to bite his nails.

Fabian. 'Excellent.'

'What d'ya reckon,' Snake asked as he caught up. "e was done in with a dagger, or a sword maybe.'

'Something sharp that's for certain,' Fabian said circling the body.

My eyes scanned the small, squalid and starkly furnished room. Something shiny caught my attention lying on the floor behind a bedpan in a corner. I leant in and picked up a cut-throat razor.

'It was felos de se,' I said with certainty.

'What?'

'Felos de se ... felon of himself ... self murder,' I repeated, rather proud of myself.

'Wha' ... how?'

'The man took his own life,' I said. 'See, a razor ... and an extra sharp one at that. He has cut his own throat and the razor has fallen from his grasp and bounced across the floor as he fell backwards.'

'Holy hen's teeth, I think you're right.' Fabian straightened up and I passed him the razor. 'A. Griggs,' he read aloud from the bone handle. 'Aye. Felos de se for certain. If you were going to slice ya own throat you'd be makin' certain ya razor was sharp. Good work Caspian. Snake, finish a short report and go see Merryweather the undertaker to come fetch 'im. Quickly now, the weather's warmin' up.'

'A crime solved already, well-done Caspian,' I congratulated myself. I slipped my fob from my waistcoat pocket, 11.10am. It was then, as I peeled the soles of my boots from the floor, that I realised I was standing in a pool of the man's blood. Self-murder was never a pretty sight.

Why was I not surprised when Fabian confirmed what I already suspected? My office, or should I say, *our* makeshift office – ten feet by twelve feet at the far end of the prison storehouse crammed floor to ceiling, wall to wall with barrels and bails – was it. A temporary wall had been erected to separate the workspace where a potbelly stove smoked lazily outside the door. Six of us were expected to work from this tiny space. Fabian nodded to my allocated desk, not much larger than the one I used at school.

'Not much to it sir?' I sighed, rolling a chary eye over my own tiny space.

'Aye,' he said poking his little finger about his pipe bowl teasing the half burnt tobacco.

'At least we have a window,' Snake remained constructive.

'I will try to get us a more spacious area in the near future,' Fabian said, 'but for now this is it. Take a pew. And by the way, call me Fabian.'

'Fabian,' I acknowledged. 'Certainly.'

Fabian returned from the potbelly stove directly outside the office with a lit taper to ignite his pipe, and caught me frowning.

'What?' he enquired.

'Well if you don't mind me asking … but you're not going to smoke your pipe in this cramped stuffy space, are you?'

'Jesus Lord!' he cursed. I heard Snake snort. 'What's with me smoking me pipe … *Caspian?*'

'It affects my breathing; my physician back in Birmingham said I have a mild asthma. So if it's not going to be too much of a problem

I'd prefer it if you didn't smoke your pipe in this confined space.'

Fabian stared at me as if I had leprosy. Eventually he put his pipe back on his desk and stepped on the taper. 'Hmm,' he muttered. 'I've been trying to stop anyways.'

He sat back on the corner of his desk and I was starting to think he would rather sit on it than at it; in his defence the chairs were less than comfortable.

'Tell me my learned twenty-seven-year-old friend, do ya drink? Rum and the like that is.'

'Yes, I don't have a problem with a strong drink or two. Although I'm more an ale or cider man.'

'Good. That's settled then. We'll visit Everret at the Hope and Anchor at the end of the day. Now, Caspian ...'

'Fabian.'

'This 'ere *Ocean Maiden*. What on earth do you think happened to the passengers and crew? Sea monsters?' he grinned.

'I really don't have an opinion at this moment,' I replied in all honesty. 'I've never encountered anything like it in my six years as a law enforcement officer in Birmingham.'

'What do *you* think Snake?' he asked the lanky constable.

'Me? Ah ... well I was thinkin' ... you know ... it could have been absconders livin' in the Strait.'

'Impossible,' I interjected.

'Oh!'

'Well how does a ship sail on its own down the coast of this island and into the Derwent Estuary?'

Fabian nodded vigorously. 'Good point.'

'Anyway,' I went on, 'the cargo was left intact, and valuable cargo at that. Rum and grain alcohol for instance.'

'What's grain alcohol?' Snake asked.

'It's alcohol, pure like, made by distilling fermented grain,' Fabian rubbed the stubble on his chin.

'Pure huh,' Snake looked contemplative. 'What's it taste like then?'

'Jesus man!' Fabian scoffed. 'Ya don't drink the stuff. It'd kill ya.'

Snake looked at me with a foolish shrug. 'It's used in solvents,' I explained.

Snake. 'Like turpentine?'

'No,' I said. 'That's made from pine resins. Grain alcohol is used to make liquids like French polish.'

'Huh!' Now Fabian laughed. 'I'd like to see ya drink a quart o' that then Snake, that'd put a shine on ya date!'

'How come you know so much?' Snake asked me while running a critical eye over his nibbled nails.

'Study,' I answered. 'I read a lot of books.'

'Well lads,' Fabian sprung to his feet. I had the feeling academia wasn't high on his list of priorities. He snatched up his pad and pencil from off his desk. "Tis near noon and the boys will be waitin' for us. Let's move it and get down to the cove and look over this 'ere *Ocean Maiden*.' He threw an arm around my shoulder, 'and see what else our brilliant young mind from Birmingham can prise from the woodwork of our ghost ship.'

We strolled at a decent pace to the Hobart Town waterfront, keeping upwind of the slaughterhouse and tannery, down past the Commissariat and Bond Store and onto the docks.

'Well firk!' Fabian swore, lifting his straw boater hat to scratch his wiry thick hair. 'Where is this 'ere *Ocean Maiden*?' Shielding eyes with our hands from the bright summer sun we searched the harbour where a dozen ships were anchored in the cove, from coastal colliers to Yankee whalers.

'She was docked at Old Wharf when I saw her last,' I said.

To the east Old Wharf was a hive of activity. The *Patrick*, a merchant ship down from Sydney, and which had sailed ahead of the *Georgette* across Bass Strait two days earlier, was unloading at the handsome stone warehouses at the end of the wharf. Here, many carts were operating to and fro along the old isthmus carriageway to the cove proper.

'No *Ocean Maiden*.'

To our right whalers were docked at New Wharf, although Fabian said it was to be called Salamanca Place after the Duke of Wellington's Battle at Salamanca in 1812. I cast an eye over smaller vessels in the docks near where we stood. The two-masted *Thistle* and the schooner *Rebecca*, in which, Fabian pointed out, the founder of the city of Melbourne, John Batman, had sailed to Port Phillip twenty years earlier.

'No *Ocean Maiden*,' I acknowledged.

'We'll go to the harbourmaster's place o' business,' Fabian suggested and strutted away full of energy.

We eventually found the *Ocean Maiden* anchored off shore further up river and now in sight of the Queen's Domain. Three constables waited for us with a tender on the foreshore.

'Ah.' Fabian slid on his boots down the dry dirt embankment creating an avalanche of pebbles. 'The three wise men,' he chuckled at the three constables Hal, Billings and Jasper who stood to attention on his arrival. The three men looked smart in their blue frock coats belted at the waist with a brass buckle that also secured a fine military issue sabre running the length of neatly pressed blue trousers. On their heads they wore the latest polished leather peaked hats, with the brass badge of the Van Diemen's Land Constabulary at the front.

All wore facial hair as if it was mandatory. Billings sported thick mutton chops that almost met under his chin; but no moustache. He looked about my age and handsome in his neat fitting uniform, which was in contrast to Hal whose girth was showing the signs of approaching middle age. Hal was clearly the oldest, alert and in his early thirties at a guess, with mutton chops that formed a beard under the chin with a thin inverted V shaped moustache joining the beard. Both men looked tanned from the antipodean weather. Jasper however, maybe twenty, was pale as an English peach with baby features and mutton chops that struggled to grow at all. Jasper had a kindly face of boyhood innocence with sagging eyelids and, I learnt when he opened his mouth, was slow of speech.

'Handsome devils,' Fabian said proudly. 'Even if I do say so meself.' He straddled the rocky shore, legs apart and with hands on hips. 'Men, meet Caspian Hunter.' There followed silence, albeit very briefly. 'I know, I know,' Fabian grinned cheekily at the troupe. 'But that's what 'is dear mother named him, "Caspian".'

Immediately the three constables smiled and returned a warm greeting. They were clearly used to their supervisor's humour. I probably should correct myself here and say two men smiled; the older one, Hal, held back and it was only after an encouraging glance from Fabian that he offered his hand.

'You've had some success already I heard my comrades say,' Billings said, with what sounded to me to be an Oxford accent. He was

distinctly from a better class than the other two.

'Yes,' I answered, secretly pleased the news had travelled so quickly.

Jasper was keen to be part of the conversation. 'Self-murder I 'eard.'

'Aye!' Fabian cut in. 'And the governor will be murderin' you firkers if we don't sort this mess out.' Fabian jerked his head towards the ghost ship anchored a hundred yards off shore.

Fabian was first on deck, swinging over the gunwale with the agility of a midshipman. The ghost ship was just that, a ghost ship. 'Ahoy,' he shouted. 'Anyone o'board?'

'Aye sir,' and a young voice with the timid undertones of a lad caught with his hand in the toffee jar called out as he tripped up the companionway.

'Well look sharp lad,' Fabian reproached. 'This 'ere is the scene of a crime and you are s'posed to be guardin' it, savvy.'

'Aye.' It was then we noticed the young soldier was having difficulty swallowing food.

'What ya eatin' then?' Fabian asked.

'Cheese sir,' he answered, the word barely audible.

'Cheese?'

'Aye. There's a big ball o' the stuff on the capn's table sir and I been 'ere since sparra fart with nuthin' to eat like so I thought ...'

'Well ya thought wrong. That's evidence ya scoffin' there ya greedy tyke. Now bugger orf and guard this 'ere ship while we do our business.'

I couldn't help but smile. The soldier was but a boy and a scrawny underfed lad at that.

Back in the stern cabin and the cannon ball sized Dutch cheese had been half eaten. 'Christ!' Fabian shook his head and rolled the mauled ball onto its side. ''e's eaten half of it. That'll block 'is pipes up for a month!'

I looked about the gloomy cabin; everything else seemed to be where I had left it. While the three constables and Snake descended to explore the lower decks, the hold and bilge, Fabian and I sat at the table and spread the log and manifest open before us. In the dim light, we became aware of the persistent buzzing of flies and at the same moment the reek of putrefying food greeted our nostrils, wafting across the table.

'Jesus!' Fabian stood suddenly pushing his chair back and an army of these filthy insects ascended from the various plates of rotten mutton – now three days old in the summer warmth. Fabian proceeded to open a cabin window and scrape the maggoty plates into the Derwent while I had a quiet smile to myself and started making notes, seeing no point in spending more time on this wretched ship than I needed to.

All cabin windows battened with canvas and board. The skylight on the cabin top raised half open.
The captain's bed unmade and wet. The water probably came in from the open skylight.
The captain's chronometer, sextant, navigation book, ship's register and other papers missing.
Note: log book and ship manifest found in first mate's cabin.

Fabian noticed the cashbox under the bunk for the first time.

'Hmm, empty. Someone took the gold and left the pennies. This harks back to piracy, sealers, bolters ...' and he looked about the cabin as if he expected Blackbeard himself to jump out from the shadows, cutlass in hand.

'Thieves would have taken the rum,' I argued. How naïve some people are. 'If not all of it they would have taken what they could carry. Besides, the sailors' possessions are untouched. Coin, tobacco, boots, clothes all were left behind in their berths ... thieves would have searched the crew's quarters and pilfered everything.'

'Maybe it was the crew.'

'What? And leave their own gold and silver behind? Doesn't make sense.'

I thought a moment then said, 'Fabian.'

'Huh.'

'There is something I should mention, for the record like.'

'What's that then?'

'Well I have a suspicion that coin chest was full ... well if not full, half full with gold and silver ... it's the ship's cashbox after all.'

'Aye, we knows that Caspian, and some bastards pilfered it.'

'But why was nothing else valuable taken? No Fabian. I have a suspicion it was removed by crew of the *Georgette*. Someone first on board, like the mate, Mr Ransford.'

'One o' the mates ya say?'

'Yes. Third mate.'

'I'll 'ave 'im arrested.'

'Well we have no proof, no evidence. That's the problem. It's merely a suspicion.' I watched Fabian pace the length of the table, his nose twitching from the lingering odours. 'I suggest we keep an eye on him,' I said. 'If he is guilty I think he'll be the man about town spending up big.'

'Aye, good deducing lad,' Fabian seemed to daydream briefly, maybe thinking what *he* would do with a pocket of loose gold. 'We'll keep 'im under observation, see if'n the bugger ain't 'round the inns and taverns spendin' 'is ill-gotten gains on gamblin', drinkin' and whorin.' Fabian's eyes shone at the thought.

I had heard enough. I gathered the manifest and log and stood. The smell seemed to cling to me and I felt my stomach churn. 'I'm finished here. I'm off to inspect the galley.'

Hatchway in the roof of the galley was off. But windows closed. Galley floor puddled with water. Once again this is probably because of open hatch.

'Strange,' I said.

'What?'

'The galley stove is off its mounts.'

I hastily wrote:

Somehow, someone or something has lifted the huge cast iron galley stove and set it back down out of place so it no longer stood on its chocks that secured each leg to the deck. Heavy water cask similarly moved from chocks.

No sign of smoke damage. No sign of rough weather.

Snake joined us as we made our way back on deck and I thought he looked a mite pale. 'Damned sinister if'n I do say so meself sar.' He shuddered. 'Ya think she be haunted like?' And he crossed himself.

'Haunted!' Fabian tittered dismissively. 'Ya don't believe in ghosts n' ghouls do ya matey?'

'Well it's downright creepy below deck sar.'

'Bah!'

'I'm just sayin' thart's all.' Snake turned away abruptly, feeling rather foolish.

'Everything has an explanation Snake,' I said not having a clue what I was talking about.

'See Snake,' Fabian grinned cheerily. 'You listen to our learned friend 'ere from Birming'am. Everything has an explanation. Now,' he nodded his head sagely, 'all we gotta do is go 'nd find out what it is.'

'I seen the binnacle has been broken and the compass missing,' Snake then said.

'Yes I already noted that when we discovered her,' I acknowledged. 'Also, interestingly enough, the wheel was not lashed alee as is normal procedure when abandoning a ship in a calamity.' I noted a horseshoe nailed to the main mast and smiled ... *superstition*. 'Someone was superstitious,' I said making a note.

Fabian paced the deck and gaped up into the rigging as if all answers awaited him there. 'How was she rigged? ... When ya first spotted 'er that is.'

I turned back the pages of my notebook and read aloud:

'Jib and foretopmast staysail set on starboard tack. Foresail and upper foretopsail shredded. Standing rigging in good order. Some running rigging missing. Masts, yards, spars and anchors in order. Stout rope of the main halyard broken and mostly missing. Main staysail lying loose on forward deck house and all other sails furled.'

Fabian leant against a gunwale rail. 'Well bugger me, cap'n firkin' Norway wasn't goin' nowhere in a hurry, was 'e?'

'Something else most important,' I continued.

'The yawl was missing too,' I remembered, and moved to the gunwale parallel to where the craft had been stowed.

'So they've just abandoned her at sea!' Fabian sighed heavily. 'Satan's blood! Why?'

'What's this?' Snake picked up a long piece of wood marked at intervals along one side with Roman numerals.

Fabian recognised it immediately. 'That's a sounding rod, for measuring water in the bilge. What's that doin' up 'ere?'

'Interesting,' I then noted deep cuts in the wooden railing *and* on top of the hatch where the yawl had been stowed. 'That would indicate that the crew had to use an axe to cut the yawl loose. They were in a hurry and had not the time to untie her properly.'

I made notes while Fabian and Snake followed me about scratching or rubbing the back of their heads.

'What do we know about the captain Caspian?' Fabian asked me, trying to appear observant as we worked the deck. I consulted my notebook of observations gleaned from the logbook.

'Brynjar Evjen was fifty-eight. The heading in his log says he was an ex-whaling captain from the Atlantic fleets. Born in Stavanger and he has been with the shipping agents Leith and Company in Southampton since 1849. His wife, Kirsten Evjen, was on board and it appears his young daughter was also on the voyage.'

'We'll have to send a report to Lloyds in London,' Fabian said. 'That's your responsibility Snake, as soon as Caspian here has the brief finished for you.'

'Aye sir.'

'And the crew Caspian, what nationality were they?'

'Mostly Norwegian it appears.'

'Hmm, … ah!' Billings, Hal and Jasper appeared from the forward companionway. 'The three wise men.'

'Sir, there's no cargo!' Hal spoke for the three.

'What?'

'No cargo. Just a bunch of broken staves and barrel hoops.'

'Are you certain?'

'Aye. There's naught below,' Hal turned to his mates. 'Eh lads?'

'Aye. Naught.'

'What took ya so long then?'

'We was searching every nook and cranny and there bein' a strong smell in the bilge 'n all …'

'Smell? What kind o' smell?'

'Strong, like a spirit o' some sort, and we was lookin' for the cause o' that before comin' to ya sir.'

Fabian eyed the three men a moment.

I had a thought. 'The bilge … how much water is there?'

'Normal, a few feet.'

'Did you inspect the bilge pump?'

'Aye,' Billings was pleased to take the credit. 'I checked it sir, and it was in perfect working order.'

'Except there was a valve missin',' Jasper was quick to add.

'Yeh, well ya gotta take the valve out to poke the sounding rod into the bilge, right,' Hal now recognised the rod in Snake's hand. 'What's that doin' up 'ere then?'

'You tell me.'

'Jasper,' Fabian said 'Go fetch that tyke.' Seconds later the young soldier stood anxiously before us. 'Has there been anyone aboard today, to unload the cargo like?'

'Aye. There be twenty men 'ere this mornin' with dray and cranes and barge.'

'What time?'

'Same time I come 'ere sir, like I said, six hours after midnight.'

'Well why weren't we told? Jesus!'

'Did they say where it was going and why?' I asked the soldier.

'Aye. They took it all to the Bond Store, for safe keepin' the supervisor told me. Said it were worth thousands and thousands 'e did.'

The smell rising from the bilge was an effluvial mix of putrefying dead rats, stagnant water and other unidentifiable effluent mixed with what I could only guess was the residue from the grain alcohol. I collected up several loose staves and saw the words 'grain spirit' painted across them in red.

'Unusual,' I thought aloud. 'Several barrels have been broken.'

'Were they broken when you found the ship?'

'Can't say exactly. Captain Slade of the *Georgette* was keen to sail on into Hobart Town. By the time I got to investigate the hold the fog was lifting and a wind picking up.'

'Well by the number of barrel hoops lying there I'm thinkin' half a dozen got wasted. Maybe they fell off the cargo pile in a storm.'

'Freak wave maybe,' Billings muttered.

'Either way the contents was wasted into the bilge.'

I'm not certain how I can describe the inns of Hobart Town. My guess is they are typical of waterfront dens along the Thames, the likes of which we don't have in Birmingham as there are fewer travellers than London and no sailors to victual and quench. Certainly the inns of the port lack any finesse, but finesse is not what the regular patron strives for in these hovels of filth and depravity.

The Hope and Anchor was no exception.

'Five quarts o' porter if ya will Everret.' And Fabian slapped a palm on the bar. 'Everret brews 'is own Caspian, it's got a nice creamy 'ead and is kept in a deep cool cellar.' Fabian watched in respectful awe as the dark beer was pumped from a keg in the cellar beneath us, while the other constables gathered around.

'This 'ere's Caspian, Everret, Caspian Hunter,' he felt compelled to say. 'Me new second-in-command to catch villains and scallywags like you tipping the slop trays back in the barrel.'

The innkeeper looked at me with an arched eyebrow as if I was already accusing him of some wrongdoing.

'I'm sure you wouldn't do that sir,' I said, wishing to gain the innkeeper's esteem.

'Nay lad,' the barman grumbled. 'And you best be watchin' ya back round 'ere lad. Thar's plenty o' ruffians what don't like law and order in these parts.'

'Now Mr Everret,' Billings said, 'don't go frightening our new member.'

'I'm just sayin', that's all.'

As Fabian sang the Hope and Anchor's praises, the mutton stew was as he had recommended, excellent. Plenty of meat and lots of juicy fat. I ate seconds with boiled potatoes, turnips and cabbage and washed it all down with more porter. A one-legged fiddler played ditties for drinks and my thoughts went briefly to Miss Rose Atwater at my lodgings and what excuses I could muster for the inquisition that was surely forthcoming. Then Fabian's buoyant voice broke my musing, 'Everret ... bring us the Geneva if'n ya please.'

Day Five – Tuesday

THE FOLLOWING MORNING, FEELING A LITTLE dusty, I washed and dressed and once more slipped out the side door to avoid the landlady. I was at the prison gate at five minutes before eight of the clock and already the comings and goings of the prison were in full swing. Maybe 'full swing' is a poor choice of words as Rosa Blossom was about to hang. My head felt as though a drummer resided within and I promised myself that I would drink less.

'Come, come Caspian.' Fabian was as excited as a hound with a ham bone. He took me by the wrist and dragged me towards the scaffold where already several hundred prisoners stood in neat rows staring anxiously at the wooden gallows. The same gallows I had watched being erected late the previous afternoon.

'No,' I said. 'I don't want to watch a woman hang.'

'Why? She's a murderer Caspian. She poisoned her husband for God's sake. The poor bastard died a slow death in agony. Firk her.'

I must confess my curiosity was piqued. I had never seen a hanging before. The nearest I had come to any experience so macabre was when my father pointed out a cadaver on a gibbet. The victim had been a highwayman, hanged for robbing a coach and his body was left to rot in an iron gibbet at the crossroads where he committed his robbery. It was in 1833; how could I forget? I was only four but I can still see the body as clear as it was yesterday. And the smell! But that's another story.

'How is *your* head?' I asked Fabian.

'What?' he answered chirpily. 'My head?'

'Yes. I've a devil of a headache.'

'Oh that. My head's fine Caspian. Just fine.' He flipped open his silver fob. 'We've another twenty minutes.'

'What?'

'Twenty minutes to the hanging. She'll be arriving soon, they're bringing her from the women's prison. Want to have a quick breakfast first? It'll fix that aching head of yours. The cook's prepared some tasty blood pudding today I've been told and we can have some fried bread with it. Wha'dya say? Hungry?' Was there no end to this man's verve? 'Caspian!'

I still gaped upon the scaffold. 'Ah sorry, what did you say?'

'Breakfast? Eat?'

But almost on cue Simeon Mead the prison superintendent was seen dragging a cane chair out onto his upper balcony. 'Best seat in the house,' Fabian said rather loudly. 'Lucky old buzzard.'

'How's Fabian do it?' I asked Snake as he joined us bidding me a good morning. 'I mean my head ...'

'He's used to it. If ya want to keep up around here ya goin' to have to drink more. Get used to it like.'

An unsettling amongst the prisoners drew my attention back to the superintendent's house – and then I saw her.

Elizabeth!

'My ...' I gasped. 'She's beautiful.'

'Aye. Told ya so.' And Fabian spat on his hand and proceeded to slick his hair back into position. We watched, the three of us, in awe as she swept down the front path of her residence twirling her parasol on her shoulder and gliding between the rose bushes in their full summer bloom. Her long wavy strawberry blonde hair reached her lower back. Her complexion was white as chalk. Her huge almond shaped azure eyes dark and mysterious. She wore an ankle high cream dress with kid gloves and pointed boots.

She was a goddess.

Elizabeth passed through the front gate into the prison courtyard and headed towards the gatehouse. A thousand eyes followed her curves.

And she knew it.

'Tasty little minx,' Snake moaned under his breath.

'Minx alright,' Fabian wheeled about to face me. 'Ya know she could easily 'ave used the entrance from the residence to the back street but that little fox wanted to tease us all.

Immediately she was upon us.

'Good morning Mr Winter,' she smiled at Fabian.

'And a top of the day to you Miss Mead,' he gushed, doing little to disguise his enchantment.

Then *our* eyes met. She ... Elizabeth ... looked me directly in the eye. She slowed in passing.

'Ah,' Fabian spoke effusively. 'Where's me manners? Ah Miss Mead, I would like ya to make the acquaintance of Mr Caspian Hunter, me new assistant from Birming'am.'

'Mr Hunter,' she acknowledged, and her extraordinary smile – directed at me alone – didn't go unnoticed by Fabian and Snake.

'Enchanté,' I greeted and kissed the back of the proffered hand. She held my gaze and I felt my heart skip a beat along with a flush. Or was that last night's gin?

'It is so nice to meet you Mr Hunter.'

'Please miss, call me Caspian.'

'Caspian then. Maybe you could be so kind as to escort me to the gate.'

'Certainly.' I offered her my arm and led her to the gate, but not before glancing over my shoulder at the incredulous faces on Fabian and Snake. Unfortunately our timing couldn't have been worse as the cart carrying Rosa Blossom to the gallows pulled alongside at the same instant. The main gate was dragged open noisily on rusty iron hinges and a gathering outside tried to enter with the cart.

'Back,' the guards jabbed bayonets towards the unruly crowds. 'Public 'angings 'ave been banned ya know,' one guard yelled. 'Now back ... all o' ya.'

The caged cart entered and I couldn't help but look directly at the wretched woman standing at the front of the cart, her wrists handcuffed and her face aged with stress, tears and fear.

'Back ya bastards,' another guard said as they tried to close the gate and Elizabeth and I stepped forward. 'Oh, sorry miss, didn't see ya sneak up on me,' he said on sighting the superintendent's daughter. 'Excuse the language but I gotta get this crowd back some 'ow.'

'That's perfectly alright Harry,' she answered the guard, and I ushered her down Campbell Street away from the crowd.

'Thank you Caspian. I don't know what I would have done without you.'

'My pleasure Miss Mead.'

'Please. You must call me Elizabeth.'

'Well,' I said rather clumsily as I backed away. 'Anytime you want assistance Elizabeth ... you know where I am.'

'That's right, Daddy made room for your new outfit in the stores didn't he?'

'Yes, and jolly comfortable it is too.' I gibbered. What was I saying? We bid farewell and I tripped back into the prison yard like an excited schoolboy.

'Yes!' I yelled and punched the air in a victory salute only to catch the eye of Rosa Blossom.

Standing on the gallows.

Eyes red raw with fear as the noose was slipped over her head.

Ashamed and disgusted with myself I hurried towards the office.

'Enchanté!' Fabian teased, feigning distaste when we caught up. 'Enchanté Miss Mead ... huh ... Caspian Hunter you old ram you.' He was clearly excited for me. 'What did ya talk about?'

'I don't know what you mean,' I replied only to be given away by an inescapable grin.

'You and Elizabeth, wha'dya talk about? When ya had 'er alone ... outside like?'

'Nothing why?'

At that moment an awful scream reverberated about the prison walls. There followed a collective groan as hundreds of prisoners gasped, then the appalling sound of the gallows trap door banging open ...

Choonk!

The noose snapped Rosa Blossoms neck breaking three vertebrae. The woman died instantly.

And may God have mercy on her soul.

A moment's silence followed.

'Breakfast?' Fabian asked eagerly. The man had a stomach of iron.

No sooner had we lined our empty bellies with fried blood pudding, fried bread in lard and steaming mugs of sweet black tea when Constable Billings found us in the prison mess hall.

'If it's not raining it's pouring sir,' Billings said to Fabian. 'We've got another mystery.'

'Oh?'

'A mystery stranger sir. A foreigner. Some cove they found wondering half naked down the coast.'

'Stranger?' Fabian wiped grease from his mouth onto his sleeve. ''alf naked?'

'Aye. He had his trousers and naught much else. And this cove doesn't know what his own name is.'

'Where was he found exactly?' I asked.

'He was found wandering along the beach on Bruny Island, all disorientated.'

'Who found 'im?'

'Whalers sir, they brought him up to Hobart Town this morning.'

'A foreigner you said.'

'Aye. He can't speak English and when they made signs to him like "me Pete who are you," and pointed at each other like, they got naught.'

Fabian finished his tea and savoured the undissolved sugar crystals in the bottom of his mug by draining it slowly into his mouth. 'So,' he finally managed, licking his lips. 'Why bother me with this?'

'Well sir. He was wearing this on his belt.' And Billings handed Fabian a dirk.

'So, 'e carried a knife. So what?'

'Read what's scratched on the handle sir.' I caught Billings' eyes wander over my plate savouring a piece of leftover fried bread. Fabian rolled the bone-handled dagger in the palm of one hand. Suddenly he sat bolt upright. 'Jesus! Where is this man?'

'In the hospital. Dr Bedford was content to have him there at Saint Mary's as long as the governor pays.'

Fabian passed me the weapon. The three-edged blade dagger was twelve inches long, pommel to point, with a bone handle, probably whalebone I surmised. I held it side on and was amazed to read the name of a ship scrimshawed into the bone.

'*Ocean Maiden!*'

'Aye,' Fabian blustered. 'Interestin' huh, my enchanting friend.'

I looked up at Billings. 'Lost his memory you say.'

'Aye.'

'It's a phenomenon known as amnesia,' I said. 'Most commonly caused by head trauma.'

'Aye,' Billings looked attentive. 'The man has a nasty cut down the left side of his head.'

'Where is this Saint Mary's hospital?' I asked.

'In Davey Street at the top of New Wharf.'

'We're best to interview this man immediately,' I jumped to my feet and looked to Fabian.

'Yes, the hospital. Best we go then.' And Fabian swaggered from the mess while I followed, allowing Billings a moment to scoff the bread off my plate.

One way to discover my adopted hometown was certainly to walk it. From the prison entrance we walked at a pace to Bathurst Street where we turned right and passed several tidy homes that would not look out of place in Birmingham. This I found interesting as the slums of Wapping were only a few hundred yards distant. Ahead stood Mount Wellington, a sphinx-like geological monster that dominates the settlement. At the third crossroad we turned left into Elizabeth Street, which sloped pleasantly down towards the wharves of Sullivans Cove. Here we passed several inns and public houses, the Old Bell Inn, The George and Dragon and the Rock Tavern, and Fabian knew them all. Indeed he had patronised every one of them he boasted.

''tis a good town for inns and taverns Caspian,' he grinned as we headed briskly south towards the waterfront. 'In fact when a stranger asks me directions I usually guide them via inns; like I'll say, "walk down Elizabeth Street 'til ya get to the Bull and Mouth, turn left and walk to the Plough and Harrow then walk right until you pass the Crown and Kettle" ... that kind of thing.'

I noticed all the taprooms were doing a good trade as at any singular day hundreds, if not thousands, of sailors from all parts of the globe could be entertained thus. At the bottom of Elizabeth Street we crossed over Macquarie Street – named after an earlier governor Snake was certain – and through a rather overgrown park or garden that delivered us to Davey Street – which Fabian assured me was named after Hobart Town's very first governor. Twenty minutes had lapsed and we finally arrived at the rather handsome sandstone hospital.

Inside was dim and pleasantly cool but I couldn't help wonder how cold and miserable this hospital would be in winter. Groans of discomfort followed us down the corridor and the air was pungent with ammonia and bleach combatting the miasma and sickness. I didn't want to be here.

Snake and I followed Fabian up the steps and down the entrance hall to the first dormitory where we were stopped in our hasty pursuit by an older nurse; a rotund specimen of the female of the species. She had black and grey curly hair that seemed to be attempting to escape from under her nurse's cap. This sat on a particularly disagreeable face adorned with unwanted hair. I couldn't help it notice her white uniform was streaked with blood. Instantly we heard a spine-chilling scream more animal than human.

'We're looking for Dr Bedford,' Fabian said with a measure of authority.

'He's busy.'

'Maybe so, but we are from the constabulary and we need to talk to him. It is a matter of urgency and,' he thought it best to add, 'it is with the governor's bidding.'

'Wait here,' she huffed, and walked off with purpose returning a moment later with a jug of hot water and clean rags. She said nothing to us in passing and hurried to a cot in a dark corner, with a screen half drawn about the bed, where we now realised some poor devil was having his leg amputated.

Another frightful scream was followed by a hollow thud. The three of us looked at each other in disbelief, then back into the vague shadows. The patient's leg had fallen to the floor, and silence followed the sounds of agony as the patient fell unconscious.

'Yes, yes, I'm Dr Bedford,' he said, ushering us to a nearby window for some air. He was a short round man with several chins, a little like the nurse, and I noted he had short legs for his body. He wiped his hands on a bloodied cloth.

'So what is so important that the governor has sent you?' The good doctor seemed impatient and in a hurry to hack off another limb somewhere in this morbid place.

'Dr Bedford,' Fabian started. 'I'm Fabian Winter and this 'ere is Mr Hunter and Constable Snake. You have a patient brought in 'ere this day, a sailor I believe, with loss of memory.'

'Amnesia,' I promptly added wishing us to appear more professional than I feared we seemed.

'Aye, amnesia,' Fabian nodded vigorously.

'Yes,' the doctor said. 'Do you know who he is?'

'No doctor, not at all.'

'When he does try to speak it's all foreign,' the doctor said. 'I haven't got a clue.'

'Oh, that'd be Norwegian,' I said.

'Oh!'

'Yes,' Fabian concurred, 'Norwegian from Norway. We were hoping you may be able to help him regain his memory, soon like, 'cos we believe 'e's off a deserted ship abandoned two day ago in Storm Bay.'

'The *Ocean Maiden*.'

'Aye, ya know 'bout 'er then, sir?'

'Good Lord man, the whole town is talking about her.'

· 'Yes, quite. Ah, we would like to see 'im please, if'n that be alright with the good doctor.'

Immediately we were confronted by the distinct stench of faeces. A nurse had stopped by the window next to us; she was holding a bed pan and seemed quite anxious for the doctor's attention but unfortunately had positioned herself in line with the fresh breeze blowing in from the street.

'What is it?' Dr Bedford asked her curtly.

'Mr Bent's stool doctor,' and she lifted a rag to present the offending turd to the learned doctor. 'There's blood in it and you told me to tell you if ...'

'Yes, yes ... take it away nurse. I'll be up shortly.' The doctor cleared his throat. 'Now where were we?'

'The amnesia patient.'

'Ah yes. You want to see him. I don't see why not. He's settled down somewhat. He was stressed earlier but I've given him some laudanum and he appears content enough for the moment.'

'Laudanum huh?' Fabian seemed to approve. 'Ya can't cure 'im with leeches then?' And Fabian hacked a laugh, but his humour failed sadly.

'No Mr Winter,' the doctor peered over the top of his glasses. 'We cannot cure the man with leeches.'

'We in the medical profession know very little about amnesia Mr Winter,' Dr Bedford told us as we ascended stairs to another ward. 'We have isolated the gentleman until, hopefully, his memory returns.'

'And when could that be?' I asked.

The doctor sighed impatiently, 'And how long is a chain I ask you?'

Hmm, point taken.

'The fact is,' he went on, 'he could regain his memory any time. It *has* happened. Then again he might remember bits and pieces as time goes by. But if he's not cured quickly he will have to be transferred to New Norfolk.'

'New Norfolk!' Fabian seemed horrified.

'What's there?' I asked.

'It's the hospital for the infirm and the insane,' Snake answered for Fabian.

'Yes well,' Dr Bedford pushed the ward door open. 'We're not a charity here you know.'

The patient was tall and slim but not handsome. His most striking feature was his long orange red hair. His head was bandaged from a wound the doctor described as a nasty strike, whether he was attacked by someone or simply fell he couldn't assess. 'But the answer is yes,' the doctor acknowledged, 'the cut was severe enough to cause this rare infliction.'

Fabian was first to approach the patient. He lay back in his cot half asleep, or maybe he was in Laudanum's Land of giant trolls and fairies.

'Sir,' Fabian said. The man jerked awake and looked terrified, digging his heels into the bed to try and sit up. Fabian introduced himself, then us. We approached offering warm friendly smiles.

'Do you remember me?' Dr Bedford asked. The man seemed comforted by the good doctor's presence.

'We are here to help you,' Fabian said loudly enough to be heard in the next ward.

'The man has amnesia Mr Winter, he is not inflicted by deafness.'

'Quite. Ah ... sir. Do you remember anything, anything at all?' Fabian was answered with a vague stare. 'Does the name of the ship *Ocean Maiden* mean anything to you?' The stare intensified. 'Do you remember where you were born, your childhood maybe, the name of your mother? Your father ...' The patient's bottom lip quivered. 'Can you tell me anything about your voyage to Tasmania ... Australia even ...'

And the quivering lip morphed into sobbing and he started talking anxiously in his native tongue. At that same moment a nurse overheard the man in passing. She was attracted by the language and recognised a little of his blabber.

'Oh dear me,' she said. 'The poor man.'

'Yes nurse,' Bedford said. 'Now if you please.' But the nurse said a few words to the man in his language. Whatever he had blabbered he repeated to her.

'What! You understand this man nurse?'

'Just a little, doctor. My Pa was Swedish but he grew up near the border of Norway, at Karlstad, and spoke Norwegian also, which he encouraged us to learn as well. This man is Norwegian.'

'Yes, yes,' the doctor said impatiently. 'But what's he saying?'

'He's distraught; he is asking why he can't remember anything. He is asking why he can't remember his name.' At that moment the man broke down in tears.

'I'll have to ask you to leave gentlemen. You are clearly upsetting the man.' The doctor took Fabian's arm and led him away from the cot. I took this moment to look the patient in the eye and saw nothing but fear and was of the opinion the man had genuinely lost his memory.

'That Dr Bedford had more chins than the Victorian goldfields,' Fabian laughed as we hit the street at a pace returning to the prison. Snake chuckled.

'We can but hope he regains his memory soon,' I said.

'Aye,' Fabian jumped from the path of a speeding buggy. 'Trot!' he yelled at the young buck in the rider's seat. 'Trot you bastard.'

He waited for us to catch up on the other side of Davey Street. 'That Norwegian cove's our only clue to unlock this mystery and if he is sent to New Norfolk it will only hamper the investigation.'

'Where's New Norfolk?' I asked.

'Half a day's ride up the river,' Snake answered.

By the time we arrived back at Campbell Street the hanging was past history. The prisoners had been sent out on work gangs about the township and carpenters were already dismantling the gallows. In a patch of ground outside the prison walls another group of men was busy digging a hole for murderess Rosa Blossom, where her canvas wrapped body would be discarded with several buckets of quick lime. There would be no headstone.

'A penny for ya thoughts Caspian,' Fabian seemed to have hit a brick wall. 'What would you do now, in my position that is?'

'Well I'd be wanting to talk to the whalers who found the sailor wandering along that beach,' I said with pause. 'See what they know. Did he float ashore on jetsam? Swim? What did he say to them when they first saw him?'

'Billings,' Fabian called to the three constables outside our tiny office sitting on barrels amongst the prison stores. Billings stood stiffly and poked his head into the room. 'Sir.'

'The whalers what brought our mystery man to 'obart. Did ya get their details?'

'Aye sir, I put a report on your desk.'

'So ya did lad, good work.' Fabian ran an eye over the paper. 'Tinderbox huh?' he read aloud.

'Aye sir, they were scouring the beach over on the island o' Bruny searching for a new location for a tryworks when they found him wandering aimless like, his head all cut open and bleeding.'

'Benjamin Bane and Polly Jones,' Fabian read from the report. 'Polly Jones?'

'Aye, Mr Bane introduced her as his half sister but ya couldn't half tell he was rogering her sir.'

'How's that?'

'Well I caught him pinching her on the arse sir.' And Billings winked like the dirty uncle at a wedding.

'Quite the detective, aren't you Billings?' Fabian grinned and called for the others. 'Hal, Jasper.'

'Sir.'

'Take two horses from the stables. I want you to ride to Tinderbox. Question the boatmen there. Here, copy these details into your notebooks.' And he handed Hal the report. 'It's just past ten. I want ya back 'ere by six, it's Wednesday and Sally's workin' the taproom at the Derwent Chop'ouse tonight and ya know what that means.'

'Boy-oh-boy,' the gatekeeper, a man they call The Priest, pushed into our humble office unannounced. 'You buggers are in real demand today.' The Priest had a frustratingly slow drawl and a limp displaying early signs of gout.

'Ah The Priest,' Fabian made to light his pipe, took a side-glance at me, and threw it back to the desk. 'What 'ave ya got for us?' This 'ere ghost ship's a real mystery.'

'No matey, that's yesterdee's news,' he stopped and stretched his back with a groan. 'You've another problem.'

'What?' We both sat up.

'Ex transport man, ah what's 'is name now ... can't think ... Jesus ...'

'Christ does it matter?' Fabian grew impatient. 'What's the problem?'

'Osmond McGregor. Aye. Thart's it. Osmond McGregor.'

'Yes ... and?'

''e's at yon gate. 'e says 'is young'uns found a body on the mount near 'is cottage.'

'A body?'

'Aye. Body of a woman. Nasty 'e says. Stabbed wiv a pitchfork 'e told me.'

Fabian turned to face me with an inappropriate grin. 'You attract business my friend,' he said, as the gatekeeper hobbled away.

'Why do you call him The Priest?' I asked Fabian as we slipped back into our coats.

'Because,' Fabian said with a smile, 'people caught in the lockup are often filled with the desire to confess to their sins when in his company.'

Violet and William McGregor were sister and brother three years apart. Ten-year-old Violet loved her little brother and above all else she loved fairy tales. And Hansel and Gretel was a favourite. The children came from a family afflicted by poverty. Their father, Osmond McGregor, was a transportee; that is he was a convicted felon sent to Van Diemen's Land in 1833 for stealing a sheep to feed his siblings. He was seventeen at the time. He told me he served his seven-year sentence, some of it at the then new prison called Port Arthur and was finally given his ticket of leave in 1840. The following year he was pardoned and he married his sweetheart, Molly Kelly, in 1843. Violet was born two years later and William joined the family in 1848.

I liked the McGregors. They were hard-working, non-drinking, god-fearing people trying hard to make a go of what was an endless battle for survival. Osmond told me he worked for Charles Tibbs, a potter in Goulbourn Street, throwing pots on the potter's wheel. But he only managed three days a week for five shillings. Times were tough.

But it is of the children I must now relate.

This morning, near the source of the Hobart Town rivulet where the town's water supply runs down the valley from the mountain, Violet was playing out her fantasy with brother William in tow. They were in search of the gingerbread house that they had been told was hidden somewhere amongst the foothills of Mount Wellington.

I should explain here that the McGregor's humble cottage, of bark, wattle and daub, is situated on the western extremities of Hobart Town near the mountain. Nearby is the Cascade sawmill and brewery where the aroma of the steam from the boiling hops is ever present in the area, about which, I would like to add, Fabian commented favourably.

Violet told me she left a trail of stale breadcrumbs – like in the fairy tale – as they walked along a track parallel with the rivulet. The breadcrumbs, she told William, were so they could find their way home. But William wasn't so gullible. He knew exactly where home was, and besides Mangy the mongrel hound was eating the bread as fast as Violet dropped it.

A quarter of a mile further up the creek the children came to a clearing. Ravens circled overhead, diving momentarily and cawing noisily. It seemed to Violet that some birds were keeping vigilance while others fed off carrion below. Carrion wasn't an uncommon sight.

Mangy barked madly and romped ahead on her long hunter's legs and instantly a dozen coal black birds, their beaks trailing intestines, escaped in a disorderly flurry.

Violet ran into the bushes after the dog. 'What is it sis?' William chased after her. But what the children witnessed that morning would haunt them for the rest of their lives.

'I do believe,' I told Fabian at the crime scene, 'that some time in the future there will be a science called forensics and it will be run by specially trained police constables.'

'Poppycock.' He didn't want a bar of it. 'Good old fashioned police work is all ya need to stay ahead o' the villains.'

'But you agree with my suggestion that we employ the services of a portrait image maker, to record the evidence for our record and to use in the courtroom.'

'Aye, I've already told ya,' Fabian shooed flies from the victim. 'There's a portrait studio in Collins Street I seen in passing. And providin' they are economic and frugal with what I'm told can be expensive materials I'll authorise it.'

I found the photographic image studio of Royle Rowley on the first floor above Mrs Jessie Adkin's Tea Rooms in Collins Street. The modest studio consisted of delightful carvers and slightly dated mahogany bergere chairs covered with red cloth upholstery. These were used for posing the subjects to have their images taken, along with various pedestals supporting indoor plants. Roman Ionic columns, made of wood by a local carpenter I would discover, framed the stage. A fine selection of theatrical style painted canvas backdrops – of gardens and old ruins – hung on the walls. I was met at the top of the stairs by a handsome woman in her forties wearing a cream cotton morning dress with red printed sprigs. The buttoned bodice was high and I saw hints that it was lined with ivory cotton.

'Good morning,' she said displaying perfect teeth and an affable smile.

'Good morning,' I answered returning the friendly greeting.

'How can I be of service to you?'

'Ah, I'm hoping to see Mr Rowley.'

'Huh!' she laughed. The woman *actually* laughed in my face. 'Oh dear,' she quickly composed herself. 'I didn't mean to be so rude.' Her smile softened any embarrassment or irritation I felt. 'No offence sir?'

'None taken madam,' and I proceeded to look about for her employer or her husband, maybe.

'You see I am Rowley!' she said. 'My name is Royle Rowley.'

'Oh gracious me,' I replied, 'I feel such a dullard.' And I meant it. 'I am so sorry … ah … my name's Caspian Hunter, I'm an officer with the recently formed constabulary at the Prisoners Barracks.'

'I see,' she offered a forgiving smile. 'So let us start again shall we. How can I be of service to you Mr Hunter?'

I explained how it was my suggestion to keep a photographic image record of crime scenes at the office, to help us with our enquiries and for evidence in upcoming trials. Mrs Rowley listened intently.

'The prison at Port Arthur is talking about making a photographic record of the prisoners instead of written records,' I continued convincingly. 'So if a villain has a wart on his nose we'll have an image of that wart on said nose instead of a remark on his file that simply reads "Wart on nose".'

For that comment I earned another pearly-toothed smile. 'So you want me to use my equipment then?'

'Well if you'll forgive me madam ...'

'Please call me Royle. Madam sounds so, so formal does it not?'

'Thank you, Royle. But I would never have asked a woman to take images of crime scenes. I mean, well ...' I paused, fishing for the right words.

'Because it's man's work!'

'Yes exactly,' I hurriedly accepted the suggestion.

'Nonsense Caspian.' And the smile vanished. 'I've travelled alone since my husband was killed at the Crimea Peninsula in '53. I sailed to Van Diemen's Land to forget, and opened this business. I bought the equipment from a French explorer I met in Sydney Town a year ago. I've seen my share of death.' She walked to her image-maker standing on a wooden tripod in the centre of the studio. 'It's an expensive business, this image taking. I trust your prison revenue will allow for such expenditure.'

'Well yes mada ... Royle.'

'Sit,' she ordered.

'Sit?'

'Yes, in that chair.' And Royle pointed to the red upholstered chair. I did as she bade. 'Now look regal.'

'Regal?' I smiled.

'Don't smile,' Royle chided. She slid what she called a dark slide into the rear of the wooden image-making box. Next she placed a photographic plate into the rear of the box and removed the dark slide. She walked to the drapes pulling them back fully, allowing extra light to pour into the room. Back at the box she removed a cover over the lens. 'Do-not-move,' she said sternly. I wouldn't dare. She counted silently for several seconds then replaced the lens cover.

'You can relax now Caspian.' The white teeth were on display once more. Royle disappeared for a moment into what she said was her dark room where she would process my portrait. As she withdrew I discreetly took advantage of the moment to appreciate her curvaceous figure. I think she noticed. A little later Royle returned.

'You make a handsome portrait, Caspian,' she said. 'Had her voice become husky?' I asked myself. 'Was this arousing woman trifling with my feelings?'

'I ... ah ... I'm mostly flattered ... I mean I'm ... thank you for the compliment ... ah ...'

'Royle,' she purred, finishing my garbled sentence.

'R-Royle,' I stuttered, 'I'm flattered indeed. When can I see the image?'

'It needs to dry. An hour maybe.'

I stood with my hat held at the front of my buttoned britches in case I embarrassed myself. She stepped in closer. 'So when would you like to have me?'

'Pardon?' I stepped aside rather hastily and bowled over one of the Roman pillars, which she was able to leap forward and catch bringing us even closer together.

'Are you alright Caspian?' she was suddenly concerned.

'Y-Yes fine. I need you to come immediately really. Is that an inconvenience?'

'I think not. But I'll need assistance to carry my equipment.'

'I'll return with a constable and a horse and trap. The crime scene is at the foot of the mountain, some distance yonder.' And I nodded to the wall that I thought most likely faced Mount Wellington. 'In one hour then?'

'One hour,' she agreed. 'Au revoir Caspian Hunter.'

I hurried down the stairs like a choirboy escaping the vestry and stepped out onto the pavement.

'Caspian!'

'Elizabeth. What are you doing here? Oh, I'm sorry, I meant, fancy meeting you here ... here of all places,' and I waved a hand at Mrs Jessie Adkin's Tearoom window where beyond the glass one could see dozens of fashion conscious women of Hobart Town supping on tea and cake.

'I'm here for tea and cake. I'm meeting my friend Penelope. Would you care to join us?'

'Ah, I'd love to actually, but I have work to do. Something dastardly has happened.'

'Dastardly?'

'Yes.'

'What may I ask?'

I thought a moment. 'Well my guess is that you will hear of it sooner or later. A terrible murder has occurred. A pregnant woman, young, early twenties, on the mountain.'

'The mountain? Who?' Elizabeth had turned pale.

'I don't know her name at this stage. The body has been moved to the morgue and I'm here to engage the services of Mrs Royle Rowley and her imagery machine to record the murder site.'

'Early twenties, pregnant ... oh dear, I hope I don't know her.' Penelope appeared around the corner and waved. 'Caspian,' Elizabeth lowered her voice. 'Promise me you'll visit later and fill me in. I want to know all the details.'

'But ...' I was blithering once more. 'It was such a brutal murder ...'

'Oh gracious me Caspian, I live at a prison do I not. Have I not seen some dastardly things?'

Reliable as always, I met Mrs Royle Rowley at her studio an hour later. I had with me Billings who had secured a prison horse and trap to convey the imagery apparatus to the crime scene and hurried up the stairs leaving Billings to watch our equipment.

'Caspian,' she purred as I entered. 'Your image is dry, come see.' And she took my hand and led me to the dark room. I had just noticed the cleavage in her ample bosom was slightly exposed when she pushed me hard against the wall and planted a lustful wet kiss upon my shocked lips.

'Oh sweet boy,' she gushed. 'You can have me ... NOW!' And she kissed me once more taking my hand and placing it between her legs.

'Oh Mother Mary sweet Jesus,' I gushed. She took me in *her* hand and I've got to say for the record, I was as hard as a rigger's fid. I thought the buttons on my britches were about to pop like corks in ginger beer bottles. With her tresses and layers of cotton raised high and her bloomers low our lustful fornication was short-lived.

'You coming sir?'

Bugger! Billings was calling out from the top of the stair. Maybe we had been a tad longer than I intended.

'Mr Hunter? Caspian?'

'Yes yes, coming.'

With the trap loaded I had a brief opportunity to tackle the delicate subject with Billings on the street. 'Not a word,' I growled. 'Not-one-damned-word. You hear me?'

'Aye sir. It's naught a problem. Mum's the word sir.'

'Fine.'

'A man's gotta do what a man's gotta do sir, you bein' at sea all them months like.'

'Enough Billings!'

Suddenly the soft voice of a woman behind me, 'What's a man got to do?'

'Miss Mead, Elizabeth!' I gasped. 'You crept up on me again.'

'Crept, Caspian?'

'Please excuse me. You … ah … *surprised* me for the second time this day.' She was immediately joined by another gorgeous creature from the tearoom. 'Ah, you must be Miss Penelope,' I said.

'Why yes,' the gorgeous creature smiled back. More white teeth. 'Have you been talking about me Elizabeth, behind my back maybe, to handsome gentlemen no less?' Penelope offered me the back of her kid glove.

I lightly caressed my lips to her glove. 'Enchanté,' I said, but not wishing to overdo things in Elizabeth's presence I kept my delivery neutral.

'The pleasure is all mine,' she answered.

'Come along then Penelope,' Elizabeth was a hint haughty. 'We must make it to Mather's Drapery before all the best oriental silks off the *Peking Trader* are sold.'

Billings and I watched the derrières wriggle down Collins Street. Our eyes met and I don't think a hurricane at sea could have wiped the grin off his wrinkled tanned face.

'So can I see your portrait then sir?' he said in an attempt to change the subject.

'What?'

'The portrait of you. The portrait made by Mrs Rowley.'

'Oh, yes of course.' I took my portrait from my frock coat pocket and had the opportunity to admire the three-inch by four-inch image for the first time myself.

'Marvellous sir. Quite dashing,' he complimented. 'If'n ya don't mind me saying so. No wonder the ladies of this fair isle wish for your company.'

Once back at the crime scene I was pleased to see the ground seemed undisturbed. Word of the murder hadn't reached the ears of the public in general as yet and no ghouls had been attracted to the site.

'Ah Royle! Um Mrs Rowley. Careful where you tread,' I called out, as the studio owner was about to drag her hem through the victim's blood, which still pooled about in a large thick puddle.

'Oh! Is that what I think it is?'

'Aye madam,' Billings stood at the perimeter with her imagery box and tripod. 'Where would you like this then?'

'Where you're standing would be fine thank you.'

It was then I noticed something I hadn't seen earlier. There were cartwheel tracks in the clayey earth. As I looked more closely I noted one was neater and smoother than the other. 'Billings,' I called out. 'Observe this.' We studied the tracks a minute. The clay had recorded a perfect image of the wheels.

'What's that say to you?' I asked him.

'It looks to me sir, like the left wheel of a two-wheel buggy has gone and lost its iron hoop.'

'That's exactly what I thought. Mrs Rowley, an image of this if you please.'

'Certainly *Mr* Hunter.' And our exchanged flirtatious glances didn't go unnoticed by Billings.

'How many images can we make?' I asked.

'Well I charge a shilling each so it's up to you and your allowance from the prison purse.'

Suddenly the most god-awful sound penetrated from the thick bushland.

'What on earth's that?' I said standing rigidly, shocked.

Billings cocked an ear. 'I think ya will find it's bagpipes sir.'

'Bagpipes! Sounds like someone strangling a cat.'

'Aye. 'tis not played well, that's for certain.'

Immediately Osmond McGregor pressed past wild blackberry bushes and entered the clearing. 'Dear god McGregor,' I called over the racket. 'What on earth are you doing?'

'Playin' tha pipes sar,' and he smacked his lips exposing several missing teeth.

'I can see that. Don't you think it's slightly inappropriate, given the sensitivity surrounding us?'

'Naw, naught a' all sar,' he answered as his instrument farted its last breath. Suddenly he spotted Billings. 'Billings ya bastart!' Then he noticed Mrs Rowley and doffed his hat. 'Ma'am.'

I looked at Royle and she seemed amused not offended.

'You know Mr McGregor?' I asked Billings.

'Aye. We were at Arthur together.'

'Port Arthur?'

'Aye.'

'Aboot '43 to '50,' McGregor acknowledged. 'Them was sad years, that's to be sure. But Billings and me, we was canny eh, we got through it, eh laddie?'

'Well I'm pleased to hear,' I said. 'All the same ... the pipes?'

'Well I thought, sar, it might scare orf the evil spirits like.'

'Evil spirits?'

'Aye. Being that dead cat 'anging in yonder tree.'

'Dead cat? Where?'

Nearby, what could only be described as a sacrifice I hadn't noticed earlier, a skun cat hung by its back legs in a tree.'

'Oh dear Lord. Now what?'

'Witchcraft sar. That lass with wee bairn was some sort o' witch's work.'

'Nonsense,' I snapped, maybe a little too vexed. McGregor responded by puffing out his cheeks.

'Right then. So if you please Mrs Rowley, would you kindly make images of ... that,' and I pointed a finger at the offending feline corpse. 'And the wheel marks and the ground where the body was found.'

Instantly something caught my eye half hidden by rotting leaves and foliage. 'Good heavens,' I said. 'What's that?'

We all stooped over what could only be described as a yard long cylindrical brass object. Billings tried to lift it but it was too heavy for one person.

'Looks like some kind of chim-inney sir, with a tank attached.' Billings said.

'Strange,' I muttered, more to myself than anyone present. The cartwheel tracks had clearly trundled over the area so it appeared to have been dumped. 'Would you kindly make an image of that also Mrs Rowley. Billings, you make certain the area is scoured well and all evidence collected.'

'Aye sir.'

'The victim was a woman with child I heard Mr McGregor say?' Royle asked, looking a little paler than when she first arrived.

'Yes Madam. And as soon as we finish here we will make for the morgue to secure a portrait of her body for the record.'

The morgue was in the basement of Dr Bedford's hospital. Until recently, Billings told me, inquests were held at inns where the body would reside in the stables or outhouse for identification. But following in the footsteps of Mother England, Hobart Town now had its very own new morgue. But on approaching, I had to admit, it smelt anything but new. Dr Bedford handed each of us a small cloth doused in perfume that, when blended with the putrefaction, made one feel slightly nauseous. He led us, puffing and panting as we followed his blubbery body down into the hospital cellars.

There were three bodies stored here this day. One, already embalmed, was the body of the young self-murder victim from Wapping. He lay on a wooden trestle looking like an Egyptian mummy I had seen in the British Museum. The second was an elderly gent who had died of loss of mind, Dr Bedford told us. He was well into his seventies and his body bloated with gases. I think he was the one I smelt when walking the long dark corridors to the morgue. As no one had been in the cellars for several hours Dr Bedford had to fumble about in the darkness. He located the wall spirit lamps and lit them with a self-igniting match. I had a quiet chuckle to myself as the lamps flared from all the methane leaking from the cadavers.

Our murder victim lay on the coroner's slab; a sandstone bed with a sluiceway carved into the stone around its entire perimeter to drain blood and other body fluids. A leather bucket, half full of a blackish substance, lay on the floor. Now I knew from where the occasional sound of a drip originated.

'We have a name Mr Hunter,' Dr Bedford said without reverence. He'd seen too much death so I forgave him his indiscretion.

''Oh, that was quick,' I said through my perfumed cloth.

'Yes. Quick … and sad.'

I looked him in the eye but only saw those layered chins. 'Sad? Why so?'

'One of my nurses recognised her when your constables brought her in.'

'And?'

'She is Miss Edith Verity Philpot.'

I heard Billings suck air through his teeth. 'You knew her Billings?'

'Aye … I know … ah knew of 'er sir. She's the daughter of Lord Marmaduke Philpot, the shipping magnate.

'You said *Miss*, doctor.'

'Yes I did.' He knew exactly what I was thinking. I looked to the corpse. The naked body had been covered respectfully in the right places but the sheet over her groin did nothing to hide the savagery we had witnessed when we first visited the crime scene. The poor lass had been pregnant and I wondered if her father knew his unwed daughter was with child. The twenty-or-so-week-old foetus had been dissected from the womb and placed between her legs, with the umbilical cord still attached. She had been brutally beaten, her once pretty face blue with bruises and her long blonde hair matted with mud and her own blood. She had been stabbed in the chest with a pitchfork, the weapon still pinning her to the ground when we found her. Her right cheek was flattened and a boot print was evident in the blood, as if the murderer had stood on her to extract the pitchfork for his second and third thrusts.

'How long had she lain there doctor?' I asked.

'I'd say she was murdered on Sunday, but maybe as late as the evening.'

I heard Royle quietly sob as Dr Bedford held a lamp over the body so we could examine her more carefully.

'Come Mrs Rowley,' I said softly. 'Let us make the photograph and leave this place.

The Derwent Chophouse was wedged in between the postal office and other administration buildings on the west side, waterfront end, of Elizabeth Street. When I arrived at half past six of the clock hansom cabs were lined up out front awaiting business and the Chophouse itself was packed with noisy hungry revellers, a good sign that the vittles were exceptional. Immediately the aromas of slow cooking pork and the agreeable smoke of grilling lamb on the bone dashed any lingering odours from the morgue and I realised just how hungry I was.

'Caspian!' I heard my name yelled across the room by the now familiar voice of Fabian. He flashed a grin at me. He had secured a table in a corner and was already joined by Snake, Billings, Jasper and ... Hal, who scowled at me like I had imprisoned his mother. I literally had to push and shove through a mixed crowd of locals, professional people, sailors and tradespeople. 'What a wonderful place,' I told myself. I had only just arrived at the table, where a spare chair awaited me, when a quart of porter was pushed towards me by a lustful wench of generous proportions.

''ere ya go luvvy, get that in ya hard workin' guts.' And the woman roared with laughter encouraged by all around her.

'Meet Sally, Caspy,' and Fabian slapped the woman's backside. He puffed on a long thin cheroot and smoke curled around him. 'Oh dear,' I thought, 'he called me Caspy. 'I hate Caspy. My aunties back in Birmingham called me Caspy.'

Sally sported long blonde hair and a heaving bosom with the arms of a mud wrestler. And what shoulders! She carried a tray with ease, holding several quart tankards and I couldn't help notice she was an attractive large buxom woman who maintained her pleasant feminine form. Her wide blue eyes sparkled and it was clear the woman enjoyed her work.

'Caspian, sit,' Fabian ordered, his hand sliding up and down Sally's derriere. I waved smoke out of my face while Fabian ignored my displeasure.

'What are ya goin' to 'ave Caspy, pig or sheep?' the wench asked, flashing her eyes at me like a moonlighter's lantern.

I must have floundered, as Fabian answered for me. 'Give 'im a bit o' each Sal, the lad looks like 'e's got a bit of a tooth on 'im.' The table laughed at my expense. 'Ya see Caspy, the Chop'ouse does soup, bread, meat, tatties, turnips and swede all fa one shillin' and sixpence. So ya may as well tuck in.'

'Fine,' I said. I was hungry after all. 'Have you ordered your food already?' I asked.

'Aye.'

'Pig and sheep cummin' up lads,' and Sally shoved through the crowd without apology.

'Wha'dya reckon Caspian?' Fabian stabbed me with his elbow as I sat next to him. 'Bit of alright ain't she?'

'I don't know what to say Fabian. She's certainly friendly enough.'

'Aye, very friendly. And I 'eard a whisper that you 'aven't been wasting ya time neither Mr *Hunt*-ter.' More laughs at my expense. I glared down the table at Billings who suddenly appeared to be preoccupied by a moth flapping about an overhead lamp.

'So how did the enquiry go at Tinderbox?' I asked Hal and Jasper, trying to bring the conversation back from the bilge.

'Nothing sir,' Jasper started. 'We talked to the whalers wha' found 'im wanderin' the beach and they did say 'e told them 'e swam ashore.'

'What Jasper means,' Hal interrupted, 'is the cove couldn't speak English, 'e's Norwegian see.'

'Yes we knew that.'

'Well 'e sort of mimed swimmin' with 'is arms like.'

'I see, well that makes sense. Is it far?' I asked. 'I mean where did he swim from?'

'We couldn't find out sir,' Jasper said, 'but the thing is if 'e did jump overboard from the *Ocean Maiden,* where you seen 'er driftin' like, it would be about three mile by our reckonin.'

'That's what the whalers say any'ow,' Hal added, staring at me with a sour face. Maybe I did imprison his mother!

'Yes, well he looked a strong man,' I recalled.

Fabian tore his eyes away from Sally behind the bar long enough to change the subject. 'So more importantly, wha' the bleedin' 'ell happened to Miss Edith Verity Philpot?'

The whole table groaned in feigned sympathy for the victim and then all took a long thoughtful tug at their tankards.

Snake spoke first. 'Poor lass.'

'Aye.'

'Aye.'

'And she 'ad a wee bairn on board.'

'Has her father been informed as yet?' I asked.

'He's not due back 'til tomorra,' Fabian said sombrely. ''e's sailin'' back from Melbourne in his own ship the *Buckingham*. Snake 'ere enquired with 'is office.' Fabian looked contemplative for a moment. 'Caspian,' he said. 'The Governor wants to see us tomorrow at eight. That's eight of the clock in the morning.'

'Oh.'

'Aye. It's not good lad. The gov'nor and 'is Lordship Marmaduke Philpot go back a ways, they was partners in Adelaide.'

'More than that,' Snake added biting a nail free, 'They's friends. Good firkin' friends.'

''ere we go,' Sally was back shoving others aside so she could place a huge tray of food at one end of our table. 'Pig and sheep, sheep and pig. Hoink, baaaaa … pig in lads.'

'Where's our soup?' Hal grumbled.

'Forget the soup,' Sally thundered. 'I got ya extra meat so shut ya gob and bury ya snout in that trough.'

No sooner had we started eating – and what a feast it was – when I spotted Captain Durward Slade, from the *Georgette,* walk into the Chophouse from off the street. He looked about, saw our table, and proceeded to push across to us.

'Caspian,' he nodded, friendly enough.

'Captain Slade. Ah … this is the captain who brought me to Tasmania everybody. Captain Slade.' The four constables looked up in unison, clearly uninterested. They grunted in concert and bowed their heads back to their plates – in unison.

'You must be Mr Winter,' Slade said, looking directly at Fabian.

'Aye, pleased to make ya acquaintance cap'n,' they exchanged greetings.

'May I …' he indicated a place at the table.

'Aye.'

'But I'll not be staying as I'm expected in the dining room of the Lord Rodney.'

I dragged a spare chair across from the next table. Slade sat, annoyingly with his back turned slightly towards me.

'Mr Winter,' he started.

'Fabian.'

'Fabian. I'll be straightforward and blunt with you. This *Ocean Maiden* sir should now be my property, after all I salvaged her and sailed her to Hobart Town, correct?'

'Aye, that's correct.'

'And her cargo, now taken to the Bond Store, that should be mine too, correct?'

'Yes captain, that's the rule o' the sea as the law stands. Finders keepers as they say.'

'Well now I'm told some charlatan foreign sailor has turned up but he can't remember if he's off the *Ocean Maiden* or not.'

'Charlatan! The man 'as amnesia Cap'n Slade, and hopefully 'e will recover 'is memory and solve this 'ere damned mystery.'

'So you're saying I have to wait, months, maybe years before I can make my claim.'

'Aye captain,' Fabian said to Slade waving a chop at him. 'That's exactly what you must do.'

'But the ship was deserted, abandoned on the high sea. I found her. She's rightfully mine.'

'That's the way it has to be, now if ya don't mind cap'n, me dinner's gettin' cold.'

'Bah!' Captain Slade stormed from the Chophouse an unhappy man, a very unhappy man indeed.

It was dark by the time we left the Chophouse. One shilling and sixpence for dinner and four shilling each for drinks.

'It's only early lads. I'm goin' to the White 'orse for a nightcap?' Fabian stood on the pavement, hands on hips, while we all watched the lamp lighter with some interest as the man lit the oil lamp with a burning taper on the end of a long pole. ''ow many firkin' whales do ya reckon we need to light this 'ere town then,' Fabian had a philosophical moment.

The lamplighter regarded Fabian for a moment. 'Ya won't 'ave to fret over no whales soon sonny,' he said. 'It'll all be gas soon.'

'Aye.' Fabian threw an arm around my shoulder. 'You may 'ave seen the chimney they're workin' on down Wapping ... that tall firker ... well that's where the gas'll come from.'

'Gas'll come from out of 'is arse more like,' I overheard Hal whisper to Jasper. Both men chuckled. 'At least Hal had a sense of humour,' I surmised.

'Now Caspy … to the White 'orse.'

It was more an order than an invite. Two nights in a row. I moaned inwardly, these colonials worked hard and played hard.

Six minutes later at the White Horse Tavern, 'Six quarts o' ya best porter Lloyd,' Fabian bawled over the crowd the moment we entered.

The Labour in Vain Inn followed. 'I love this place,' Fabian roared as we crashed through the door into the taproom like a lynch mob after the barrel. 'Did ya shee the firkin' shine out front?' Fabian's speech was deteriorating. So was his language. I *had* noticed the sign as it turned out. Between the words *Labour in Vain Inn* was a painting of a white woman washing a black baby. 'She's tryin' to wash the bairn white, can ya believe it, firkin' hypocrites!'

Fabian swivelled about the busy bar looking for someone. 'Uh-hah! There 'e is.' And Fabian barged between drinkers spilling tankards and causing a kerfuffle.

'King Billy ya old bastard!' And Fabian threw his arm around a man who I could only imagine was an indigenous islander. The lads followed and I felt obliged to do the same.

'Come 'ere come 'ere,' Fabian was clearly excited. He grabbed me by the shoulder and pulled me close. 'Thish 'ere black devil is an ol' mate. King Billy. 'e's real name ish William Lanney and Christ knows what 'is native name is but I'm reckonin' 'e likes to be called King firkin' Billy, eh my friend.'

The Aboriginal nodded and smiled warmly. He had a pleasant round face under thick tightly cropped black hair and someone said he was twenty but he looked a lot older.

'Works the whalers 'e does,' Fabian slapped a palm on the counter. 'Seven quarts Vernon,' he yelled across the noisy room at the barman.

The Steam Navigation Hotel wasn't as busy so we downed a hasty quart each, bid farewell to the owner Ernest and ploughed onto the George and Dragon where innkeeper Baldwin treated Fabian like a long lost friend. Barton at the White Hart Inn was less friendly however, only because, Snake warned me, the publican caught Fabian up to mischief with his wife in the washhouse a week earlier.

'I wash doin' 'er a f-favour,' Fabian assured us by the time we crashed the bar at the Black Prince. I was starting to slur myself and things only became worse when Billings returned to our table at the Bull and Mouth with six gins on the house from Dwayne who was keen to do the constabulary a favour while the innkeeper was away for the night.

'Thish is Jennifer ... ah Geneva ... I 'ope,' hiccup, 'Bill-Billings,' Fabian garbled.

'Aye sir, only the best from Dwayne thar.'

Happenings are a little vague after the Old Bell where Marty Brigham the innkeeper decided to join us on the Geneva. He closed his doors at two of the clock in the morning, thereabouts, and I seem to remember seeing Hal, Billings and Jasper in a disorderly line urinating on a shop window before we wobbled clumsily arm in arm into the Crown and Kettle, where I watched Fabian's eyes cross over just prior to me missing my chair as I sat.

Day Six – Wednesday

Eight o'clock of the morning. Government House,
Hobart Town waterfront.

FABIAN TOOK SMALL STEPS. CAREFULLY, ONE FOOT in front of the other and one foot at a time. He was still inebriated and with each tread his head thumped. I was no better. We passed the guard at Government House gates – a neat, refreshed and attentive lad of eighteen – with groans of self-pity.

Fabian and I sat in the anteroom outside Governor Henry Fox Young's office. The room was deadly quiet except for the incessant monotonous tick tock from the long case clock near the door.

Tick tock tick tock …

It chimed quarter past the hour of eight. The governor was late. *Suit me if he never showed.* I looked to Fabian. He was leaning forward, his elbows planted on his legs with his face in his hands. I'm certain I heard a moan. If it was any consolation I knew the man felt worse than I did.

'Never again,' I muttered, the words inaudible and pasty as my mouth felt like the inside of a night cart driver's sock. 'I'm never drinking again.'

Another groan.

I took a moment to look about my surroundings, hoping some brain activity would help me regain some sobriety. I knew the house had been built by Governor Macquarie nearly forty years earlier in 1817. Fabian had told me the two-storey residence was fourteen rooms of badly built brick, wood and stucco and as I sat fighting my suffering I could appreciate the building was in disrepair and how the new colony desperately needed the new mansion, now being erected on the Queen's Domain.

Suddenly heavy boot steps on the oak floorboards and the voice of Mr Samuel Wheaton, governor's secretary, took our minds from our wretchedness. He was a tall but scrawny, insipid man with sunken dark and narrow eyes perched too close together for my liking. His clean-shaven lower face divided two long thick disorderly grey side-burns that terminated inches below the point of his chin with receding hair swept to one side in a vain attempt to hide his pate.

'Ah, Mr Hunter,' he singled me out from across the room. 'I would like to apologise once more for not meeting you earlier, but we will catch up soon.' I stood and nodded.

'Mr Winter. Mr Hunter,' his aristocratic voice resonating off the plastered walls with a subtle hint of superiority.

'Aye!' Fabian stood groggily, struggling to focus on the older gentleman through his blood red eyes. I didn't fare much better and had the foresight to avoid eye contact.

'His Excellency is ready to see you now. This way gentlemen,' and Wheaton's nose twitched and I had the distinct impression that the anteroom smelt like a brewery.

'Gracious me,' the governor sat back in his handsomely carved desk chair. The man was a picture of good health and spritely for this early hour. *Wretch!* 'You both look positively scandalous.'

We stood before his desk, hands behind our backs, while he scrutinised our attire, hooking his thumbs behind braces under the charcoal grey waistcoat of his immaculate three piece suit.

'You look like you've had a hard night at it and slept in your clothes!' He seemed quite shocked peering at us over the top of wire rim reading glasses. And he wasn't far wrong.

'We've been awful busy of late Your Excellency,' Fabian said and even *I* caught a whiff of his breath. 'Workin' long hours like, with the *Ocean Maiden,* now this 'ere young lass being brutally slaughtered.' Fabian nodded to Royle Rowley's images on the governor's desk. *Good.* Royle had delivered them last evening as I had instructed.

'Yes quite,' the governor scattered the cards about and was clearly sickened by the one of Miss Philpot's body, the silver grey image seeming ghostlike.

'No words can describe how sickened I am gentlemen …' and he paused a moment battling to find a suitable word. 'Sickened. The animal that did this *must* be brought to justice and hanged.'

'Aye sir,' Fabian managed. ''anging's too good for the swine.'

'Nevertheless a hanging is what he'll get.'

'May I enquire, Your Excellency,' I asked, 'when His Lordship, Mr Philpot is due to arrive back in Hobart Town?'

'Some time this day, he sails from Melbourne on his ship the *Buckingham*. He has business interests in the goldfields of Victoria.' The governor pushed his chair back noisily and walked to the window. 'This is a monstrous business,' His Excellency said quietly. 'Monstrous. I know His Lordship well; we've been friends since Adelaide when I was governor there. I've known Miss Philpot since she was twelve. Delightful child, heart of gold, never hurt a fly, now ... now this.'

'Shocking sir.'

'Lord knows how Marmaduke ... ah, His Lordship will take this.' Instantly the mood changed and the governor swung about to face us. 'I want this ... this murderer caught quickly. He is to be brought to justice smartly. I will have words with the magistrates and judge. He is to be hanged without delay.'

'Sir,' I ventured.

'Yes?'

'What of the ... ah ...'

'Ah what man? Spit it out!'

'She was with child Your Excellency.'

'Do you think I'm not aware of that?'

'No sir, not what I meant. But ...'

'But nothing, Mr Hunter, that is to be kept quiet at all costs. His Lordship couldn't possibly have known.'

'So who will ... ah ... break the news like?' Fabian asked.

The governor looked at the polished floorboards. His shiny-toed shoes shifted anxiously and his voice dropped to a whisper. 'That will be my severe duty Mr Winter. Leave that to me. And for God's sake keep the matter of the child a secret.'

'One more thing sir,' I enquired.

'What is that, Caspian.'

'Do we know who the father of the child is?'

'Oh for God's sake!'

'Well he could be part of the answer to this crime sir,' I persisted.

'Then the answer, I'm afraid, is no. I thought her a woman of virtue, I had no idea she was a woman of the world. His Lordship will be devastated to hear otherwise.' The governor looked us in the eye, individually. 'You *must* find this animal gentlemen, you *must*.' His eye cast over the images once more. 'Kindly take those with you.'

I collected up the images, which I shuffled into a neat pack and said, 'We will have to ask His Lordship questions sir.'

'No! I mean ... well not immediately, give the man a chance to mourn his loss.'

'Sir,' I pressed on. 'In all my experiences back in Birmingham I always found it prudent to move quickly. The first days are crucial. The murderer could still be amongst us.'

There followed a heavy sigh of defeat. 'Very well, but wait until this evening. Give me a chance to explain the procedure to His Lord-ship.'

Back at the prison Snake and the other three weren't faring any better. They stood huddled about a potbelly stove in the store each handling a mug of thick, black, stewed coffee heaped with sugar. Fabian wiped dregs from two spare mugs and poured coffee for us both.

'Whose idea was it to paint the town red?' he finally grumbled.

'Actually it was your idea sir,' Billings eyes were redder than most.

'Aye,' Fabian managed a chuckle. 'I think ya right. Argh! But it was a merry time what we 'ad eh lads?'

'And how was Mrs Winter this morning?' Snake asked.

'Now that be a subject we need not talk about Mr Snake.'

'You're married?' I asked Fabian, incredulous.

'Aye, ya not know that lad?'

'Ah, no,' and I had flashes of Fabian's hand rubbing the generous backside of Sally the wench at the Chophouse.

'Well it be true, married six years now, got a bairn at two years and a girl five,' Fabian said flipping pages in his notebook.

Billings caught my eye and whispered, 'His wife told 'im it don't matter where 'e gets 'is appetite long as 'e eats at 'ome.'

Fabian sipped his coffee, sighed like he meant it and then worked at regaining some respect. 'So lads, we got a murder to solve, and it ain't pretty.'

The next hour was spent recuperating and delegating duties. Jasper was to go about every blacksmith and wheelwright in the township to see if anyone had had a new hoop fixed to their buggy or trap lately.

Billings was to visit cobblers around town, establish what kind of boot would leave its distinct mark on a blood soaked cheek Hal would have to make discreet enquiries if there were any witches in Hobart Town; anyone practising black magic. But first he was sent to Lord Philpot's mansion to arrange a time for Fabian and me to interview the devastated man. Meanwhile it was agreed I was to secure more images from Mrs Rowley.

'Mr Hunter, Mr Hunter … Caspian!' I turned on the street to catch Dr Bedford puffing and panting and sweating profusely as he waddled up Elizabeth Street towards me dragging his copious flab along with him. 'Thank goodness I caught you,' he wheezed.

'What is it?' I asked. The man looked positively distraught.

'It's the Norwegian … the sailor …'

'What of him?' I asked.

'Well we were preparing to send him to New Norfolk for recuperation and one of my nurses, Beatrix Sprite … you met her … the one who understands a little Norwegian, she had a Swedish father remember … and he was …'

'Doctor! You were saying the Norwegian patient …'

'Yes, he regained some memory.'

'Wonderful.'

'Nurse said he suddenly became terrified. He snatched Beatrix's arm and told her he thought a sea monster had come to get them. He remembered the ship shaking like it was going to fall apart.'

'This is great news. I'll come with you to the hospital now.' 'At last a breakthrough,' I thought.

'No point Mr Hunter.'

'Oh! Why?'

'He's dead!'

'Dead?'

'Yes.'

'How? I mean how is he dead?'

'He was found dead this morning. Died in his sleep.'

'Died in his sleep. How is that possible?'

The doctor took a silk handkerchief from his coat pocket and mopped the sweat now trickling through the crevices between his chins. 'It does happen from time to time. Some people simply expire in their sleep.'

'Old people doctor, not fit sailors. I'll accompany you to the hospital now. Is this nurse, Beatrix, still at her duties?'

'Yes.'

The Norwegian's body was already laid out in the morgue where I was becoming accustomed to its dark, dank space redolent of man's extinction. I stood with Nurse Beatrix and Dr Bedford a moment in respectful silence and stared at the body, which lay on the coroner's slab. The odours of death teased my senses and I felt my stomach, weakened by last night's revelry, start to churn.

The Norwegian was bare-chested but still wore the britches he was found in. Sadly, I couldn't help but consider, the man was about the same age as me. Miss Philpot, I noticed, had already been prepared by the mortician and her bandaged body placed in an open coffin.

Even in the warm yellow lamplight the sailor's skin was a pale waxy white. His eyes were peacefully closed and to all intents and purposes the man looked asleep. His hands lay at his side. Rigor mortis had set in and I noticed his right fist was balled tightly shut.

'They say the only guarantee in life is death,' Dr Bedford muttered, looking on through the eyes of medical wisdom. I waved the nurse's lantern over the body. It was then I noticed marks, bruises, about the man's throat.

'What's that?' I asked.

'What?' Dr Bedford shuffled his flab closer.

'That, doctor?'

Bedford studied the light purplish marks around the Norwegian's throat and neck from his jawbone to his clavicles. 'Well I never.'

'You didn't notice that before?' I asked astounded.

'Well, no, Mr Hunter. I did not.' He turned to Beatrix. 'Nurse?'

'No doctor.'

'That man was strangled,' I insisted. 'He didn't die in his sleep at all.' And indeed the marks were indicative of a murder victim. Admittedly the marks were faint, the light poor and the head bandage had fallen loose about the body.

But all the same.

The doctor peeled back the man's eyelids. 'Oh dear, how could I miss that?' The eyes were blood red. 'Subconjunctival haemorrhage,' he muttered.

I had seen this before in Birmingham. 'So you agree doctor, it was murder?'

'Yes, I'm afraid so.'

I ran the lantern back down the body and hovered over the balled fist where something caught my eye. Something poked out from his vice-like, clenched fingers. I tugged at it; it was a leather strap.

'Here,' I said to the nurse. 'Hold this please.' She took the lantern while I prised the fingers open; with much effort I would like to add. Rigor mortis was a force to be reckoned with but as macabre as it may sound, it had to be done.

'Well well,' I smiled, feeling one clue closer to the man's murderer. 'I believe this is a love token.' I held the copper disk up to the lantern light. 'Yes indeed.' The halfpenny had been beaten smooth with a hole drilled for the leather strap so the medallion could be worn about the neck. Such items, engraved with the name or initials of their loved one back in the old country, were common amongst prisoners and particularly transported felons who treasured them. I held the coin high by its broken strap and watched it spin and unravel before me, excited to learn its secrets. Finally it stopped before my eyes and I read aloud the token's inscription, stippled into the coin in tiny dots with a sail needle,

'R. D. ... 1844. Forget me not. Betty. Free Sept. 17th 1851.'

'Our sailor here has torn this from his murderer's neck in his struggle to survive,' I told the other two. 'I'll wager that the culprit didn't realise he had lost this until it was too late. Which means our man here put up a struggle.'

I examined both hands, fingers and fingernails. 'Uh huh!' The other two looked closely as well. 'See that? Skin and blood under the nails. Whoever attacked this man has some nasty scratches to show for it, possibly to his face.'

'Tell me nurse,' I asked once we were back amongst the living – and the barely living – outside the wards on the ground floor. 'Exactly what did our man say to you last night?'

'He got awfully excited sir, like he was scared. He spoke of monsters under water. He said the ship shook and he thought King Neptune himself was coming to get him.'

Did he say anything about the crew or passengers ... about what happened to them, why the ship was deserted?'

'No sir. I did think to ask him a few questions but he got awful anxious and panicky. I gave him laudanum like the good doctor ordered and last saw him asleep when I left for home at nine o'clock.'

'Thank you nurse. If you think of anything else you know where you can find me.'

And weighing the evidence in the palm of my hand I hurried to meet Fabian.

'Where the 'ell 'ave you been man?' Fabian was annoyed. 'We have to interview His Lordship. I sent Hal to secure us an appointment and we're now late. 'e wanted us there at noon.' I instinctively jerked my head skywards; the sun was directly overhead and I wished I had brought my hat.

'Aye,' Fabian noted me looking to the heavens. 'It's noon already. Now hurry.'

'Wait!' I grabbed his arm. 'You won't believe what's happened.'

'Tell me on the way.' It was then I noticed Fabian had a hansom cab waiting. We climbed into the coach of the two-wheeler and were underway in a flash.

'Lord Philpot's residence,' Fabian barked at the driver. 'And an extra sixpence if'n ya halve the time.'

'Yah!'

We were both thrust back into the studded leather seat.

'So. What's so important?' Fabian asked.

'Our *Ocean Maiden* sailor's dead!'

'No!'

'Murdered!'

'No!'

I gave Fabian the brief and showed him the love token on the way up Davey Street towards the mountain where magnificent stately homes were in abundance. By now Fabian's brow was lined. 'Was it the stress of his work or the night before or both?' I wondered?

'His Lordship is waiting in the study,' butler Mr Quincy Ambrose took Fabian's hat and ushered us along a wide foyer where a spiral wooden staircase snaked its way to the upper floors. We walked down a cedar wood-panelled passageway lit from skylights glazed with multi-coloured lead glass. The effect was stunning. On either side of the passage there were what I could only guess were busts of ancestors chiselled from marble and sitting on Corinthian-style pedestals of the same material. Carved cabinets of elaborate design lined both sides of the wide passageway. They were filled with antiquities the likes of which I had only ever seen at the British Museum in London. I recognised Roman, Greek and Egyptian cultures on exhibit amongst others I could not identify. I was about to comment when Fabian elbowed me reminding me of the seriousness of our engagement.

'Wait here please gentlemen.' And Ambrose knocked and entered the study before he was invited to do so. There followed low voices, the butler opened the door wide and peered around. 'Please come in.'

His Lordship Marmaduke Philpot sat at his huge mahogany desk with his back to the window; a position I find quite irritating on a sunlit day as it is difficult to interpret a visage silhouetted by back-light. Looking about I couldn't help admire the room full of a master mariner's nostalgia. Ship models stood proudly in glass cabinets, their detail meticulous; the rigging, the anchors, the tiny hand carved blocks. The figurehead off a scuttled ship stood sentry in one corner, eyeing us across the room as we entered. She wore a tiara of sorts, with one hand shielding her eyes from the sun as if she was surveying the horizon, while the other hand rested on her belly. I so wanted to ask His Lordship about her but now, clearly, wasn't the time.

'Come in come in,' His Lordship snapped. Impatient. Curt. Croaky.

'Your Lordship,' Fabian spoke for the two of us. 'I'm Fabian Winter sir and this is my colleague Caspian Hunter.'

'Damn it man I know who you are. You should be down in that festering village catching my daughter's murderer, not wasting your time here.'

'Agreed sir, but we need to start our enquiry somewhere, we need to know your daughter's movements before the … before she met 'er death.'

The Lord stood abruptly and turned with his back to us and with clenched hands behind him he stared out the window towards the magnificent River Derwent. It was then I noticed he was only just over five feet tall. A small man by any standards, clean-shaven and from the bright light pouring in the window I would say he was bald and wearing a wig.

'Ask questions then if you must, but be quick about it. I'm a busy man.' He was understandably upset but this rudeness ... *Bloody aristocrats,* I wanted to yell, and saw Fabian shared my sentiments.

'Ya recently sailed to Victoria on your ship the *Buckingham* on business did ya not?' Fabian first asked. 'Arrived back last evening.'

'Yes,' His Lordship twisted about angrily and for the first time I noticed his hairless face with black pea eyes popping under a furrowed brow. 'What's this got to do with my daughter's death?'

'Sorry sir, I just need to make me notes. Does, ah did, ya daughter live 'ere with you?'

'Of course, where else would she reside?'

'Did ya see your daughter before ya left for Melbourne?'

'Yes. We dined in the observatory. Breakfast.'

'Right. Did Mrs Philpot join you?'

'Christ man, didn't you do your research before coming here? Mrs Philpot died four years ago, pleurisy.'

'Oh, my condolences,' Fabian's awkwardness was palpable. 'What did you talk about ... at the breakfast table?'

'I ... I hardly remember ... small talk. My daughter wasn't interested in the family business. Oh she was keen to spend my money but showed no desire to help accumulate it.'

'Did your daughter talk to you sir, about any problems she may have had. In particular any people she may have been afraid of? Anyone who may have wanted to do her harm?'

'Don't be ridiculous. My daughter was an angel.'

An angel? She was with child out of wedlock!

'Ah ...' Fabian cleared his throat. I knew what was coming and thought, 'This'll be good.'

'I know this is rather delicate Your Lordship, but Miss Edith was with child, she had a suitor I assume.'

'Lord have mercy on me!' Lord Philpot's face reddened as he salivated and shook; his black pea eyes now pomegranate seeds. He slammed a fist to the desk. 'I will not stand here and have my daughter ... my little angel's reputation slandered sir, no ... I will not. This business of this ... this bastard child must be kept secret. Do ya hear me?' Both Fabian and I took a step back from his wrath. 'If this information gets out around Hobart Town I'll have your posts terminated. Do you understand?' he seethed. He positively sizzled.

'Do-you-understand?'

'Aye sir.'

'Now leave.'

'Excuse me Your Lordship,' I dared to speak, 'but we need to see your daughter's bedroom sir, before we leave.'

I sensed Fabian facing me. 'We do?' I looked at him poker-faced. 'Aye ... we do,' and Fabian looked back at Lord Philpot who had collapsed back into his chair, his face silhouetted once more and his wig crooked.

'Aye,' Fabian backed my decision. 'We do indeed. If'n that's alright with you sir ... before we go like.'

'Do as you must.'

At that moment the butler walked into the study with a silver tray sporting a silver pot with a Coalport tree pattern teacup, sugar bowl and cream jug. 'Ambrose will direct you to Miss Edith's room.' It was an order not a request.

I was about to turn on my heels when I remembered, 'There is one more thing I must ask you Your Lordship.' Fabian shot me another side-glance. *There is?*

'What?'

'Would you like to post a reward, say a hundred pounds to encourage possible witnesses to come forward?'

'No! I certainly would not. You men are paid handsomely to do your work, now get to it!'

Stepping into Miss Edith's room was like stepping into a field of lavender. Besides the perfume it was clear the young lady had a passion for the colour lavender as well. The four-poster bed was draped in a mauve bed spread with lilac trim, the curtains were a shade of purple and violet and when I glanced in her giant rosewood wardrobe I noticed many of her garments were mauve or the colour of lavender.

But the room came with a chill. I felt her spirit hovering nearby and harboured guilt fossicking in drawers and cupboards. Quincy Ambrose stood at the doorway and watched us with mistrust, especially when I opened a cherry wood jewel box with a highly polished lid and ran a finger through the baubles, gold and jewellery studded with gemstones.

Immediately something caught my enquiring eye. A cream coloured card – five inches by four – lay face down under the jewellery that I recognised from Royle Rowley's portrait studio. I plucked it from the box and turned it over. It was a portrait image of a rather handsome young man, a little younger than me, wearing white britches held with a wide leather belt and brass buckle, and a waist length coat I imagine was blue with a stitched leather buttons. His shirt was horizontal stripes and he wore a cravat under neatly cropped hair. His right leg was stepped onto a short plinth and he rested a straw boater on his knee. He appeared to be in his Sunday best.

A studio portrait and a gift, especially for Edith. Was this her secret lover? I flipped it back over and now read the print.

From the photographic studio of J. Bishop Osborne. 68 Murray Street Hobart Town. Written in handwriting on the bottom was *Love forever and always, Nathaniel.*

Fabian saw my interest in the image and gave me the nod before stepping aside and drawing the butler's attention away from me long enough for me to pocket the card.

'What a whoreson,' Fabian grumbled as we walked the driveway from the mansion to the street, our boots crushing gravel underfoot to a most satisfying crunch.

'Who's the whoreson,' I asked when I realised our hansom cab had deserted us. 'The cabbie or His Lordship?'

'His Lordship Marmaduke firkin' Philpot … horse's arse!'

'I have to agree,' I said. 'And it doesn't matter how much money you have, a wig is still a wig.'

'Aye. And Marmaduke!' he spat. 'Who the firk calls their bairn Mar-ma-duke?'

'The same sort of mother that calls their son Caspian,' I grinned.

'Aye! Point taken. Hey, the Greyhound Tavern's just down the road, we better drop in and see ol' Tristram me mate the innkeeper and 'ave a quart to quench ourselves before the walk to the barracks. Hair o' the dog an' all that.'

Back at the prison office Jasper had a grin on his face like a poker player with a royal flush. He had had success of sorts with the hoopless cartwheel at the murder scene.

'Good lad. So what 'ave we got then?' Fabian sat on the corner of his desk while Snake chewed at a fingernail.

Jasper took out his black leather notebook and flipped the cover over with an air of professionalism; God bless his holey woollen socks.

'Yesterdee afternoon,' he read from his notes, 'a buggy belonging to a certain Mr Lynch Savage was brought to William Cobb's smithy shop in Brisbane Street for a new iron hoop to his left wheel.'

'You've done well Jasper,' and Fabian leapt to his feet and slapped the boy on the back. 'Now … who the firk is Lynch Savage?'

''e's a tavern keeper sir. Gotta public 'ouse down Kingston on the Browns River a ways … least that's wha' the smithy says.'

'Oh. And what's this 'ere establishment called?'

'The Sea o' Graves sir.'

'Sea o' Graves huh. Aye, I've 'eard of it, but never been like.'

'That was a first,' I thought, 'an inn Fabian hadn't visited.'

At that moment Billings returned all hot and bothered.

'Billings,' I greeted. 'How did you fare?'

'No luck I'm afraid. I talked ta two cobblers and they both says the same thing,' and he threw the drawing of the boot print sketched from the bloodstained print on Miss Philpot's cheek onto the desk.

'It's a hobnail boot, every prisoner wears 'em and 'undreds of free villains also.'

'Bugger!'

'Aye.'

I picked up the sketch and studied it more carefully than previously. 'Hmm … interesting.'

'What?'

Ignoring the others for a moment I took the image from the file to confirm my suspicion waving a magnifying glass over the card. ' Hmm …'

'What fa firk sake?' Fabian grew impatient.

'Well look closely. It's not the clearest of boot prints but if I'm not mistaken there's a nail missing from the left row near the heel.'

'Aye! You're right Caspy.' Suddenly Fabian was cheerful once more. 'We'll go visit this tavern keeper Lynch Savage and see what 'e's wearing on 'is hoof.'

'Right. Now if you'll excuse me Fabian,' I said enthusiastically,

'I've got some poking about to do of my own.'

'I bet you have you old dog you. Off for some hanky panky in the dark room huh?' And he and Hal had a good snigger. I shot Billings a disappointed glance and he looked for another moth anywhere in the room.

'Actually, *sir,*' I answered with a touch of sarcasm, 'I'm going to the prison library to research a theory I have on the *Ocean Maiden.*'

'Not now ya not. Ya can read them books tomorra. You, Snake and me's gonna pay the Sea o' Graves a visit. Jasper, fetch irons and muskets from the armoury … Snake go ahead to the docks and enlist the services o' one of Master Lucas's cutters. Tell 'im we want ta sail to Browns River within the hour.' Fabian unlocked a small iron cashbox and took out a gold guinea. ''ere,' he tossed the coin to Snake. 'And get me a receipt.'

'Aye.'

There was no point arguing. I looked to Hal who was grooming his moustache with forefinger and thumb. 'Hal,' I instructed, 'I need you to take this to the prison administration and comb the records for a *R.D.* who was transported here in '44.'

He lost his smile as I passed him the love token.

'But that's fifteen year ago,' he groaned. 'It'll take ages.'

'It's *eleven* years ago actually and yes it will take ages. But it's our only clue to the sailor's killer.'

Hal looked at Fabian for support.

'Now! If you please.' I grew angry at the man's insubordination. Fabian jerked his head towards the door and Hal begrudgingly left the office. 'Why don't you 'elp 'im,' Fabian ordered Billings.

'I don't think he likes me,' I said to Fabian when we were alone.

'Aye, it seems that way. But it's just you're a new lad and 'e's older than you and don't like takin' orders from a junior.'

'Junior!'

'Ya know wha' I mean Caspian. You're much younger than 'e be.'

'Yes, and far more qualified,' I huffed. 'I can't help it if the man's a dullard constable still at thirty.'

Whilst Kingston and the mouth of the Browns River – where it empties from the mountain into the River Derwent – are only six miles from Sullivan's Cove, it is nonetheless remote. The River

Derwent at this point would be two miles wide. We tacked against a southerly breeze, with the salty spray stinging faces and clearing heads. We passed a square-rigger, probably from England and full of immigrants our skipper said, and a fishing boat, the *George Bridges*, sailing towards the harbour with a full catch. Soon we rounded the headland and set course for Browns River.

A magnificent schooner, the *Revenge*, was anchored in shallow water. This, I was informed, belonged to Lynch Savage, the Sea o' Graves' innkeeper and local entrepreneur extraordinaire.

I snipped open my fob. It was four hours past noon by the time the sloop *Urchin* anchored off the mouth of Browns River. Master Lucas himself and one deckhand transferred us to shore in a tiny clinker dinghy that felt like she had more holes in her than a crumpet. We stepped ashore onto the beach of a handsome cove where Master Lucas pushed immediately back away from the shore like it was some leper colony.

'One hour,' Fabian called after our skipper. He answered with a vague nod.

'I guess he'll wait out at anchor,' I said with reservation, checking my issued Tower pistols were loaded, the powder dry and that my cutlass was secure on the hip. We turned our back on the *Urchin* to get our bearings and Fabian pushed out his chest and whistled.

'Look at this place will ya.'

The beach was strewn untidily with marooned vessels of all shapes and sizes. A regular bone yard where we had learnt Lynch Savage the tavern keeper also ran a tight business of second-hand chandlery stripped from the abandoned and wrecked craft. Several tents and huts were distributed along the sands and a number of people seemed to be doing a brisk trade.

'Ah, so this 'ere's where ya come if'n ya lost an anchor or lookin' for some rope eh?' Snake perused the landscape and popped two fingers into his mouth for a nibble.

To the right of the mouth of the river, wedged in a crevice on the side of a steep hill and perched halfway up on a steep embankment, was the Sea o' Graves inn. It was built from the wreckage of a whaler said to have been beached here after being rammed and holed by a rogue whale just off the shore. With plenty of blood, sweat and tears the bow was block and tackled up the hill and the midships section and stern dismantled and rebuilt resulting in the novel tavern. It was a testament to man's determination. To a naive traveller it looked like the abandoned effort of a tsunami. The stern cabin had been rebuilt 'arse about,' as Fabian described it, so the stern windows faced over the bow beneath it and back along the beach.

The bow jutted over the embankment edge, its bowsprit snapped above the figurehead – the figurehead of a rampant wolf. The stern nameplate was nailed over the doorway, a low hatch at the port bow facing the Derwent. It read *Sea Wolf* but painted along the hull were the words *Sea o' Graves.*

The Sea o' Graves was a gathering place for lawless rogues and villains, sealers, absconders, whalers and lost sailors we were told. There was naught a vice a man could not find to pleasure him here, as long as he had coin in his pocket.

'Ya can see why they named it Browns River,' Snake grumbled as we waded across the brackish inlet to reach the inn.

'No,' Fabian laughed. 'Master Lucas told me it was named after a botanist, Robert I think 'e said ... Robert Brown, back when Collins landed 'ere.'

'Well why is it shite brown?'

'Probably oozing outa the inn privy,' Fabian waded ahead and shot me a cheeky grin. 'Nay lad,' Fabian went on. 'It's the tannin from dead plants up river.'

Jokes aside, I don't think Fabian had noticed the arses hanging from medieval-style garderobes hidden in the shadows of the starboard bow where waste dropped into the river. 'Tannin indeed,' I thought to myself, climbing quickly from the other side.

We crossed a precarious gangplank from land to ship and stooped to enter the inn. The low deck-plank ceiling, once whitewashed but now stained brown from smoke, was supported by heavy ship beams. The taproom was dark and smoky and filled with drunkards, all with clay pipes grasped between yellow rotting teeth. Whores fed the debauchery like burley to sharks. Fabian stood a moment, orientating himself. His eyes adjusting to the gloom and darting about like school fish when he spotted the whores.

'Ah, filles de joie,' he sighed and his chest rose considerably. 'Big ones, small ones, fat and skinny, young and not so young, chinks, wogs and niggers. My God it's a banquet!'

'Ah Fabian,' I hissed just loud enough for him to hear me.

'What?'

'We are here on a police matter remember.'

'So we are lad, so we are.'

And that's when the fiddler stopped playing, the taproom went quiet and a few dozen rugged heads turned to face us.

'Maybe it's the guns!' Snake muttered from the corner of his mouth while biting a nail. But Fabian would have none of it. He sauntered to the bar like a regular.

'Three porters lovely lady,' he ordered and tossed a crown on the bar. Slowly, ever so slowly, the conversation and revelry picked up again.

The bar wench was a half-caste aboriginal woman I guessed, in her early twenties; the product of a drunken liaison no doubt. She wore a green silk and satin crimped ankle high dress – a patched hand-me-down – with modified bodice to expose her breasts. *Her mother'd be proud!*

She wasn't the most attractive specimen I've seen but as Fabian whispered to me, 'She has youth on her side.'

We three leant an elbow on the bar, nursing a pewter tankard of porter each and turned to face the crowd; a desperate bunch of reprobates, blackguards and scoundrels if ever I have seen one. Even if we felt out of place, armed as we were we certainly blended in; there was enough weaponry in this place to re-enact the Eureka Rebellion I had read about in the Hobart Town Gazette.

'Well hello sugar.' A siren approached, singled out Fabian immediately and pushed herself hard against him.

'Well hello back,' Fabian slipped an arm about her waist. Now it was my turn to sigh. She eyed off Fabian's change on the bar and purred, 'I'm Fannie Peach.'

'Why of course you are,' Fabian grinned back, flash as Lucifer.

'Ya wanna buy a girl a drink?'

'Aye, why not.' And Fabian shot me a *not now* look.

Instantly another soft voice over my shoulder. 'Me thirsty too.' An oriental beauty emerged from the shadows like a carp to a worm. She was extremely desirable and I was only wondering what it would be like to bed an oriental when she said, 'Me Soo Yung.'

'Me Snake,' Snake pounced, his mind clearly not on police business.

'Oo … Snake,' she giggled, stepping around me to nibble the man's hairy salty ear. 'Why you call Snake?'

'I'll show ya if 'n ya like me little pickle.'

'Oh please!' I groaned; then bawled across the taproom. 'We are here to see Lynch Savage.'

Instant silence.

Instant eerie silence.

I suddenly felt ill at ease and wondered how long the silence would last. Less than ten seconds as it turned out. I heard a chair scrape across the deck as one man, amongst the dozens of rogues, stood purposefully and walked slowly towards me with angry sunken black eyes. He stopped inches from my face rolling a splinter of oak, like a toothpick, from one corner of his mouth to the other. He stared at me, massaging his gold earring between forefinger and thumb as if it itched. I held his gaze defiantly, reminding myself that the earring was a talisman for superstitious sailors against drowning. And by the smell of this man water was to be avoided at all costs, while his breath stank worse than bilge water.

'You together?' he rasped, his eyes glued to mine as he jerked his head to Fabian and Snake who both remained strangely quiet. *Thanks crew.*

'Yes,' I finally managed with a croak.

'And why would ya be wantin' ta see Mr Savage?'

'What the hell I told myself.' I stood proud and to his credit Bilge Breath stepped back. 'We're here on police business.'

There was a collective gasp and it was with some relief that the fiddler started playing again, one of my favourites as it turned out – 'Farewell to you, ye fine Spanish ladies'. Fabian and Snake inexplicably found themselves unattached once more and I had the distinct feeling they would want to have a chat with me later. Bilge Breath rolled the splinter about his gums with his tongue.

'Follow me,' he ordered.

I don't know whether the drinkers were nervous of Bilge Breath or whether it was his foul breath that made them part like the Red Sea. But part they did. A moment later found us at a heavy, arched oak door, sitting crooked – like all the doors I noticed – and studded with iron bolts. Bilge Breath kicked it open with his boot and ushered us into a cockfight.

We stepped onto a landing where we could peruse the room at leisure. Here a stair descended to a purpose-built pit within a hall made of shipwreck flotsam fifty feet by fifty at a guess. It seemed to be wedged into the steep hill that had been excavated for the purpose. Around the cockfighting pit were another thirty or forty ruffians, all vying for the best position, shouting encouragement or screaming out bets while two powerful roosters tore each other apart.

'That's Lynch Savage, the big cove with the red velvet feathered hat.' And Bilge Breath pointed to a rather slovenly, obese, middle-aged man sitting back in a tall-backed carver made of whale ribs and other bones. He wore a tailor-made red frock coat with a wide belt held with a huge brass buckle, tartan style trousers and knee high boots. On his head he wore an old-fashioned red velvet tricorn hat festooned with ostrich feathers.

'Firk me, it's Cap'n firkin' Morgan the firkin' pirate!' Fabian fell about laughing.

'Oh I wouldn't do that if'n I was you,' Bilge Breath warned.

'Eh?'

'Don't laugh squire. It ain't no laughin' matter. Ya see Mr Savage is a patron o' the arts see, 'e likes the theatre and 'e dresses rather flamboyant like 'cos 'e likes to. So ya may jest sir, but ya cannot 'ide be'ind the Queen's name if'n ya upset Mr Savage. Savvy?' And the wiry cove tapped the side of his nose with his forefinger.

'Right then.' And Fabian regained his pride by leading down the stairs. We jostled our way to the cockpit and waited while Bilge Breath made his way to the colourful innkeeper, as a cockfight was about to start.

The combatant owners held their roosters by tail and feet, facing each other off, while they riled the birds to pique their anger. At the sound of a bell the birds were dropped to the ground where they wasted no time fighting to the death in a flurry of orange and black feathers and testosterone. With bodies arched and chests out the flightless roosters flapped their wings wildly and kick-boxed in a fashion, clawing at each other with their talon-like spurs. It was primitive and I drew no pleasure from watching this blood sport. In less than a minute the winning cock had ripped the throat out of his competitor.

Bilge Breath shoved between us. 'Mr Savage'll see ya.'

Lynch Savage turned awkwardly in his throne to face us, his jowls and chins jelly-like and wobbling from the movement. His rich dark brown eyes were large and his globular visage displayed some traces of a handsome past. Although his frock coat was specially made and extra large, his grossly overweight belly put strain on the brass buttons. As he spoke I noticed shiny mutton fat around his mouth and realised why the cuffs of his ample coat were glossy with grease.

'Well,' Savage's voice was slow and deep. 'What brings the constabulary to Sea o' Graves?' Although he had lived in Van Diemen's Land nigh on twenty years he still maintained a trace of a Yorkshire accent.

'I won't beat about the bush Mr Savage,' Fabian said, his eyes on the next fighting pair of feathered rivals, as the crowd grew restless. 'But can ya explain to me and me colleagues 'ere what ya cart was doing up behind the Cascades in 'obart Town recent like?'

I caught Fabian out the corner of my eye slip a sixpence to the bookmaker.

'Me cart,' Savage shouted over the racket. 'Me trap ya mean?'

'Aye.' At that moment the next cockfight was under way and the crowd became as noisy as ever.

'We have evidence it was at a crime site sir,' I had an urge to say.

'Crime site!' And the handsome eyes narrowed. 'Ya didn't come 'ere to accuse me o' mischief I 'ope?'

'Well Mr Savage,' I persisted. 'Please explain.'

'You're not too smart are ya?' was his answer.

'Pardon me.'

'I says, ya not too smart lad.' He sniffed and wiped his nose on the back of his hand. 'Sure I 'ave a cart in 'obart Town. But there ain't no roadway I can ride me cart down 'ere to Browns River on, at least not the last time I looked, is thar now?'

Rogues and gamblers in earshot sniggered at my expense.

'Well no, Mr Savage. But the fact is you do own the said trap and it was at the scene of a brutal murder.'

'Murder! Who may I ask?'

'Miss Edith Philpot, the daughter of ...'

''is firkin' Lordship Philpot!' Savage blurted.

There followed an unearthly cry and we all looked at the combatants. One cock stood on top of the other plucking at its eyes, while the sad creature underneath hopelessly struggled with a gash in its guts.

'Aha! You knew 'er then?' Fabian, who was now a sixpence shorter, was forced to juggle his attention.

'Yes I know her, who doesn't? She's the daughter of that bastard Marmaduke Philpot ... lord indeed!'

'So why, Mr Savage, was your trap at the murder site?' I asked.

Immediately the huge man became more compliant. 'I don't know lad. That trap resides at Mr Cumming's residence up north end o' Campbell Street. Cuthbert Cummings 'is name is. That trap is for me when I'm up in port, to take me 'bout town like. But I don't make it there a lot these days, not with me arthritis and gout.'

That, I could believe.

'And,' he went on, 'I knows that Cummings rents me trap out to all and sundry ... oh 'e doesn't think I know but the truth is, ya can't pull the wool over Lynch Savage's eyes.'

'Campbell Street ya say,' Snake finally took out his little black notebook. 'Cuthbert Cummings ya said?'

'Aye, a stone cottage opposite the cemetery on the east side.'

'And what is Mr Cuthbert Cummings' craft, may I ask.'

'Why 'e's a brewer. A brewer for Mr Cowburn at the Jolly 'atters in Melville Street. It's 'e what brewed me ales and porters when I first started 'ere.' A thought clearly crossed his mind. 'Speaking o' ales and porters, it's near teatime lads, why don't you gentlemen join me and me coves for a bite in me cabin. I got a big fat emu slow roastin' on the spit with wild berries, bush 'erbs an' spices.'

I was about to remind Fabian that Mr Lucas and the *Orphan* were waiting for us when Fabian's taste for porter took hold. 'Aye ... well it is tea o'clock is it not? Thankee Mr Savage, that sounds mighty generous o' ya sir.'

Sir now?

'Call me Lynch ... ah ...'

'Fabian, Lynch. And this 'ere's me colleagues Caspian and Snake.' Lynch answered with a nod.

'Didn't it occur to Fabian that Lynch just wanted to extract more information about the murder from us?', I questioned myself, rather vexed, and paid a young'un twopence to run down to the beach and send skipper Lucas on his way.

'I didn't think there were any emus left on this island,' I made small talk as we made our way painfully slowly to the stern cabin via a back stair that could accommodate Lynch Savage's sedan chair. It was especially built to cart him about, and was carried by four of his faithful crew. 'There is no way he could have murdered that young lady,' I thought.

'The emu, Caspian, come from up the east coast,' the big man told me. 'There's whalers up there what render blubber ashore and they know of me penchant for the exotic.'

'Sounds delicious,' Fabian was content to grovel, as long as there was a drink in it for him.

'Aye. I also nabbed me a French cook recent like; 'e's orf the *Chasseur de la Mer*, a Frog trader what was in 'obart Town. Crossed 'is palm with gold and filled 'is bed with whores. 'e's as 'appy as a pig in shit, as they say.'

The stern cabin, perched arse about as Fabian put it, nestled rather precariously over the bow, which, I had noted on the approach earlier, sat on the edge of a cliff. Mind you, the view was stunning looking along the beach towards the southern point of the safe cove. 'A nice place for families to bring children for a swim,' I pondered, 'if there weren't so many villains about.'

I drew Lynch's attention to the schooner moored in the bay. 'She's yours I believe.'

'Aye, beautiful ain't she?' he said with a tear in his eye. 'Won 'er I did. On a game o' dice with a cove what made good at Ballarat.'

'Why the *Revenge*?' I asked of the schooner's name.

'Sir Francis Drake had a ship called *Revenge* at one time. The name appealed to me. 'cept 'e had forty eight guns to my four little six pounders.'

'I'm surprised you'd need guns on her,' I said, still admiring the sleek two-masted gaff-rigged schooner.

'Oh aye lad, there's still lawless villains 'bout these islands, that's for certain.' And he flashed me a wink. I was beginning to like this man.

Lynch Savage sat at the head of an old oak table, 'a heirloom' as he put it, 'left me by me granddaddy in Penzance.' From here he could keep an eye on all the comings and goings on the beach and I had the impression he knew every transaction occurring down yonder, and estimated his cut forthwith.

Four of what I could only describe as his henchmen sat around the table, where there was plenty of food for the most ravenous of scoundrels.

The emu was superb, rubbed with native herbs and spices. It had been slowly spit roasted for five hours; the lean meat basted with mutton lard Savage explained. Jean Parton, the pirated cook, served the meat with tatties fried in duck fat with garlic and onions and cabbage he said he had acquired from one of the increasing number of Chinamen settling on the island. A couple of roast ducks were also quartered and smothered with a sticky apple sauce.

'This is awfully generous of you Lynch,' Fabian spoke with his mouth full. '"You can't teach an old dog new tricks" my grandma used to say. And this 'ere wine is most toothsome.' Fabian shot the fat innkeeper an affectionate grin.

The huge man answered by nudging the bottle closer to Fabian with the back of his fat hairy fingers.

'So tell me more about this dreadful murder Fabian,' Savage wanted to know. 'How was Edith killed?'

'Here we go,' I thought, 'Savage is going to play you like a flute.'

'Not a great deal I can tell ya really. Only she was stabbed through the chest with a pitchfork,' and Fabian swilled the burgundy like it was on tap. He went on to volunteer the information about the cartwheel hoop, the witchcraft angle with the dead cat hanging from the tree and the photographic image of the suitor in the jewellery box. *Well done sir.*

The conversation eventually swung around to the *Ocean Maiden* and all at the table knew of the ship and all had their own theories. Ghosts, sea monsters, strange lights in the sky, piracy. At least I could console myself with the fact I had a theory, a practical solution, which I would keep to myself, for now. But I must confess, after a few more wines I too started to harbour thoughts of the unknown.

'The *Ocean Maiden's* cargo ya say,' Lynch Savage looked Fabian in the eye conducting the conversation with a meaty bone, 'was rum ya say, with some grain alcohol as well ya say?

'Aye!'

'Are ya sure now?'

Fabian drained the bottle into his wine glass. 'What are you implying Lynch?'

'Well, 'ow can I put this? Ah ... ya can't tell a book by its cover. Aye. That's it.'

'Are you suggesting smuggling Mr Savage?' I asked.

'I'm not sayin' nuthin' laddie, I'm just sayin' ... that's all.'

The pewter chargers were cleared to a chorus of crushing bones at our feet as mongrel dogs under our table gnawed and chomped and sucked. But it was when sweetmeats were served that I caught a glimpse for the second time of the tattoo of a mermaid entwined in a chain. It was etched in the same place as Snake's, between thumb and forefinger. The wearer was a scrawny varlet with rat-like features, short and wiry and slippery-looking to boot. He wore slop trousers fastened about his thin waist with rope and a calico blouse laced at the front. He wore the gold earring of a Jack Tar and padded the decking with gnarly bare feet. He spoke little but when he did I noticed several teeth had gone AWOL. He answered only to Couta and he aroused my naturally suspicious and inquisitive mind.

Lynch Savage reached over to the silver salver piled with sweetmeats. He danced blubbery fingers over the pyramid of sticky bonbons before plucking the largest piece of marzipan from the middle of the mound, causing a mini avalanche.

'Do you partake of the theatre Fabian?' he managed to query before cramming the confection into his mouth.

'Theatre? You mean stage, curtains and whatnot?'

'Aye ... theatre,' as he macerated between ulcerated gums.

'Can't say I do,' Fabian stretched across the table to tease a half bottle of burgundy away from Snake, who sat and listened, nibbling his fingernails and contributing naught to the conversation around the table.

'Why's that?' Fabian asked.

'I was just thinkin', that's all. Mistress Ruby Blood is the main attraction this Saturdee night at the Theatre Royal near Wappin' and I was thinkin' o' goin' to see 'er, being me favourite performer an' all that, havin' seen 'er last year in Melbourne like.'

'Hmm. Can't say the theatre's ever really tempted me Lynch.'

Fabian thought a moment and I watched his eyes with interest as they followed a large ball of what I recognised as Edam cheese, with its dark red wax skin, being placed on the table with crusty bread.

'I visit inns for me entertainment,' Fabian said. 'Ya know wha' I mean. A good fiddler, accordion and a drummer playin' a lively tune an' I'm a happy man, 'appy man indeed.'

When the opportunity arose I followed Couta into the galley where he scraped food scraps out through a gunport. Below, where I imagined the keel lay, I could hear ducks from the river quarrelling over garbage and had a vision of them waddling amongst the turds from the garderobes, one deck below us, to get their vittles. Suddenly my stomach cramped when I remembered eating duck an hour earlier.

Couta cleared my thoughts. 'Wha'dya want?' His subserviency had deserted him once away from his captain.

'That tattoo, what's so special about it?' I asked.

'Sod off. I don't 'ave to talk to no constable.'

'No, you don't but your silence will fuel my curiosity and make me think you are guilty of something.'

'Bah! 'tis a talisman for a Thames gang back in London over ten year ago. Nuthin' untoward like. We was just kids bangin' 'round the waterfront, making a shillin' best we could.' He paused a moment to run a wary eye over me before breaking into a smile of sorts. 'Death Rattlers we called ourselves,' and he chuckled quietly at the memory.

'You're a transportee aren't you?'

'Aye.'

'What was your felony?'

'Stole a watch from a cove at the Isle o' Dogs. Bastard caught me red 'anded. There was a constable I didn't see right near.' Couta cleared his throat and hawked out the gunport. 'Another reason to never eat duck again,' I told myself.

Captain Lucas and his sloop *Orphan* had long gone and it took a half sovereign and some searching around the cockfighting pit before we found a punter with a boat that had lost on the roosters and needed money. But sharing a bottle of rum on the three-hour journey back to Sullivan's Cove left Fabian with a raging thirst.

'Anyway it's only nine!' he said jumping from the bow to the dock directly in front of five inns on New Wharf. 'Come on Caspy, you've gotta meet Bonnie Nettles.' I must say here that the rum had improved my spirits and the lively music lured me across the docks like a rat to cheese.

We walked into the Sailors' Rest to be confronted by a drunken sailor playing a piano with his penis! *Yes, dear reader, think about it, I had to!*

'Nice place huh?' Fabian had to shout over the racket. At least twenty revellers – a mixed company with dubious moral standards – stood about the piano singing a vulgar ditty to a tuneless rattling of ivory keys.

Bonnie Nettles pushed through the crowd. 'Fabian Winter ya whoreson,' she bawled over the rumpus.

Slap!

'Jesus Bonnie! What was that for?'

'Ya still owe me ya bastard.'

Fabian took out his purse and slipped Bonnie a sovereign. Then she took Fabian by both cheeks and threw a sloppy and wet kiss full on his lips. I looked at Snake but he simply jerked his head towards the bar. I followed.

'What was the sovereign for?' I asked Snake at the bar.

'Expenses,' was all he said, and he tapped his nose knowingly with his forefinger.

Bonnie Nettles, I was to find out, ran the best whorehouse in Hobart Town. The taproom was packed with merrymakers revelling in all sorts of drunken behaviour, but it was in the backroom and upstairs where the real action took place – for a price of course.

Bonnie Nettles took Fabian by the hand and led us to the first floor where we had a plush front room to ourselves overlooking the docks. Rum and mugs soon joined us along with half a dozen of the most desirable tempting vixens I had ever seen.

'Wha'dya reckon Caspian?' Fabian grinned at me like the cat that scored the cream. 'Penny for ya thoughts lad.'

'Ah … I …' I gaped open mouthed at the line of pink, purple and ruby attire barely covering bloomers, stockings, garter belts, corsets and naked flesh.

''alf price tonight Caspy,' Fabian laughed slapping Bonnie on the backside and slopping rum into pewter.

''alf price over my dead body,' Bonnie snapped, but her smile spelt otherwise.

''Oh, that can be arranged,' Fabian fired back and slipped his hand up Bonnie's dress.

Oh, how Hobart Town is growing on me!

About two hours after midnight, it must have been the sea air, because I let my guard down miserably. I remember feeling my way back down the stairs, one step at a time while holding the banister. On reaching the ground floor I remember a door flying open to a rear room and I stumbled through. The room was dimly lit with oil lanterns struggling to illuminate through the wretched smoke. I seem to remember there were four tables; cards, dice and something else I couldn't see properly. Then I saw *him* ... just before I smacked the deck headfirst.

Day Seven – Thursday

ILAY IN BED, MY HEAD THUMPING ... AGAIN! AND watched a tiny spider crawl to and fro across the ceiling. My head was filling with questions. Who was Nathaniel? Why was Lynch Savage's cart at the murder scene? Why was the dead cat there? Then I wondered what Snake and Couta's gang were like and why, in particular, did they not acknowledge each other yesterday. 'The Death Rattlers,' I thought over and over and made a mental note to ask Snake about it.

Hang on a moment!

I sat bolt upright in bed and immediately wished I hadn't. But memories of last night flooded back as fast as the blood pumping around my brain. The Sailors' Rest! I remembered the face at the gambling table, Norvin Ransford the third mate off the *Georgette*. That was it. And he was cashed up. He had a pile of gold in front of him ... well several hundred pounds worth anyhow. 'So where did he score so much wealth?' I asked myself, 'Not gambling I'm sure.' And then I remembered Fabian giving Bonnie Nettles a sovereign from his purse. I remembered Snake tapping his nose and saying 'expenses.' 'What is it with this town and gold?' I wondered?

I crawled from my bed, my head pounding and realised it was to be another warm day. I noticed my sheet was damp from sweat and then I smelt bacon crisping in the pan. I splashed my body with cold water and towelled down, cleansed my mouth with my favourite Gosnell's tooth powder and vowed to avoid the inns and taverns as I dressed.

My landlady at the Red Rose Cottage – whom I had persuaded to give me a key to a side door as I '*worked*' late and odd hours in my profession as a crime investigator – had prepared me a hot fried breakfast. But the moment I entered the kitchen with my blood red eyes, she lectured me on the sins of Hobart Town. I tried to explain how my detective employment took me to seedy addresses, but she didn't want to know. And that was the reason why on day three I had found a bible on my freshly made bed.

Fabian was early at the office. He's dependable, I'll give him that. Billings, Hal and Jasper had moved out into the prison storeroom for
extra space and sat like naughty school boys at their respective desks
arranged around the potbelly stove where they overindulged in the
one item that had no budget restraints: thick black coffee.

Jasper looked the worst for wear. He looked gaunt and white.

'You alright Jasper?' I asked.

'Not really sir.'

Then Hal spoke for Jasper. ''e's had a right nasty ol' night.'

'I'll say,' I commented, thinking I didn't feel too chipper myself.
'You look like you've seen a ghost.'

''e did an' all. Seen a ghost like. Didn't ya Jasper ol' mate?'

It eventuated Jasper had talked his way into a séance, although
it had cost him a guinea, which Fabian promised to reimburse him
from the office cashbox.

'So what happened?' I asked, forever the sceptic of such showmanship, having witnessed fraudulent and deceptive operations in
my work back in Birmingham.

'Well it were at the residence of Mrs Camilla Celeste at the top
end of 'arrington Street sar. I seen the séance advertised on posters
in the township like and went along at nine in the evening as you
ordered I should find out more 'bout the spiritual word, witchcraft
and the like. I thought I might get a contact 'ere see.'

'Did anyone know you were from this 'ere office?' Fabian parked
his backside on the edge of his desk. 'That you was a law enforcer and
detective like?'

'No sar, no never.'

'Right. So what 'appened?'

'Well she give us drinks on arrival, in a very posh front room in
the 'ouse ...'

'Drinks?'

'Aye.'

'Like what, sherry?'

'No, more like gin it were. She said it was to relax us for what we
was about to experience.'

'Hmm. Drugs,' I thought.

'Any'ow we was taken through to the parlour in the next room ...'

'We?' I asked. 'How many?

'There was eight of us sar, eight and two o' them ... Mrs Celeste and another cove, bit o' a toff 'e was. Black frock coat and a bowed tie, bit of a ponce really.'

'So you're in the next room feeling relaxed, describe the parlour.'

'Very dark sar, lots o' drapes 'round the walls, big round table in the middle covered with red velvet and ten chairs.'

Fabian. 'Dark ya say?'

'Aye. Just a coupla candles in the corners like and a small oil lamp on the table.' Jasper looked at each of us individually, crammed into our claustrophobic office and I had the impression he was enjoying the limelight.

'Anyways, the toff sits at one side o' the table and the clairvoyant, as she called 'erself, sat opposite and she got us all to 'old 'ands like. But the thing that got me most was one o' the other patrons what turned up late and joined us at the last minute. I could 'ardly see 'im proper in the candlelight but 'e looked a blackfella ...'

'Native Tasmanian?'

'Nay sar, a nigger. African blackfella. But 'is 'air and skin was white as you and me.'

'Interestin'.' Fabian played with his clay pipe. I sensed a sideways glance and the pipe slipped back into his pocket.

'Tell them about the ghost Jasp,' Billings said impatiently.

Hal. 'Aye.'

'Well, we're all 'oldin' 'ands like and she ...'

'The clairvoyant?'

'Aye. She goes into a trance like and 'er partner – the toff that is – says 'Mrs Celeste's body now gives access to the afterlife.' and she speaks all this mumbo jumbo and she asks one o' the coves sittin' at the table if 'e knew 'is Auntie Lil was present ... "Lillian," she says, "I 'ave a Lillian present." And the cove at the table got all flustered and said, "Yes I 'ave a Aunt Lil." and then firk me if'n she don't appear in the armchair against the drapes. Sittin' there starin' back at all o' us. She was white and transparent like ...' Jasper shuddered at the memory. 'She 'ad 'ollow eyes and then all this stuff come out o' Mrs Celeste's mouth ...'

'Ectoplasm they call it.' I had seen it myself in Birmingham.

'Thart's it ... ectoplasm.'

'Then what?' Hal shook his head slightly in disbelief.

'She disappeared and quick as a flash.'

'Smoke 'n mirrors lad,' Fabian pinched his lips in thought.

'But this white Negro?' I said. 'Why was he of interest to you?'

'Well 'e was different sar, the way 'e carried 'imself, the way 'e dressed ...'

''is aura eh?' Billings suggested.

'Aye ...'is aura.'

'Sounds like the gin was a strong'un.' Hal grinned.

'Right, then it wouldn't hurt to follow up on Mrs Celeste, if that is her real name,' I said. 'And the white Negro. Now to other business.'

I put the portrait image of Miss Edith Philpot's lover on the desk along with my notebook and other papers.

'Where'd that come from?' Billings asked immediately. He picked up the card, turned it over.

'You know him?' I asked with sudden excitement.

'Aye,' he said reading the inscription on the back. 'Says 'ere ... Nathaniel.'

'But you know him?'

'Aye, like I said, Nathaniel ... Nathaniel Rudder 'is name is. 'e's a store clerk at the Commisariat. At the Bond Store. Where'd ya get this?'

'Well as far as we can tell he is Miss Philpot's suitor ... and the father of her child ... we think.'

'Aye. 'e always had a bit of a reputation with the ladies. Anything in a skirt really,' Billings looked at Fabian but decided against saying what he was thinking ... *a bit like you ya dirty bastard!*

'Right. Billings,'

'Sar.'

'Take Jasper. Get down to the bond store and bring Nathaniel Rudder back here for questioning.'

'Hal,' I summoned. No answer, just a scowl. 'I take it you haven't had any luck as yet with the token.'

'No ... No I ain't.'

'Then return to prison records, I ... ah we, need to know who it belonged to.'

The moment Hal withdrew another constable stood in the doorway. He cleared his throat for attention.

Fabian. 'Yes.'

'I'm from Government House sar,' the lanky constable said in a timorous voice that clearly annoyed Fabian.

'What is it?'

'This sar.' And he passed Fabian a folded parchment secured in red ribbon. Fabian brushed the man away.

'Thank you,' I acknowledged.

The enveloped velum was opened and the contents spilt onto the table. 'Two one pound notes issued by the Bank o' England!' Fabian pushed them aside and read a dispatch from Governor Fox Young.

To Mr Fabian Winter Esquire of the police detecting agency, Hobart Town.

Find herewith two notes recently circulated in the colony. You will observe, I trust, that both notes have been forged. It is with great urgency that you apprehend and incarcerate this forger with all haste.

We will discuss the matter in the near future but for now I send you these as evidence.

Signed His Excellency Henry Fox Young

'Damn, ain't we got enough to do already?'

I picked up one of the banknotes. It was almost perfect. I had seen forgeries back in Birmingham, but not as perfect as this. 'Now that the payee's name doesn't have to appear on the note and that the cashier doesn't have to sign, these notes can be exchanged for goods anywhere.'

'Aye. So how are we to catch the bastard?'

'We can only do our best,' I shook my head in frustration.

No more than half an hour later and the two constables, Billings and Jasper, hurried back to the office and I was summoned from the prison library.

'Nathaniel Rudder's absconded sar ... done a runner.'

'Oh?'

'Aye. We spoke to the overseer at the Bond Store and 'e said 'e hasn't seen 'im for three days.'

'Damn,' Fabian paced the office. 'We've got to find him. He's our man.'

'Start by finding out where he lives,' I added. 'Billings, Jasper ...'

'Aye.'

'Talk to neighbours. Make notes. I want every detail recorded.' I wheeled around to Snake who was having a problem tearing a torn fingernail free. 'Snake. Go to the docks, check all outgoing vessels this day. Check he hasn't boarded a ship. Take the image with you, show it around.'

'Aye sir.'

I looked at Fabian for a reaction.

'Ya doin' grand lad, just grand,' and he smiled like the proverbial Cheshire cat.

'I'll be in the prison library, I've a theory I'm trying to follow about the *Ocean Maiden*.'

I caught up with Snake in the prison storeroom. He was slipping into his jacket, belting on his cutlass and placing two pistols in his belt. 'Snake,' I said.

'Aye.'

I waited until Jasper and Billings had made their exit. I took a moment, wishing to gauge Snake's reaction. 'What do you know about the Death Rattlers?'

'Th… the Death Rattlers sar?'

'Yes. You were a gang member in London years ago were you not?'

'Well … I … ah … I …' I walked directly to him and took his left hand with mine and with my right hand I rolled back his cuff. Suddenly I gasped. Not only did I reveal the gang tattoo, but the man had a badly scratched arm and the more I looked the more obvious it was that the wound was caused by someone clawing at him.

'What's that?' I asked.

'Nuthin' sar. Just a scratch.'

'It's more than a scratch Snake.'

He looked at me a moment and although the light was poor I noticed the man's face redden. He looked beyond me to the office to see if Fabian was in earshot. He lowered his voice and a sparkle appeared in his eye. ''twas a whore sar, she got stuck into me like. Think she was enjoyin' it too much.' And he grinned, as if reliving the memory. I held his gaze. It seemed innocent enough but I had a niggling suspicion it was more. 'Alright then. So what of the Death Rattlers?'

'We was young sir. Stupid young'uns rulin' the roost about London's docklands, making a shillin' as best we could ... thievin' mostly and standover stuff, I'm shamed to admit.'

I nodded. 'Thank you for being honest with me ... now go find this other villain Nathaniel Rudder.'

The Prisoners Barracks library was a small one, nonetheless with an invaluable set of Encyclopaedia Britannica amongst its collection. *Marvellous.* 1826 edition. Only thirty years old and dog-eared from use, but I soon found tantalising information that gave me a clue to what may have happened to the *Ocean Maiden.* I was quite absentminded and reading over my notes as I dawdled from the library across the yard in front of the superintendent's residence, when a soft voice called out. 'Caspian.'

'Elizabeth,' I answered, pleasantly surprised. She wore blue today, an ankle length dress with pink and blue bodice and a sky blue bonnet with her long blonde hair curling in spirals down her back.

'Your hair looks wonderful,' I couldn't help the compliment, but hastily added, 'if you don't mind me saying so.'

'Not at all,' she gushed. 'Caspian. What terrible news about Miss Edith Philpot.'

'Shocking. Dreadful,' I said and displayed a suitable expression of sorrow and disgust.

'Caspian,' she said and took my arm before she realised it. She stopped briefly, looked about. We were alone. 'I need to talk to you ... about Miss Edith.'

'Oh!'

'Yes, can you meet me?'

'Certainly, what did you have in mind?'

'Well, Daddy's gone to supervise works at the Oatlands gaol. He won't be back for two days so maybe we could meet at my residence.'

'Oh,' I must have sounded shocked.

'We could meet elsewhere if you prefer. It's just that I thought we could talk in private.'

'Of course, of course.'

'Noon then?'

'Noon it is.'

Elizabeth surreptitiously looked about once more, lifted her skirts to cross the yard to the gate when she stopped and said quietly, 'Oh, and use the Melville Street entrance. We don't want these dastardly guards gossiping.' And she smiled and disappeared. I opened my fob, two hours to noon!

I watched Elizabeth swan through the prison gate and out onto Campbell Street and was lost in pleasant thoughts for a moment when Snake's face replaced the vision, passing her at the entrance.

'Nathanial Rudder!' Snake said, looking rather pleased with himself, 'I found 'im sar.'

'Wonderful!' I looked over his shoulder expecting to see our prisoner in irons.

''e's in the morgue!'

'What!'

'Aye sir. 'e was found face down in the rivulet up creek in south 'obart Town. All bloated 'e was, full o' maggots like, reckon 'e's been there for days.'

'When was he found?'

'Only this mornin' like sir. Me mate Harry Bull the sausage maker told me 'e was found by some woman doin' 'er washing in the rivulet.'

'Damn and blast. That's a lead lost and another crime to solve. Lord help us.' Suddenly my headache returned. 'How did he die?'

'Murder. Bullet through the 'ead, clean as a whistle 'twas. Small calibre, single ball sar.'

Instantly I saw Hal returning across the yard from prison administration. He walked through the door without greeting or salutation but wore a smile of sorts.

'Good news I hope,' I said.

'Aye, I got 'im alright.' And he thrust his notebook at me open at the page where he had neatly sketched the coin. I was impressed. Under the sketch he had written: *Robert Dodds, transported for larceny April 11th 1844. Ship The* Dolphin. *Ticket of leave February 1851. Full pardon. September 17th 1851.*

'This is wonderful news. Do we know where he is employed, where he resides?'

'Aye we do … 'e resides in Port Arthur.'

'Port Arthur?'

'Aye.'

'Not as a prisoner, surely?'

'Well no cove would go there for a holiday would they now …
sir?'

'Lord help me.'

''e got 'is ticket like, then goes orf and gets caught nicking a pair o'
britches from Samuel Page the dressmaker.'

'No!'

'Oh aye. Got another seven years as a re-offender. 'e was be'ind
bars when that sailor got strangled.'

'It can't be the same man that owned the token.'

'But it is Caspian. The initials and the dates all the same and 'e left a
wife back in Lancashire called Betty! Same name what's on the coin.'

'Another false lead, damn their eyes!'

Billing and Jasper entered at the double. 'Ya won't believe what we
just found out sir …'

'Nathaniel Rudder is dead …' I said.

'Aye and he has been dead for da …'ow did you know sir?''

'Snake just told me,' I said unenthusiastically.

'But I bet Snake didn't have a suspect sar,' Billings grinned across
at Snake.

'A suspect,' my interest rising, 'a murder suspect? Murderer of
Nathanial Rudder?'

Jasper. 'Aye …'

Billings. 'An old woman was seen hanging about his cottage up
top o' Liverpool Street.'

Jasper. 'All suspicious like she was …'

Billings. 'And the day 'e disappeared.'

'How do you know?' I asked.

'They said they hadn't seen young Nathanial since Tuesday,' Billings said.

'A day or two after Miss Edith was murdered,' I thought aloud.

'We talked to neighbours like ya said to.'

'Good,' I praised. 'Very good.'

All the excitement drew Fabian from his desk. The pressure was
showing and I observed a whiff of brandy as he passed. He had heard
everything.

'Firstly we need to send someone to Port Arthur to talk to this Robert Dodds,' Fabian said. 'Find out how, why, when he misplaced his token. There's a government cutter leavin' in the mornin', at sunrise. Why don't you go Caspian, have a look at Port Arthur. Take Jasper here.' Jasper beamed. I sensed I was being fobbed off.

'Fine,' I said. 'Then Snake and Billings should follow up on the old lady angle,' I suggested.

I felt somewhat awkward approaching the prison superintendent's residence from Melville Street, a public thoroughfare that terminated at the prison. But as Elizabeth insisted I be discreet I obliged, even to the extent of tilting my boater hat to an unnatural position to aid my disguise. I was on time. Elizabeth was watching out for me. The large cedar door opened silently like some hidden machine device was operating it. Elizabeth's delightful face appeared around the corner and her eyes darted about, up and down the street, before her greeting.

'Come in, come in,' she said with some urgency and I felt my heart beat faster as I slipped into the cool dark hallway.

Elizabeth wasted no time telling me she was a friend of Edith's, or rather a well-known acquaintance. 'For an aristocrat she was happy to mingle with the riffraff.'

'Riffraff?'

'Yes, the commoners, you know the sort.'

'Well not really, why don't you explain yourself?'

'Well Nathanial Rudder for one. A lowly clerk at the government Commissariat and Bond Store.'

'You *know* of Nathanial Rudder?' I was surprised; Elizabeth seemed to know everything.

'Of course,' Elizabeth said. 'The lustful zealot with a passion for young blonde ladies.'

'Ladies?' I raised an eyebrow.

'Where did they meet, do you know?'

'At the Theatre Royal. Edith went with her father to see *Hamlet* by a Sydney troupe and Nathanial made himself known to her while her father was absent a moment. She was a terrible flirt and an adventurer.'

'So you are suggesting Nathanial wasn't Edith's first ... ah ... lover?'

Elizabeth answered with a disarming smile. 'Not all young ladies are prudes Caspian.' *What was she suggesting?*

'Lord Philpot was awfully protective of Edith, especially after Lady Philpot died a few years ago. He was heartbroken. He still has all her clothes in her wardrobe you know – Edith told me. Frocks, blouses, dresses, gowns, shoes, wigs ... All still there as if she were coming back at any moment.'

'Elizabeth ... was Edith interested in witchcraft, did she ever mention it?'

'Witchcraft! Good heavens no.'

'Maybe Nathanial was.'

'Was?'

'Pardon.'

'You said *was*. How do you know of Nathanial's death?'

'Death! What are you saying?'

'Nathanial's body was found in the rivulet only this morning ... how could you possibly know about it?'

'Oh my God Caspian, I had no idea. I said *was* because Edith is past history, to put it rather bluntly.' Elizabeth looked me in the eye. 'May I ask how he died?'

'Murdered. Shot.'

'Oh dear,' suddenly Elizabeth looked even more serious. 'And what were you accusing me of ... Mr Detective?'

'Nothing, nothing at all. I just wondered ... that's all.'

'Well now you owe me Caspian.' The smile had returned with a vengeance.

'Owe you?'

She stared into my eyes a brief moment and her chest rose as she sighed, 'Take me!'

'Pardon ... wha ... ?'

'Take me Caspian. I know you've wanted me since the moment we set eyes on each other.'

'Elizabeth!' But I wasn't that convincing. 'Are you serious?'

'I have never been this serious in my entire young life.' And she took my hands in hers. 'Come, I have Daddy's Madeira ready and poured in my room. We can have an all afternoon dalliance should you wish.'

'*Dalliance* ... I ... I ... ah ... I ...' I was gobsmacked, shocked, but smartly took hold of the situation and said, 'Where are the servants?'

'It's their half day off. Old Quincy always visits his sister in New Town and the maids always treat themselves in the town, flirting with the sailors.'

'My goodness!' Elizabeth gasped. My unpretentious arousal thrummed before me, pointing towards her lying on the bed in expectation. I folded my britches neatly, dropped them on the floor and mounted the lustful vixen like a ploughman in a barn.

The Madeira went untouched.

'Caspian!' she groaned.

'Elizabeth,' I whispered in her ear between nibbles.

'Caspian, oh Caspian.'

'Elizabeth.'

'Daddy!' she suddenly cried out.

'What, what?' I was only half way through first course.

'Daddy!' she called again, and threw me off her.

'Oh sweet Jesus!' It hit me hard, like the lead ball that put Nathanial Rudder face down in the rivulet. The bedroom door had been left open in our haste and I heard the hollow sound of an iron key in the lock.

Car-lick!

It echoed up the stairs.

'Daddy's home ... quick ... you must go. Go! Go!'

'Eliz-abeth,' the prison superintendent sang from the hallway. 'Sweet pea ... are you in your room?'

Footsteps hit the boards. He was climbing the stairs. Elizabeth gathered up my clothes and heaved them out her bedroom window and onto the veranda that just happened to face the prison yard. I was unceremoniously pushed out after them. Naked!

'There you are sweetheart,' I heard his deep voice resonate out on the veranda.

'D-Daddy, you're home ...'

'Yes we only just travelled past Pontville when we were held up by bushrangers, can you imagine that, bushrangers. John Quigley they think it was. We're not going to Oatlands now until the villain is caught.' The superintendent had sudden concern in his voice. 'Elizabeth!'

'Daddy?'

'You haven't taken up drinking in my absence have you?' He was staring at the Madeira and two neglected glasses.

'Goodness me no … Quincy must have put it there thinking it was your room Daddy. Silly man. He's getting old and dithery.'

'Yes your right.' And he sat on the bed! Damn!

'Well now Elizabeth, I must tell you about these bushrangers, rogues and thieves, wait until I have them here at the prison, we'll make them do the hangman's jig at the end of the rope, what.'

My mind raced. If I waited on the balcony, naked as the day I was born, I would be discovered from the prison grounds; and sooner than later. Then, as the day was warm, Elizabeth's windows and door were open; her father could stroll onto the porch at any moment. I had little choice. I slipped into my clothes and slipped down a veranda post. I rushed along the rose-lined path to the gate. The prison yard was free, the only guards, twenty yards away, shared a pipe and conversation with their backs to me. All good. I opened the gate, stepped out, closed the gate behind me and scurried across the yard towards the storeroom.

And there they were. Fabian and company, mouths wide open, noses pushed up against the glass and gaping out from the office window at me as if I was a unicorn.

'Everything all right sar?' Billings was the first to speak, rolling his tongue about in his cheek and trying not to laugh.

'Fine,' I said, all serious like,' Just fine.' I wasn't certain they had *actually* seen me on the porch.

'Very nimble,' Fabian said. 'Very nimble indeed.'

'Nimble?' I asked all innocent.

'Aye lad. Ya scampered down that post fast as a ship's rat ya did.'

'Aye,' Hal grinned. 'Fast as a ship's rat.'

It was early afternoon by the time the government dispatch cutter *Porpoise* docked at Norfolk Bay on Tasman Peninsula. Jasper, who was born in Van Diemen's Land, warned me the weather would change, and true to his prediction we saw all signs of a squall brewing.

However we were in a calm bay on the lee side of the peninsula, away from the wild Tasman Sea off to our south.

Here Commandant Charles O'Hara Booth had built a railway that ran from Norfolk Bay overland to Long Bay – a distance of around seven miles – just north of the settlement of Port Arthur. But this was no ordinary railway. This novel railway, operated under manpower – namely the prisoners – shortened travelling time somewhat, at the expense of the wretched convicts. No sooner had we disembarked at a wooden pier than we were seated by Sergeant Avery of the Port Arthur guard, in carriages a little like mining skips. Four passengers to a car and pushed along a wooden rail fastened by iron bolts to logs for sleepers. The sheer brute force of four prisoners soon had us rattling along at tremendous speeds – up to eight miles an hour I was told. Faster speeds were achieved on the downhill runs when the four prisoners, legs chaffed by irons, would jump aboard for the descent. One man at the rear could lock a wheel with a wooden crowbar should we need it but I had the distinct impression these seasoned operators were out to shock their passengers. Occasionally on a corner at speed, the men would have to lean out for balance for fear we would roll.

'We had a carriage with a public official on board roll off the tracks and into a ditch recently,' Sergeant Avery told me later. 'The railway men set him to his feet and dusted him down brushing the dirt off him, apologising profusely all the while relieving him of his watch and purse,' he chuckled.

From Long Bay we had to walk the mile to Stewarts Bay and the prison settlement. I was told horses weren't available on the peninsula for fear of absconders making off with them.

We walked through thick bushland, rich with the smell of eucalyptus, and down a hill into the prison village; for that's exactly what it is, a village complete with church, neat streets, cottages, a massive granary, guardhouses, barracks, chapel, hospital, and prisoner barracks.

We were directed immediately to the granary overseer's office where Mr Bert Wilberforce, the overseer, served us refreshments and bade us wait until our prisoner, Robert Dodd, had completed his time on the wheel.

'The wheel?' I asked.

'The treadwheel,' Bert Wilberforce looked at me as if I had failed first grade arithmetic. I was still none the wiser so the pock-faced man in his fifties – with his sour breath, straggly beard and teeth yellow from tobacco – explained it to me.

'Prisoners what misbe'ave within the prison system get extra punishment,' he said. And I suspected the smile on his face was not for my benefit but caused by the delight the extra punishment gave *him*. 'Sixty men at a time tread the wheels what grind the corn for the Commissariat 'ere.'

Now I realised what the incessant rumbling sound was, like continuous low thunder reverberating in the very walls.

'The wheel itself resembles the floats on a paddle steamer wheel ya see,' he went on. 'For the *treaders* it's like ascending stairs exceptin' the difference bein' the steps pass under 'em as they's turnin' the wheel. Very tirin' owing to the want of a firm tread,' the overseer chuckled with his tongue hanging out.

'I see,' I said. 'So how long will our Mr Dodd be do you think?'

'Oh, another thirty turns I reckon. Ya see each turn of the wheel, men step down from the left side, and everyone takes two steps to their left along the line, so after one hour ya get a break. And let me tell you squire, one hour of the wheel and ya fucked proper, if ya knows what I mean.'

Robert Dodd was ushered through to the office in irons. He was breathing heavily and dripping in sweat. I eyed him carefully. He was understandably lean, who wouldn't be after a week or two on the wheel. I introduced Jasper and myself and explained the situation. Until now he hadn't uttered one word.

'Well it weren't me sir, ya knows that,' he happily volunteered.

'Yes. That is quite clear. That's not why we are here. We want to know how your token found its way into the clutches of a murdered man,' I told him. Dodd looked back at his guard and Overseer Wilberforce, who were clearly entertained by the enquiry.

'Gentlemen,' I said. 'Would you kindly leave us alone for a moment?'

Wilberforce must have been of the opinion that I was about to torture the prisoner because he shot me a wink before dragging the guard out by the arm.

'I can't see why I should keep me gob shut,' Dodd spoke up immediately. "twas that bastard Richard Dart, it was 'e what took the coin to 'obart Town.'

'Please explain.'

'I lost the coin at the cards.' I must have looked confused because he quickly added, "e's initials are the same as mine see ... R.D. ... Robert Dodd, Richard Dart. And 'e's mother's name was Betty, like my Betty, too. So 'e was keen to take it to cover me debt like.'

'But Betty was your true love,' Jasper seemed genuinely upset. 'Why would you gamble with your token? Your only connection to your lady?'

'She ain't me true love no more trooper.' And Dodd's face grimaced at the thought. 'She made off with another cove back in Dover.'

I returned a suitable nod of condolence, and asked, 'Where is this Richard Dart, do you know?'

'Aye. 'e is in the employ of some sea captain, 'e's a manservant like. More a dogsbody I'm thinkin', 'e always was a shifty bugger.'

'Who's the sea captain?'

'Dunno squire, 'onest I don't. Can't be too 'ard though for smart coves like you, to find out in little ol' 'obart Town.'

The threatening squall petered out but gave us a decent blow back to Sullivan's Cove. We sailed into the harbour with its magnificent Mount Wellington backdrop and a sunset bathing the eastern shores with brilliant orange light. My silver fob read eight exactly.

We tied up in Waterman's Dock, only to be greeted by Snake looking pleased with himself.

'Fabian's waitin' for you at the Rodney,' he said without so much as a *how was the trip?*

'The Rodney?'

'Aye. The Lord Rodney 'otel. Two doors from the Sailors' Rest.'

The Lord Rodney demanded a tad more respect than The Sailors' Rest next door. Indeed it seemed strange that the two establishments could co-exist in such a close proximity. Fabian waited for me in the lounge bar where oak panelled walls supported oil lamps behind etched glass and one walked on Persian rugs. Most fashionable.

'How was your trip?' Fabian asked cheerfully. *Christ, does the man never tire?*

'Good thank you,' I answered, staring at the glass of amber liquid on the bar in front of him and wondering what it held. He gestured to the barmaid to pour me a glass of the same while protests fell on deaf ears. Fabian raised his glass.

'Bottoms up,' he said like a gentleman, more becoming of the respectable Lord Rodney after last night's swill.

I drank. Shuddered. 'Quite nice. What is it?'

'Madeira,' he answered.

'Oh!' I thought. 'So that's what Madeira tastes like.'

'Richard Dart is the man we're after,' I finally said and explained the love token initials and how Dart is a manservant to some sea captain about town. "I've told Jasper, first thing in the morning, to locate this scoundrel.'

'He could be back out at sea.' Fabian suggested, drained his glass and banged it down for another.

'I don't think so, I am of the impression he is a manservant employed in the captain's household.'

'I see ... Wendy ... ah Wendy. Two more if ya please ...'

'No no really, not for me,' I protested.'

'Nonsense. Fill 'em Wendy.' And he threw a half sovereign onto the bar.

'Fabian,' I had to ask.

'Aye.'

'If you don't mind me asking ... you ... ah ... well, you always seem to have gold in your pocket.'

'Expenses old chap, expenses.' And I was answered with the old finger tap on the nose.

Four Madeiras later and Fabian asked. 'Say, have you eaten?'

'Ah, no ... but I ...'

'Good. It's oyster night at the Marine.' Fabian drained his glass and turned for the door. 'And don't forget ya hat.'

• • •

'Ah, oysters, vinegar and stout,' Fabian roared at me over a packed dining room of happy eaters at the rear of the Marine's taproom. 'It doesn't get any better than this.'

I had to admit I was hungry and the stout excellent.

'O' course ya know what oysters and stout do to ya, do you not?' Fabian said with a cheeky countenance.

'What?'

'Get ya pecker up.'

I was about to ask, rather naïvely, how the mechanics of *that* would work when the innkeeper was at our side.

'We got a beef and mushroom 'otpot what's flavoured with marrow bone jelly tonight Fabian.' Phineas Arvel leant over the table and lifted the pewter charger of empty oyster shells with one strong hand. Fabian caught me staring at the innkeeper's stub where his right hand once was.

'Beef and mushrooms eh Phineas,' Fabian said. 'Better get us two plates I'm thinkin'. Oh aye, this 'ere is me new offsider from Birming'am, Caspian Hunter.'

'Pleasure ta meet ya young man,' the old fellow had a happy face; round and red, probably from partaking too much of his own brew. He wore a leather apron over a calico shirt with slop trousers and a cloth slung over his shoulder. 'I'd shake ya hand lad but I lost a paw as I'm certain ya already spied with them big 'ealthy eyes o' yours.'

'Phineas was an 'arpooner on the *Beetle* out o' Nantucket,' Fabian filled me in. 'But 'e lost 'is mit when it got caught in the harpoon rope as the whale dived. Ain't that a fact Phineas?'

The innkeeper nodded. Now I realised the significance of the retired harpoons pinned to the stone wall over the fireplace.

'Nantucket,' I said. 'I thought you had an accent.'

'Aye lad. The *Beetle* had a full hold o' oil, over three thousand barrels. We sailed into the cove 'ere and I thought to meself, "Aye Phineas, you 'ave enough saved, and along with ya share from this voyage, to buy an inn 'ere." An' 'ere I am.'

The beef followed along with more of the finest stout I have had outside of Ireland. Then the rum bottle landed on the table and Fabian muttered something about *peckers up* and *maybe we should visit the Sailors' Rest*, but I excused myself to pay a visit to the latrine and kept walking … to Red Rose Cottage.

Day Eight – Friday

FEELING SLIGHTLY BETTER THAN MOST OTHER mornings of late I convened a meeting early at our prison office. For once Fabian was late. He sauntered into the office looking slovenly, like he had slept in his clothes.

'Fabian,' I said, 'do you want to chair the meeting?'

'What? Chair? No! ... ah you take it lad.' He clearly had something on his mind.

'Right.' I looked at the other four who had dragged their chairs into the office and sat gaping at me holding coffee and notebooks with enthusiasm. Well, all except for Hal who made it clear his dedication leant towards Fabian and not me.

'We have one deceased daughter of a Lord, Miss Edith Philpot,' I started. 'You have all seen the portrait; I've been told they call them photographs. Edith was killed with a pitchfork through the chest. We have a cart to investigate ... ah ... a Mr Cuthbert Cummings of Campbell Street. We have a boot to find with a hobnail missing from the left row near the heel. But we do not have a motive. Any suggestions?' I asked.

Jasper sat bolt upright. 'Sacrifice!' he offered. The others looked at him waiting for him to elaborate. 'The skun cat! Wasn't the skun cat an offering, for the devil like?' And I swear he shuddered.

'Nar, I say it's money,' Hal directed his suggestion to Fabian. *I really don't know why he dislikes me.*

'Then explain,' I said.

'Well,' he shuffled about in his chair and continued to look at Fabian. ''er daddy is one o' the richest merchants on the island.' This he said with a heavy dose of resentment.

'She was brutally beaten,' Snake said biting a fingernail like he'd missed breakfast. 'Maybe it was revenge for somethin' 'is Lordship done earlier, to someone else like.'

'Possible,' I said. 'So we need to re-interview His Lordship, ask if he has any enemies he would like to tell us about.'

'Then there is the shame,' Billings added. 'She was with child remember ...'

'Or jealousy,' Fabian had a second wind. 'If she was a little ... how should I say ... free with her affections, she may 'ave upset another suitor.'

'Jealousy,' I repeated and jotted the word into my notebook. 'Every possibility. The problem is we have the governor looking over our shoulder on this one too, he and His Lordship are good friends, I'm led to believe.'

'Now we 'ave Miss Edith's lover, Nathanial Rudder. Dead!' Fabian sat on the corner of his desk.

'I just remembered something,' I said.

'What?'

'Well Elizabeth Mead told me ...'

Suddenly suppressed laughter stopped me dead.

'Oh to be a fly on the wall!' Fabian chuckled. ''Ow is the little honey any'ow?'

'So you are feeling better then, *sir*.' I blushed at Fabian. 'Would you care to take over?'

'No Caspy, no. Ya doin' just great ... go on ... Elizabeth Mead told ya ...'

I took a breath. 'Elizabeth Mead told me Nathanial Rudder worked as a clerk at the Bond Store.'

'She did, did she?'

'Yes, she did. Then he was shot in the head with a single ball, small calibre from a small pistol that fits with a suspicious looking elderly woman seen at his cottage by neighbours just prior to his murder.'

Fabian. 'So where was he shot and 'ow did he turn up in the rivulet, dead?'

'More friggin' questions,' Snake muttered.

'Now,' I sat at my own desk and flipped the pages of my notebook. 'The *Ocean Maiden*.'

Groans.

'*The-ghost-ship*,' I reiterated. 'And the murdered seaman who we know swam ashore from the ship but conveniently had amnesia ...'

'And then got 'imself strangled!' Fabian interrupted. 'I've gotta say Caspy, you certainly brought some work with ya when ya stepped on our fair shores. We 'aven't 'ad this many mysteries for months. I mean a few pickpockets nabbed. A burglary ... Ah Wong Sing the grocer was bashed and robbed two weeks ago, but this, phew!'

'You 'ad an idea didn't ya sir,' Jasper asked, "bout what 'appened ta the *Ocean Maiden*?'

'A wild theory only. I need more time in the library. But what we do know is that the man who killed our seaman was ex Port Arthur man Richard Dart. We need to locate him as quickly as possible.'

'What 'bout that Lynch Savage cove tellin' us to check the barrels off the *Ocean Maiden*,' Snake asked.

'Yes, that was strange and we need to follow up on it,' I said. 'Fabian ...'

'Aye.'

'May I suggest you and I re-visit His Lordship then investigate the contents of the barrels off the *Ocean Maiden* stored at the Bond Store. Snake, you follow up Cuthbert Cummings, check the soles of his boots for the missing nail. Find out what his movements were the day of the murder. Jasper ...'

'Aye sir.'

'You continue on the witchcraft angle, I want a full report on covens, if any, in Van Diemen's Land. Billings, you hunt down this Richard Dart, and beware, he's dangerous; you should take Hal with you. Place him in irons and bring him in.'

'Well delegated Caspy,' Fabian rubbed sleep from his eyes. 'We'll nail these villains in no time with you at the helm lad.'

'Wait,' I said to Fabian. 'I've just had a thought.'

'What?'

'Captain Slade hassled you about taking possession of the cargo of the *Ocean Maiden,* right ... at the Chophouse?'

'Aye.' Fabian's eyes widened. 'Finders keepers, law o' the sea an' all that.'

'Yes. So doesn't that make him a prime suspect? I mean if that is not incentive to murder the only known survivor of an abandoned ship at sea to make one's claim on the cargo, what is?'

'Jolly good lad ... who's free?' He was met with furrowed brows and the scratching of scalps. 'Hm, Jasper,' Fabian snatched the boy's arm. 'Forget the witchcraft angle for the moment and bring in Slade. I believe his estate is in New Town. Go check at the Town Hall.'

Jasper ginned madly. 'Bring 'im in fa questionin' sar?'

'Aye.'

'On me own like?'

Fabian looked at the scrawny twenty-year-old a moment. 'Yes you're right. Tell the gatekeeper to send two guards with you.'

'But I thought this Richard Dart cove done it for sure,' Billings looked confused.

'Aye,' choroused from the others.

'True, but Captain Slade also has a motive. We need to question him. Maybe he is in cahoots with Dart.'

Suddenly the third mate from the *Georgette* flashed back into my vision.

'That's right!' I said aloud.

'What?'

'I just remembered, the night before last when we were at the Sailors' Rest …'

'Aye, good night that'n … wha' about it?'

I had the impression Fabian had forgotten the night completely and I must confess here that much of what happened was a bit of a blur for me too.

'I distinctly remember seeing the third mate off the *Georgette* playing at the gaming tables in a room behind the taproom …'

'You shifty dog Caspy,' Fabian grinned. 'I didn't know ya liked a wager.'

'I don't,' I answered sharply, not meaning to appear indignant. 'But Norvin Ransford was there with a pile of gold in front of him.'

'So 'e got lucky.'

'No. Our eyes met and he looked mighty guilty.'

'What are ya suggestin'?' Hal actually looked at me, probably hoping I had made a mistake.

'I was with the second group to board the *Ocean Maiden* that morning and we all agree there were no, sealers, thieves, pirates involved. The ship was abandoned in haste and valuable cargo left on board …'

'Aye.'

'But it always bothered me that the ship's cashbox, the captain's coin, was found empty and slipped under a bunk in the main cabin.'

'Oh,' Billings said. 'So you're suggestin' this 'ere third mate, what's 'is name …'

'Norvin Ransford.'

'Aye, Norvin Ransford, thieved it.'

'Exactly.'

'Alright,' Fabian jumped to his feet. 'We'll bring him in too. But 'e'll have ta wait 'til we sort these others out.'

It was only ten in the morning. The hansom cab cantered up Davey Street and along the gravelly path shaded with oaks and a walnut tree in full bloom leading to Lord Marmaduke Philpot's main entrance. As the morning was already sultry and the sun washing his estate with warmth the man himself was taking a late breakfast on the eastern porch. Having noted this, we strolled through the garden and approached His Lordship unannounced.

'Dear God!' Philpot's face reddened. 'Could you not have waited for Ambrose?' His Lordship sat in silk trousers and matching smoking jacket of an oriental pattern, open at the chest; it was after all shaping up to be a hot summer's day. His head was as bald as the day he was born. He sat with the *Hobart Town Gazette* and a pot of tea, milk and bowl of dark sugar, waiting for his hot breakfast no doubt.

'Sorry Ya Lordship,' Fabian said. 'But as we saw ya 'ere like we thought we'd save Ambrose the trouble.'

Philpot grunted.

'And you 'ave met Mr Hunter, the other day sir.'

'Yes yes, what do you want?'

Immediately Quincy Ambrose, His Lordship's butler and manservant, stepped through the open double doors from the drawing room onto the porch carrying a rattling tray of silverware and food. He rolled his eyes at Fabian and myself and burst into an apology. 'Oh I am sorry Your Lordship, I didn't know these gentlemen were ...'

'Just put the tray down and leave us.'

Lord Philpot's mood was reflected in the look of displeasure on the butler's face, which he directed at us. For Ambrose, it seemed he would be enduring another day of nitpicking from His Lordship. The tall slim butler, in his mid fifties, already had a fine bead of sweat across his brow from the three-piece long-tailed suit he wore.

We were not offered refreshments, nor did I expect it. But we were not even offered a seat in the shade.

'I trust you have come to tell me you have a lead on my daughter's killer,' Philpot said without looking up from his breakfast tray; creamy scrambled eggs with smoked herring. He spread soft butter onto thick pieces of toasted bread, which he liberally piled with egg and herring.

'I'm afraid not sir, not as yet,' Fabian's stomach rumbled loud enough for all to hear. 'But we will. Have no fear ...'

'Oh but I do Mr Winter. I do fear you will never catch this wretched animal.'

'Your Lordship,' I said, 'it is most important that we ask you some more questions ... well ... ah ... do you have any enemies sir? Anyone who would wish revenge on you enough to do something so dastardly.'

The man chewed at another fork of egg and herring, sipped his tea and looked up at me. 'Young man, in my line of work there are always enemies. Where there is money involved there are winners and losers and it's the losers one must watch out for.'

'Then do you have any names sir, for us to follow up. Any leads here in Hobart Town?' He held my eye and I felt I was connecting with the man at last. After all he didn't get where he was being soft hearted and I knew he judged Fabian by his coarser grasp of the English language.

'No Mr Hunter, no one comes to mind.'

'Then sir, it pains me to ask, but were you aware of a Mr Rudder, Nathaniel Rudder?'

Philpot turned to face his breakfast; he paused a moment pushing the food about his plate like a spoilt child preferring cake all of a sudden. 'I've heard the name, yes.'

'Then you are aware, sir, that he was acquainted with your daughter, Miss Edith.'

There followed an uncomfortable pause, as if the man was composing himself.

'Yes Mr Hunter. My Edith was a force to be reckoned with. She took it hard when her mother died.'

'So did you, I believe,' Fabian said without reflection.

'Of course I was upset,' Philpot's vitriol spat across the table along with specks of egg and herring. 'What a stupid comment, man.'

'Sorry Your Lordship ... I ...'

'But Edith took it really badly. She started clandestine meetings with lowly people I didn't know about, but Hobart Town being a small place I heard things, as you can imagine.'

'Did you ever meet Mr Rudder sir,' I asked.

'No. Definitely not. Why should I?'

Fabian thought briefly. 'Did ya know ya daughter was 'aving his child sir?'

'You have a wonderful way with words, Mr Winter, don't you?' And he shot Fabian another sharp look.

Silence.

His Lordship took a deep breath and sighed heavily. 'Yes,' he finally answered. 'I suspected as much.'

He looked away, as if ashamed. 'Now if you gentlemen don't mind, I would like to be alone.'

Palmed with a shilling to remain in the shade and wait, our hansom cab then delivered us to the waterfront, namely the Commissariat and the Bond Store. The handsome two-storey sandstone building was one of the first built in the colony, so Fabian informed me. Behind the Commissariat on the dockside and running parallel is the Bond Store, a sturdy four-storey warehouse built to hold stores in bond by the government, until taxes are paid to release them. After scrutiny from the guard we entered the courtyard between the buildings and through a delightful arched stone entrance, where we met the chief clerk, Hilbert Roswell, a tired looking man in his forties who walked with a limp.

'The upper floors sirs,' the chief clerk told us, 'are for grain and the like and the lower floors, includin' the vaults, are for the barrels o' meat, foodstuffs, grog, rum and the like.' The five-foot-six chief clerk scratched his groin and caught me watching.

'These woollen britches make me knackers itch like buggery,' he said, genuinely irritated.

'Ya need some cotton undergarments,' Fabian said with cheer.

'Christ no,' he shook his head adamantly. 'The wife complains washing these every fortnight, let alone an undergarment.'

'So where will we find the cargo from the *Ocean Maiden* Mr Roswell?' I asked, dreading to imagine what calamity was underway in his britches.

'Follow me.' He eyed the manifest for the first time and took a lantern from its sconce and read aloud while we descended into the vaults.

'Sixty barrels o' brandy, twelve 'undred barrels o' rum, fifteen barrels o' grain alcohol … oh yes.'

He stopped a moment and turned to face us holding the lantern high to see us clearly.

'I don't knows whether you gentlemen realise but nine barrels o' that grain alcohol were damaged on voyage.'

'Aye,' Fabian said. 'We know that.'

'Aye.' Roswell thought a moment and blinked like he had dust in his eye. 'They was stored above the rum see, in the ship like, and some 'ow theys cut loose and nine of 'em smashed open. The alcohol would 'ave drained into the bilge. Jeezus!' He suddenly looked animated. 'Could ya imagine if'n some tar down there lit 'is pipe. Kaboom! Firk! There would be nuthin' left I tell ya.'

'Yes,' I agreed. 'But we've surmised the spirit evaporated before any damage could be done.'

'Aye. I reckon ya hit the nail on the 'ead there lad … now, where was we? Ah yes … forty salted pork, ten barrels o' pickled beef, twenty barrels o' tea, ten o' preserved fruit … now *that* gentlemen, I do like, and the wife … them preserved prunes 'specially.'

'Aye,' Fabian concurred. 'What else we got?'

'Ten barrels o' baccy, five coffee beans, ten crates o' pomades and apothecary medicinals … says 'ere bear's grease, tooth powders and assorted creams and ointments and last o' all five crate's o' anchovy and bloater paste. Hmm … all them was stored down 'ere three day ago and eighty barrels o' 'ouse'old fixtures destined for the ironmongery are stored on the first floor.' We three stood while the chief clerk held the lantern high in an attempt to throw light across the mass of barrels.

'Total value,' Hilbert Roswell said with a flourish, 'five thousand four 'undred guineas … not bad find for lucky Cap'n Slade.'

'You know Slade?' I asked.

'Only fru 'ere like, 'e's been pesterin' the clerks 'bout getting' it released so 'e can sell it orf.'

'Well he knows he has to wait until after the inquiry,' I said bluntly.

'Oh, we knows that squire …'e's just been a pest like, that's all.'

'Is there another lantern 'ere abouts?' Fabian asked.

'Aye.' Roswell took up another lantern, lit it with a taper from his own, and passed it to Fabian.

'Thankin' ya my friend, now ya can leave us to do our commission if'n ya please.'

'Certainly sirs, if ya need anythin', anythin' at all I will be up with the clerks.'

He handed me the manifest and his lantern and I watched with some amusement as his shadow formed a ghostly configuration on the stone wall ahead of him while the light from our lanterns ushered him back up the steps towards the daylight.

The barrels were stored on their sides in long rows from one end of the building to the other, stacked on top of each other, six high with wedges to hold them in place.

'Lookin' pretty much intact ta me,' Fabian sauntered between the first and second rows swinging his lantern nonchalantly. 'So what's Lynch Savage on about then, suggestin' the Norwegian captain was smugglin'?'

'Don't know,' I said, casting an eye over the markings on the closest kegs. 'But if anyone knew of any illegal goings on, it would be the likes of Mr Savage.'

'Aye.'

We worked our way methodically amongst the barrels and checked off the customs markings against the kegs.

'Well accordin' ta the manifest it all looks present and correct.'

'Hmm.' I stood at the end and perused along the rows, my ever-suspicious mind trying to imagine nefarious scenarios.

'Must be time for midday refreshments,' Fabian said stepping ever closer towards the exit. 'The 'ope's across the road, Caspian.' There followed a moment's silence while I was lost in thought. 'Caspian!'

'Sorry. What?'

'The 'ope and Anchor's across the road, refreshments?' And he took out his fob. 'Half eleven,' he reiterated.

'One moment!'

The man's off duty interests were starting to annoy me. I had an idea and pushed my generous girth into a tight opening between the first row of barrels closest to me and the stone wall of the vault.

'What is it?' Fabian watched me squeeze along the narrow passage. I held the lantern ahead of me and had penetrated almost to the end, where I would have to twist about and return, when suddenly I stepped in something soft and pliable; spillage from a barrel perhaps? I manoeuvred the light to see.

'What's up?' Fabian called along the gap.

I leant over with some difficulty and pinched a sample to smell. 'Tea!' I finally answered.

'Tea huh,' Fabian sounded disappointed.

'Yes. But why has dried tea leaves spilt from a barrel that is perfectly sealed?' I had an instant thought. 'This barrel has been opened and sealed again.'

'Oh?'

'Yes. I need something to open these barrels with.'

Moments later I heard Fabian mounting the barrels level with where I waited. Soon his head appeared over the top from near the vault ceiling and he peered down at me like some explorer in an ancient tomb, his mischievous grin troll-like in the eerie shadows.

''ere,' he rasped from lying on his stomach, and he dropped an iron bar with a claw on the end that I caught just in time. The storeman's crowbar easily prised the lid of the suspect barrel. It fell at my feet and tealeaves instantly poured about me.

'Whoa!' I gasped. Immediately a face appeared from the blackness; waxy and white, like that of the strangled sailor in Dr Bedford's morgue.

'What is it?' I fancied Fabian was about to slither in excitement from the top of the barrels towards me, like some great lizard, when Snake's desperate voice located us in the vaults.

'Thank God, thar ya be,' his voice echoed about the store. 'Come! Come quick,' his voice was panicked and out of breath.

'What?' I jerked to my feet cracking my head on a barrel overhang. 'Jesus Christ!' I blasphemed before I realised.

'What's goin' on Snake?' Fabian slid off the barrels on the far side. 'What is it man?'

Snake was clutching his sides gasping for breath. He had clearly raced to find us.

'It's-that-Mr-Ransford,' he puffed. ''e gone knifed Bonnie Nettles.'

''e what?'

''e's gone deranged sar, 'e's taken Bonnie 'ostage. 'e already stabbed 'er in the chest an' 'e's holdin' 'er hostage at the window o' the Sailor.'

'Damn! Come Caspian,' Fabian shouted. 'Hurry.' Truth was it took me some wriggling to squeeze out from behind the confines of the barrels.

Completely forgetting our waiting hansom cab, we ran across the docks to New Wharf where a crowd had already gathered on the docks. They were mostly concerned regulars of the Sailors' Rest, but some drunkards were yelling abuse at the ship's mate who was clearly mentally unstable and not handling the insults too well.

'There,' Snake pointed to the first floor window. 'Like I said, mad as a hatter 'e is.'

Norvin Ransford, the third mate off the *Georgette*, a man I thought I had gotten to know on the voyage out from England, was standing at the open window with a pistol to landlady Bonnie Nettles' head. He looked bedraggled and quite intoxicated.

'Is he drunk?' I asked Snake.

But a man standing next to us said, 'Drunk, aye, and he's had opium too. 'e's been up all night on the cards and dice, lost 'undreds o' pounds 'e has. He's accusing Bonnie of cheatin' him.'

'Damn.'

'Any ideas?' Fabian turned to me. I was flattered.

'I'll try and talk to him.'

'Atta boy lad,' and Fabian crossed his arms and leant back, content to let me sort out the problem.

I pushed through the crowd until I stood directly under the window. 'Norvin,' I cried out, but he had already been watching me approach. It was at this moment I saw the landlady's wound clearly. She appeared to have lost a fair amount of blood in a stab wound to the left side of her neck and chest and looked listless.

'Norvin,' I called up. 'What are you trying to achieve? Don't do this, if Bonnie dies you will certainly hang. Now throw me the gun.'

'No Mr Hunter.' He sounded sober enough. 'She cheated me at the tables. Took all me gold.'

I wanted to say 'the gold you stole from the Ocean Maiden' but thought better of it.

'Go fetch a surgeon,' I said quickly to a distraught woman next to me who I recognised as one of Bonnie's whores. 'Hurry now.' She scampered away.

'Norvin, please,' I went on. 'Surrender to me and I'll see you are treated fair and square.'

'Fair me arse!'

Someone cried out. 'Hang the firker!'

'Aye. Hang the bastard. He be a bad loser, the worst kind.'

'Norvin. At least let me come up and talk to you in private. Let me get a surgeon to Bonnie. I'll come up, alright, just me on my own and we'll talk in private … you and me …'

Karboom!

The musket ball slammed into the mate's face pulverising his head in a flash of blood, brains, skin and hair. As wounded as Bonnie was, she managed a weak scream before both she and her captive collapsed, disappearing behind the window ledge. I spun about on my heels to see a dissipating cloud of smoke spiralling away from the muzzle of an assassin's rifle, elevated in the ratlines of a ship a hundred yards distant. I yelled to Fabian and Snake who raced to the ship while I sprung for the stairs three at a time. The door to the first floor room was locked but I couldn't wait for a key and ploughed my boot into the lock fitting. The door splintered open on the second kick.

'Bonnie!' I called and rushed to the poor creature crumbled on the floor where she fell with Norvin Radford's bloodied and near headless corpse lying across her.

By the time Dr Bowling arrived to take Bonnie to nearby Saint Mary's Hospital Fabian and Snake had the assassin in irons – handcuffs and leg irons loaned from the adjacent guardhouse. The killer was a giant of a man, unrepentant, morose and sullen, sitting in a hired cart. We sat in silence and exchanged little conversation until we arrived back at the prison where the killer was placed in the gatekeeper's lockup.

'Well that was unexpected,' I sighed. The day was warming up in more ways than one.

'Aye,' Fabian wiped sweat from his brow with his sleeve. 'Can ya believe it? Christ I 'ope Bonnie's goin' to be alright.'

'I never seen a man's 'ead explode like that before,' Snake looked a little disconcerted.

'Well I'm thinking he was guilty of stealing the ship's coin on the *Ocean Maiden*. We need to find out where he was lodged and search his belongings.'

'Aye, we'll send Jasper.' Fabian pondered a moment. 'Where did we send Jasper again?'

'To bring in Cap'n Slade, sar,' Snake replied, still haunted by the memory of the exploding head.

'How did ya go with Cuthbert Cummings?' I asked Snake, remembering it was his duty to find the brewery worker and ask him about Lynch Savage's cart.

''e wasn't 'ome at his cottage in Campbell Street but the lady next door said 'e was at the brewery ...'

'The Jolly Hatters?' I said.

'Aye. I found 'im there in the factory; 'e' one o' the chief brewers for their aerated waters ... ginger beer and dandelion ale.'

'Firkin' ghastly stuff that dandelion I gotta say,' Fabian complained.

'So, the cart, man,' I said growing impatient. 'Did he say he had the cart wheel repaired and why?'

Suddenly a commotion caught our attention and Jasper stormed into the office looking proud as Punch. 'I'm 'ere sar!'

'So ya are lad,' Fabian looked slightly surprised. 'What's up?'

'I got Cap'n Slade in the gatekeeper's. 'e weren't 'alf angry sar ... when I arrested 'im like ... well me n' two guards that is.'

'I said bring 'im in for questionin', not arrest 'im!'

'What's the difference ... sar?'

'Jesus lad, go fetch 'im 'ere.'

Captain Durward Slade was not a happy man ... 'Especially when you send this young cock to fetch me ... and in public!' He waved a hand at Jasper. 'No I'm not happy sir. I'm damned humiliated!'

The captain looked to me for answers. We had got along pleasantly on the voyage out on board his ship the *Georgette*, now this. It was awkward for us both.

'My apologies Captain,' I answered. 'But the lad's fervency displays his dedication to his employment.'

'So to what do I owe the pleasure, Caspian, of being dragged here, *here* of all places, for an interview?'

'Do you know a Mr Richard Dart Captain,' I asked.

Captain Slade was taken aback. 'Why, yes, of course, he is my manservant at my home in New Town.'

'Manservant!' Fabian jumped up like an opponent had called 'checkmate'.

'So you're the sea captain Port Arthur prisoner Robert Dodd was talking about.'

Slade's jaw dropped open. 'Port Arthur, what … who?'

I explained the connection and then showed Slade the token.

'Well goodness gracious, I … ah … do not know what to say.'

'You knew the man was a convicted felon when he was assigned to you, did you not?' I asked.

'Yes, yes. *All* decent hired help are ex-felons in this colony.' That was true I guessed. 'But I can't imagine the man killing anyone, no sir, not at all,' the captain shook his head adamantly.

'The fact is, Captain Slade, that you sir, have a motive to eliminate the Norwegian sailor from God's earth so as to maintain the mystery bestowed on the *Ocean Maiden*,' I said. 'Without the threat of him, the dead sailor, regaining his memory and assisting in laying claim to the ship's plight, you sir, have a lot to gain,'

'Aye,' Snake decided to throw in his two bobs worth. 'The cargo alone is worth over five thousand guineas we're told.'

'Now we discover the murderer, Richard Dart, is in ya employment, rather coincidental wouldn't ya agree?' Fabian looked pleased with himself.

'Well yes,' the captain said. 'But I can assure you neither Richard Dart nor myself had anything to do with this crime. And if you are going to arrest me I say now I want the services of a legal representative.'

'Where can we find this manservant of yours, Richard Dart, now captain?'

'Why he's at my residence. He's critically ill and confined to his bed in his quarters.'

'Ill! With what may I ask?'

'Stomach cramps, excruciating pains,' and Captain Slade screwed up his face as if he was experiencing the agony himself. 'I fear he has the cancer.'

Fabian shot me a glance and tipped his head towards the door.

'One moment please captain,' he said, and he promptly walked out into the privacy of the store. I followed and had a silent chuckle at Jasper standing erect and ready to pounce on *his* prisoner should the man move.

Fabian out of earshot. 'We've naught to hold him.'

'I agree.'

'There's no doubt about this 'ere Richard Dart though, we can arrest him ...'

'Not while he is bedridden. We would come across as heartless beasts.'

'Aye, ya right. And 'e ain't goin' nowhere' while 'e's that poorly. But we'll still 'ave to go see for ourselves.'

'Ya free to go Captain Slade,' Fabian said without apology back in the office. 'Ya don't plan on sailin' anywhere too soon I 'ope?'

'No sir, I do not.' Slade stormed off humiliated, ushered out by Jasper.

'Jasper,' Fabian said on his return.

'Sar.'

'Go finish this witchcraft angle and I'm holdin' you responsible for keepin' an eye on Cap'n Slade and the welfare of 'is ailing manservant.'

Fabian looked at me and sighed, 'You and me will 'ave to pay a visit to the Slade residence.'

Immediately footsteps drew his attention to the door.

'And look what the cat dragged in,' Fabian chuckled at the sight of Hal and Billings returning.

'Firkin' wild goose chase,' Hal grumbled, standing in the doorway, leaning on the mull posts and sweating from the afternoon sun.

'Would that be because that Richard Dart is mortally ill?'

'Aye, how did ya know sir?'

'Because we just had a visit from his guv'nor, Captain Slade.'

Billings pushed past Hal 'Oh. So you know then sir, that Dart is Slade's manservant?'

'Aye. Jasper 'ere is goin' ta keep an eye on the both of 'em.'

'So Snake,' I finally managed to ask, 'Cuthbert Cummings, the Jolly Hatter brewer, what was the outcome?'

''e's clean Caspian. I'd bet me life on it. 'e was devastated when I told 'im about the murder sar,'

'He hadn't heard?'

'No.'

'He must be one of very few who hadn't then.'

'I made 'im take 'e's boots off an' all. To see if'n a nail was missin'.'

Nar, nuthin'. Bit cranky 'e was.'

'And what of the cart wheel?'

''e says he took it to the smithy to get a new 'oop fitted. 'e was cranky 'bout that too 'cos it cost 'im half a sov. He has an alibi for all night the night of the murder ...'

'Who?'

''is wife.'

'Ya see 'e's been lettin' other coves use Savage's cart for two bob a day, when 'e's not usin' it for Savage's business like.'

'Cartin' barrels o' grog to the wharf?'

'Aye.'

'Yes, Savage said that he knew about that,' I said. 'He also thought Cummings didn't know he knew.'

'Aye, that's why Cummings was a bit cagey, but when he knew it was at a murder scene he told me everythin'.'

Fabian's impatience showed. 'So pray tell man, who did 'ave the firkin' cart Sunday night?'

'Aboubacar.'

'Aboo firkin' what?'

'He's an African here with a dance troupe playing at the Theatre Royal this week with Mistress Ruby Blood.' Snake looked at us all staring back at him and wondering. Wondering where this was all heading.

'There's more sar,' Snake rolled out his bottom lip scraping his teeth with his tongue.

'Well?'

'Aboubacar is an African albino!'

Jasper screwed up his face. 'What's that?'

'It means he is a white black man,' I answered. 'A negro who is born white ...'

'That's the cove I seen at the séance.' Jasper interrupted.

'Aye, sounds like 'im.'

'Yes,' I said. 'They're very rare. And I hate to say this but they are considered medicine men and quite often dabble in black magic ...'

'Like witchcraft?'

'Yes.'

'I need a drink,' Fabian slipped off the desk and snipped open his fob watch, 'Goodness gracious, is it that time already?'

'I would like to confirm Richard Dart's malady,' I said. Fabian eyed me briefly.

'Of course ... yes, yes,' he muttered. 'You're right ... we must,'

Fabian spun his boater deftly between his fingers throwing it onto his head in one well rehearsed rakish manoeuvre. 'So Jasper ... witch-craft ... Aboo ... Aboo ... firkin' bacar, track 'im down, you know what to do. Snake.'

'Sar.'

'Find out where that dead'un, the third mate ... ah ... Ransford ... yes Ransford. Find out where he was lodgin' and search his room. Billings ...'

'Sar.'

'You go to the morgue and see if Dr Bedford has completed the autopsy on Edith Philpot's lover Nathanial Rudder. Get me a report. And Hal, you return to Rudder's cottage and find out more 'bout the old lady seen 'anging about the night o' his murder. Savvy?'

'Aye.'

Fabian caught up with me at the prison entrance where Corporal Aldrich opened the door in the gate leading onto Campbell Street. The afternoon sun was high in the cloudless sky and there would be no shade for an hour or two. The guard was sweating profusely in his blue woollen coat, with perspiration running down both cheeks from under his shako. He made a cursory inspection up and down the deserted street, leant on his rifle with both hands, raised his chin with importance and said artfully, 'I 'ear ya got ya man already, squire.'

'What?' Fabian was rather abrupt with the man who had little else in his weary life to amuse him.

'Ya gone caught ya murderer I 'eard, a sea captain no less.' He stepped back to scrutinise us attempting to wet his lips with a parched tongue.

'No we have not,' Fabian was irritable; I think he really did need that drink. 'You must take care not to spread gossip Aldrich.'

'Eh?' the guard was not giving up that easily. 'What's this I 'eard 'bout some nigger witch then?'

'Jesus man, do you believe everything you hear?'

I managed to attract the attention of a hansom cab driver outside the Royal Exchange Hotel some hundred yards distant. He trotted towards us.

'Imbecile,' Fabian spat as we walked away. 'If we're not careful rumours will spread 'round 'ere faster than the pox at Bonnie Nettles's whorehouse!'

The two-wheel cab pulled into a turning circle at the front of Dover House where we were greeted by a relaxing melody from a cast iron fountain cascading waters over its many faceted sides. The top tier was adorned with a naked cupid firing his arrow. Three King Charles spaniels came scuttling off the balcony yapping at the horse, which responded by pawing nervously at the pathway. Captain Slade's residence was a one-storey sandstone affair, yet of grand Regency design with an east and a west wing. It was spread out generously and surrounded by manicured gardens fit for royalty. I guessed the building to be around thirty years old with its slate roof and wooden shutters. Shutters that Fabian informed me were originally for security, when bushrangers were a problem in the area.

'Aye lad, on the inside of each window is a wide sill that is 'inged. When ya lift it there's solid wooden shutters what is on a pulley like so they can be raised up in front o' the glass in an emergency. Bit like a Norman castle drawbridge... well sort o.'

Instantly Captain Slade was drawn to the veranda by the yapping dogs. 'Really,' he shouted. 'This is too much ... simply too much. I barely return to my home and you are here ... I can honestly say you are less than welcome.'

'I understand undoubtedly cap'n,' Fabian jumped from the buggy. 'But we're here to see Richard Dart. And in the name of Her Majesty Queen Victoria, I would like to add.'

Slade bit his lip and skulked back into the shade while I dismounted the hansom cab and ordered the driver to wait. The three-mile walk back to Hobart Town would otherwise be an arduous task in this heat.

'This way!' Slade whistled to his dogs and strolled off ahead leading us around the outside of the residence to the servant's quarters.

'We don't get to see inside His Majesty's palace then,' Fabian said to me not too softly.

'The man has worsened I'm afraid,' Slade said in a hushed voice as we entered a small cottage at the rear of Dover House next to the kitchen. 'You won't be able to talk to him but you can confirm what I told you, the man is dying, and then kindly leave.'

We entered the room that had been shuttered for shade and coolness; however the air was stuffy and foul smelling from vomit and diarrhoea. The woman attending to him introduced herself as Peg, his sister. There was no doubt the man was mortally ill, his countenance was sallow and devoid of the colour of health. Richard Dart was delirious and falling in and out of consciousness; appearing in all ways to be at death's door.

'Seen enough,' Fabian said discreetly pinching his nose with his fingers. I nodded silently.

'That is ... was ... our only suspect,' I said as we trotted in the cab back up the hill and past the Queen's Domain towards the township.

'A malignant growth of the stomach Slade says ... huh!' Fabian was clearly annoyed. 'Is that God's way of punishing the man?'

'We must be getting back to the Bond Store,' I said.

'Aye!' Fabian's eyes widened once more – and it wasn't over the female form or a quart of grog. 'You made a discovery. I totally forgot with all the goings on ... what was it lad?'

'Well I saw a ...'

But destiny had other plans. A red-coated soldier, whom I recognised from the grounds of Government House, bailed us up at the crest of Argyle Street before the hill rolls back towards the cove. He reined in his stallion before us, forcing our hansom cab to a halt.

'Mr Winter and Mr Hunter I presume,' the guard looked at us carefully, finally recognising Fabian.

'Aye.'

'The governor would like to see you on a matter of importance,' he said sternly, his back military straight. We must have looked a little confused; we were after all ensconced in our conversation.

'I was told at the Prisoners Barracks you would more than likely be found on this road,' he added in response to our bewilderment.

A pleasant afternoon sea breeze had picked up by the time we alighted our ride at the gate to the crumbling Government House. The Union Jack snapped in the wind, its rope smacking the flagpole with rhythmic slaps while the fountain water misted onto the pathway.

We followed Mr Wheaton, the secretary, down the passage where an unattended door slammed shut in a flurry of air and a small piece of plaster fell from the ceiling crumbling on Fabian's head.

'Jesus!' he hissed. 'What's that?' He ground crumbs of plaster between his fingertips.

'1820s I'm guessing,' I said stifling a laugh.

'1820s? ... right ... jolly funny bastard ain't ya?'

Mr Wheaton led us out the door and along another veranda and into the garden on the cove side of the house where the governor sat in a sheltered gazebo groaning under the weight of a canopy of string beans. An artist painted His Excellency's portrait and both men were deep within their own thoughts. The secretary cleared his throat rather unceremoniously to win attention. The artist, deep in concentration, looked up from his easel where already, I observed, the portrait was a brilliant likeness of the governor.

'Gentlemen,' Governor Fox Young's eyes sought to track us while his head remained firmly posed, gazing with theatrical intelligence across the garden. 'Please come over.'

We stepped up into the gazebo, stooping low to avoid the beans, and into the welcome shade. The governor's eyes turned back to the artist.

'You can relax Your Excellency,' the artist said with a strong Scandinavian accent.

'Thank you Mr Bull,' the governor faced us with an appreciative sigh. 'This is Knud Bull gentleman,' he said to Fabian and me. 'The celebrated Van Diemen artist whom I have recently had the pleasure of meeting.' We made his acquaintance.

Fabian told me later the man had recently been given his free pardon after being convicted in England for being involved in forgery of Bank of England bank notes. Fourteen years transportation. He was sent to the infamous Norfolk Island Penal Colony and later to the coalmines of Saltwater River here in Van Diemen's Land where he finally received his freedom two years earlier.

'He's a great artist and it's that that has kept him in good stead,' Fabian advised me.

Knud Bull nodded to us over his easel and I couldn't help think what a sad face the forty-four-year-old artist had. His red wavy hair was turning silver, as was his full-length ginger beard and his sullen eyes looked as though they had witnessed much misery.

Governor Fox Young turned to the artist once more; words weren't necessary and the man collected his coat from the back of a chair and took a stroll through the vegetable gardens where he sat by a rather handsome folly of a miniature castle gatehouse. The governor caught me staring. 'You like my folly Caspian?'

'If that's what it be sir, yes I do.' The structure was made of wood but painted to look like stone. It stood some twelve feet high, eight feet wide and with a crenulated roof to resemble battlements. A flag-pole poked from the top, proud and erect with halyards and flag snaps to accommodate the Union Jack.

'My wife, Lady Augusta, had it built for me. When we entertain, the men usually retire with cigars and brandy. My wife, you see Caspian, can't abide the smell of smoking tobacco so we are delegated to the folly. The flag though, well that was my idea. Being so far from the main house, all us gentlemen have to do when we require drinks is raise the flag for the butler. Clever, what?'

'Indeed sir.'

'Well down to business,' the governor took a kerchief from his trouser pocket and wiped beads of sweat from his brow, 'I have some interesting news for you gentlemen.'

We stood with our hands clasped in front of us – for want of not knowing where else to place them – and waited in anticipation.

'I had morning tea with Mr Anthony Buckminster, the director of the Bank of Van Diemen's Land.'

He stopped and thought a moment. 'I'm wondering if they will change the name to the Bank of Tasmania when we officially change the name of this island in the near future? Anyhow, I digress ... Mr Buckminster informed me that our shipping captain, Captain Durward Slade, is in debt up to his crow's nest.'

I smiled at the notion.

'How much sir, do you know?' Fabian asked.

'Five thousand pounds. Enough for a motive to kill someone?'

'Aye, an' that's close to the value o' the *Ocean Maiden's* cargo. He stands to lose his ship.'

'The *Georgette*?'

'Yes.'

'I got to know her well on my voyage out here. Your Excellency,' I ventured. He looked me in the eye. 'Our prime suspect in this Norwegian sailor murder, Mr Richard Dart, is critically ill.'

'I was about to ask why you haven't arrested him?' Henry Fox Young sighed and his brow furrowed. 'How so?' he asked.

'Bedridden sir,' I was quick to reply. 'With the cancer, Captain Slade has proposed.'

'Captain Slade!'

'Yes sir, Dart is Slade's manservant …'

'Yes, yes, but why isn't he at a hospital if he is so indisposed, critically as you suggest?'

I had no ready answer.

'Then is his bedside being supervised by a physician?'

'It appears, Your Excellency, 'e is being succoured by 'is sister,' Fabian said.

'I would like a full report if you please, the sooner the better. And keep me informed.' The governor sat back and wiped his brow with a neckerchief. Our interview was over. 'Please let Mr Bull know as you leave that I am available to continue with this … this tiresome process.'

'Tiresome sir,' Fabian stepped in front of the easel and took a moment to admire the artist's work. ''e makes you look mighty 'andsome Your Excellency, if'n ya don't mind me sayin'.'

'Possibly Mr Winter,' Fox Young saw humour in Fabian's typical colonial familiarity not witnessed in the old country. 'But this is of my wife Augusta's making, not my vanity I will have you know. And it's costing a pretty penny too I might add. Ah! Speaking of money how is your investigation advancing with the forged one pound notes?'

'Ah … well … yes sar,' Fabian floundered while I took the opportunity to enjoy the view of the harbour.

'Well?'

'Not good ya Excellency. Ya see we're a wee bit under-manned.'

'Well it's a priority Mr Winter, a priority sir. We cannot have forged notes circulating, it could ruin our already fragile financial circumstances.'

'I know sir. We'll give it our best shot Your Excellency but we 'ave little to go on.' Fabian thought a moment and then added, 'Sir.'

'Yes.'

'This 'ere Mr Bull ... ah ...'

'Ah what Mr Winter?'

'Well ya don't suppose 'e's up to 'is old tricks do ya? I mean knockin' out a few quid ... forged notes like?'

'I doubt that very much. He knows he would not escape the hangman a second time if he were to be caught. Besides he is charging an arm and a leg for this portrait. He has a waiting list. The man is making a fortune.'

The Bond Store an hour later.

'What do ya mean they come and took six barrels?' Fabian flew into a rage. The chief clerk at the Bond Store, Hilbert Roswell, stepped back with his dodgy leg, almost falling down the stair well.

'They come with a magistrate's order sir,' he squealed in a high voice. 'It was all legit like.'

'What'ya firkin' talkin' about, legit? It belongs to the crown until cleared.'

I followed Fabian three steps at a time chasing the lantern light down into the vault. The clerk scampered off to find the paperwork.

'No!' Fabian yelled, angry and flabbergasted. And so was I. 'Of all the firkin' barrels they took the ones we was lookin' at earlier!'

Fabian rounded on me thrusting the lantern into my face. 'What did ya see in that barrel any'ows?'

'A face ... a carving I think ... all white and staring back at me through tealeaves.'

Fabian's angry eyes narrowed. 'A face?'

'Yes, the light was bad, I think it was the head of an older man.'

''ere, 'ere ya go,' and the clerk hobbled awkwardly down the steps shaking the creases out of the parchment keen to clear any impropriety on his own behalf. He held it up for us both to see with the aid of a second lantern. Fabian snatched it away and straightened the document out over a keg.

'Well I'll be rogered backwards,' he snarled stabbing a finger at the signature. 'Magistrate Bellamy,' he spat. 'A shady rogue o' the courts if'n I ever knew one.'

'Who came for the barrels?' I asked the shaking clerk.

'Some cove what called 'imself Maxwell and three big buggers what moved these 'ere barrels as ya can see to get at the six down the bottom what were marked with the clearance on that there parchment.'

'Markings?'

'Aye, they 'ad a small red stamp, of a springing deer I think it was, on the side like.'

'Yes,' I remembered seeing the markings.'

The chief clerk shifted on his dodgy leg. 'But there was somethin' strange squire.'

'What was that?'

'Well them kegs was s'posed to be full o' tea but they was too 'eavy for that. Oh I seen tea spilt on the ground but ...'

'That was me,' I said, 'well some of it anyhow.'

'You opened one sir?'

'Yes.'

The clerk gave me a look of reprimand but thought better of it. 'Well as I said, too 'eavy fa just tea in my 'umble opinion.'

'So did you recognise any of these men?' I asked.

'Well funny ya should say sir, but I 'ave a tipple at the Shades now and again.'

'Shades?'

Fabian looked alert. 'Shades is an inn under the Theatre Royal,' he explained with the knowledge of a street map.

'Aye,' Roswell continued. 'But I only imbibe the one or two drinks mind, 'cos I live close by in Wappin'. Any'ow I seen one o' them coves in there many a time.'

'Oh!' Fabian held the lantern higher. 'Description?'

'Not too good lookin' with a scar on 'is left cheek, curly brown 'air, pointy nose, bushy eyebrows and 'e loves 'is pipe 'e does. Always got a pipe hangin' from a gap o' missin' teeth in his lower right jaw.' Roswell pinched his lips like he was thinking. 'Oh aye, 'e always wears a black patched coat, white shirt – when it's washed – and a thick bowed tie done up 'round 'is neck, like 'e's hidin' somefink.'

'Thank you Hilbert,' I said. 'You've been helpful.' I jotted the description into my black notebook.

'Well we've done the full circle this day my friend,' Fabian had that look in his eye after Roswell parted. 'And 'ere we are back at the Bond Store. I suggest we reconnoitre at the 'ope and Anchor 'cross the street and partake of refreshments while we nut this thing out.'

I could hardly argue as I myself felt as dry as the parchment we held in evidence.

The Hope and Anchor, directly across the road from the Commissariat in Macquarie Street, was doing a good trade with rough and ready seamen.

'Two ships come in this mornin',' Audrey the barmaid in the taproom told us while pumping two quarts of porter up from the keg cellar directly below us. 'One whaler down from Twofold Bay and a merchantman from Batavia.'

Audrey blew unwanted froth aside and thumped the heavy tankards in front of us. I pressed a shilling into her waiting palm.

'Cook's gone done some nice wallaby stew if'n ya hungry,' she said with her eyes wandering over my generous waistline.

'Sounds good to me Rose,' and Fabian was about to order when Snake pushed between noisy seafarers.

'There ya are!'

'Christ Snake, we just got 'ere,' Fabian muttered. ''Ow did ya know we was 'ere?'

'The clerk 'cross the road.' And he tipped his head towards the open corner door. 'Anyhow I've come to inform you our suspect Richard Dart is dead.'

'Dead!'

'Aye, dead as a door nail.'

'But we was with 'im only a couple o' hours ago.'

'But he did look pretty sick,' I acknowledged.

'Aye, that 'e was.' Fabian took a long draft on his porter and licked the froth from his moustache with a practised tongue.

'We need to see that autopsy,' I said. 'Remember the woman who poisoned her husband? Dart was violently ill, Slade may have poisoned him.'

'Aye.' Fabian belched and took another well-earned guzzle.

'Billings was onto it, wasn't he?' I reminded him.

Fabian nodded, before burying his face in his tankard once more.

'How did you go with our other dead villain,' Fabian asked Snake after he came up for air. 'Norvin Ransford the third mate on the *Georgette*?'

'Found his lodgings sir, in the Victoria Tavern in Murray Street.'

'And?'

Snake instantly wore a broad smile. He pulled a small package from his coat pocket, unwrapping the brown paper carefully for us to see.

'Oh my!' I gasped. 'It's beautiful.'

'Aye and worth a pretty penny an' all,' Fabian smiled. 'That was in 'is room I take it?'

'Aye sir,' Snake crowed. 'Hidden with some other baubles and two half sovs that I'm thinkin' was all that was left o' what 'e thieved from the *Ocean Maiden* captain's money chest. And lookee 'ere.'

Snake turned the Italian cameo in his rough fat fingers. It depicted a bacchante in a heavy gold frame, where we clearly read the engraved name *Ingunn Evjen* on the back.

'That's the Norwegian captain's wife's name,' I remembered from the manifest and log. 'Well done Snake,' I said. 'That's enough to hang the thieving blaggard.'

'Aye,' Fabian drained his tankard and delivered a disarming smile at the bar wench. 'Enough to 'ang 'im if 'e didn't already 'ave 'is face blown off this mornin'.'

'And what of the sniping assassin Snake, have you learnt anything about him?'

'Aye. His name is Quillon, he's the bosun off the *Albatross*, a whaler out o' Twofold Bay.'

'Quillon?'

'Aye. Just Quillon, no other names like. 'e was smitten with Bonnie Nettles sar, smitten 'e was.'

'Enough to murder a man, damned waste.'

'They's sayin' the magistrate'll go lenient on 'im 'cos 'e probably saved Bonnie's life.'

'I hope so,' I said. 'I really hope so.'

I failed. Failed bitterly. The truth of the matter was the past few days had been so stressful and the weather so unusually hot, that I imbibed on more porter than I intended, with Fabian's encouragement I might add.

It was after six in the evening when Snake arrived back to the Hope and Anchor from the morgue to let us know Richard Dart had been poisoned and over-bled with leeches, a common enough cure, but not when pints of precious blood are removed, drawn out by their three razor sharp blades for slicing the skin.

'Richard Dart was definitely murdered sir,' Snake nodded sagely and drank his first quart.

'Then we musht arrest Cap'n Shlade, gentlemen,' Fabian slurred. 'Drink up Shnake, we 'ave work ta do.'

'Oh, can't rush it sir, I'll get indigestion.'

'Then two more 'ere Audrey, we may as well 'ave another Caspy, while we wait for this young man.'

And Fabian laid a crisp one pound note on the counter to settle our wallaby stew and porter lunch account.

• • •

Armed with our service pistols and Fabian's favourite twenty-year-old blunderbuss loaded with rusty nails and slag from the blacksmiths, we rode back to New Town. We travelled on the Iron Widow, as Fabian insisted on calling the prisoner transport cart with its iron lockup; a cumbersome four wheel cage. Fabian was at the reins while Snake and I rolled about in the cage in complete discomfort.

With the benefit of courage from an afternoon's drinking, Fabian took the Iron Widow through the front gates and *over* the carriage turning circle at the front of the Captain's residence – rather than around it. After barely missing Cupid's fountain he trampled over a flowerbed in full bloom and climbed onto the Widow's roof with a brass speaking horn and his blunderbuss.

'Strange,' I said. 'The house is all shuttered up.' But on further observation one window on the east wing was unprotected.

'Cap'n D-Durward Shlade,' Fabian wheezed alcoholic fumes through the megaphonic device. 'You are unner arrest shar.' No answer. The residence looked deserted. 'You are unner arresht for the murder of your servant Mr R-Richard Dart ...'

An amplified belch escaped.

'And the implication for the murder of ...' Fabian swayed about on the cart roof and I swear I thought he was going to topple off.

He dropped to his knees on the roof and peered down at us. Blood rushed to his head.

'Wha' was that sailor's name, the cove what was s-strangled.'

Snake poked his head out from the open cage. 'No name sar.'

Fabian straightened with difficulty. He put the horn back to his lips. 'For the implication of the murder of N-Norwegian sailor no name sar!' He was half way through a giggle when a shot rang out and Fabian's hat was plucked from his head. 'FIRK!' Fabian fell back to his knees and I thought he'd been shot.

'Fabian!'

'Wha'?'

'Are you alright?'

''e took a shot at me, the firker!' he said, slightly sobered.

Snake poked his head out the back once more. 'Get down sar.'

'The f-firker took a shot at me!'

Boom!

Another musket ball shredded the wooden frame of the iron cage. 'Jeshuz!' Fabian fell from the roof landing heavily in the flowerbed, like a sack of potatoes.

Boom!

The blunderbuss discharged, peppering the marble statue of Cupid with nails.

'Ouch, that's gotta hurt!' Fabian snatched a mouthful of air, wheezing a laugh.

'Are you hit?' I jumped from the cart.

'No!' Fabian was more shocked than anything.

'Get in the back,' I took him by the arm and dragged him behind cover at the same time discharging my pistol towards the house.

Boom!

Kashatter!

It was some time since I had fired a pistol and the recoil kicked like a mule. I daren't see where my shot had gone, but it sounded like my ball hit a window.

'Atta boy Caspy!' Fabian was impressed. His shoulder hurt from the fall, otherwise he was not injured. He drew his Tower pistol and fired a shot loosely. Another boom and a billow of smoke were followed by the sound of smashing glass.

'FIRKER!' he shouted. I picked up the speaking horn from where it had fallen. 'What ya doin'?' Fabain glared.

'I sailed with the man, I know him well.' I held the horn to my mouth. 'Mr Slade sir … Captain …'

All was quiet. Eerily quiet.

'Captain Slade!' I went on. 'If you come out now I will see you are treated like a gentleman …'

'Pig's arse you will, I'm goin' ta pop a ball in 'im first,' Fabian threatened, picking up his hat from the garden and wiggling a finger through Slade's neat bullet hole.

'Captain Slade … we know you are in there,'

Silence. No one heard the patter of feet sneaking through the apple trees on our left flank. No one saw the movement of bushes near the grand gate entrance.

'Captain Slade … you are making this difficult for yourself sir …'

'Sir?' Fabian grimaced. 'Cur more like!'

Suddenly a voice boomed from behind us. 'Stand to!'

'Christ!' We spun about to see Captain Slade standing ten feet away levelling a six-barrel pepperbox pistol at us.

'Captain Slade!' My voice must have sounded unnaturally high. 'What are you doing?'

'Doing, I'm pointing a gun at you, that's what I'm doing.'

'Don't be a fool man,' and Fabian took a step towards him.

Boom!

A lead ball splintered the cart between us and Slade twisted the next barrel under the hammer. 'Next one's in your heart. I have five shots left, more than one each. Now get to the back of the cage.'

'Wha …?' Fabian was still unsteady from his fall.

'I-said-get-to-the-back-of-the-cage.' And Slade waved the pepperbox about like it was a flag at a coronation. 'I've five more shots and I can't possibly miss from here.'

'Do as he says,' I told Fabian and Snake. 'He's not worth dying for.'

'That's correct Mr Hunter. I'm sorry to do this to you, I quite like you sir. But at the same time I will not hang, no sir.'

Captain Slade forced us to throw our weapons to the ground and padlock ourselves in from through the bars.

'Now throw me the key if you please.'

And that's the moment I realised it was going to be a long night as there were no neighbours within shouting distance of us.

'Handy weapon, those pepperbox pistols,' I said as we watched Slade disappear from sight on horseback. 'I nearly bought one from a gunsmith in Calais. That one was French you know. I recognise the silver lion's head on the handle …'

'Shut up!'

Yes, a long night indeed.

Day Nine – Saturday

'WELL WELL, THERE YA BE.' THE WELCOME VOICE came from Sergeant Caldwell of the prison guard. He rode onto the property with another soldier, both men fresh from a night's sleep and erect and proper in their neat red coats and shakos.

'I said to Cedric 'ere,' the sergeant said. 'Mr Winter and 'is team haven't returned from that arrest last night.'

'Would you just get us out of here please sergeant?' Fabian was not in the best of moods. The sergeant walked around the property, soon returning with an iron bar, which he used to prise the lock from the cage door.

'Thank you,' I said rather humbly, speaking for the three of us, as I crawled out and stretched.

'Not a word,' Fabian threatened our saviours. 'Ya hear me. Not a bleedin' word to anyone, right?'

Sergeant Caldwell looked to his uniformed partners then back to Fabian. 'Me lips is sealed sir,' he said biting his bottom lip in an attempt to maintain a straight face.

'Foolish man,' I said into my mug of steaming thick black coffee back at the prison. 'He had everything. The beautiful residence, a merchant ship and he murders people all over greed.'

Snake blew on his brew in a vain attempt to cool it. 'Aye, but 'e was in deep debt was 'e not?'

'Yes, but you don't kill for it,' I was unforgiving.

'Some do lad,' Fabian sniffed his armpit; there was no chance to retire and wash. 'Some do … ah Hal …'

'Sir.'

'See to it that a guard is put on the *Georgette*, she rides at anchor off Hunter Wharf.'

'What will happen to her I wonder,' I thought aloud.

'Bank o' Van Diemen's Land will lay claim to her, you mark my words.'

Hal, Billings and Jasper were clearly deep in contemplation. Fabian could see that they wanted to know what had happened to us, for we obviously hadn't spent the night in our beds; yet we were sober.

'Don't ask,' Fabian glared at Hal. 'Any'ow Hal, how did ya go with the old lady enquiry in the laneway outside Nathanial Rudder's cottage?'

'Two cottages down from the deceased's abode, a Mrs Nora Evans told me she seen an old woman 'angin' 'bout suspicious like on Mondee night.'

'The night Rudder was murdered?'

'Aye. She says it was awful dark but she thought the woman to be about five-an'-'alf-feet tall and a bit on the chubby side.'

'Chubby?'

'Fat sir.' And heads turned in my direction.

'Don't look at me, gentlemen,' I reprimanded, making a mental note to lose a few pounds.

'Oh ... and there was somethin' else,' Hal continued.

'What?'

'She said she went out lookin' for her cat, Mrs Evans that is, 'cos 'er sick daughter was frettin' 'bout it ... and 'ow she said good evenin' like, a greetin' in passin' to the woman in the dark laneway and the woman grunted back ...'

'Grunted?'

'Aye, just a grunt. But she said she was dressed like a vagabond, like a destitute ya know, but she didn't smell.'

'Smell! Good heavens why should she smell?'

'Well street people usually stink sar, unwashed like.'

'Oh, of course.'

'But she did notice the woman smelt clean and of soap, too.'

'Right.'

'Billings,' I asked, 'what about you? What did Dr Bedford have to say about Nathanial Rudder?'

'Shocking sir, Christ didn't he half stink. Four days 'e's been face down in the rivulet. I'm surprised no one found 'im sooner. All blown up with gas and maggots 'e was and ...'

'Yes, yes, spare us the details thank you.'

'Well Dr Bedford says 'e was bludgeoned *and* shot sir. His head was broke above the right ear. 'e reckons the murderer whacked 'im one, but 'e escaped from his cottage to the rivulet before the killer put a lead ball in 'is 'ead. Small calibre, like one of them pocket pistols 'e reckons, which have become popular for travellers.'

'What of Richard Dart, did Dr Bedford have time for an autopsy?'

'Ah! I nearly forgot, yes,' Billings said, looking rather pleased with himself. 'He found ground glass in Dart's lower bowel.'

'Ground glass!' I was incredulous. 'So Captain Slade was feeding Dart ground glass in his food while the man was weak from being bled by leeches and on strong doses of laudanum.'

'Aye,' Snake shook his head. 'Slade drugged Dart with laudanum first, so he wouldn't feel the pain ... and people said he was heartless.'

'We still have nothing on Edith Philpot's killer, do we?' I looked back to Jasper. 'So tell me what do we know of Aboubacar, the albino Negro who we know hired the cart the night of the murder?'

'Aboubacar!' Jasper groaned. 'He's a dark one sir.'

'No 'e's not, 'e's an albino,' Fabian chuckled at his own joke. Snorts of laughter buzzed the room.

'What do you mean, a dark one?' I asked.

'Well 'e is part of a magic show,' Jasper went on. 'A troupe what's travelling around the colonies. They are playin' out their show at the Theatre Royal, sir, the past week, but ya know what I think?'

'What?'

Jasper's chest pushed out with pride. 'Well the star of the show is a beautiful lady ...'

'I wouldn't call 'er a lady!' Billings interrupted.

'Beautiful woman then ... she's like a white witch, in the stage act that is, and Aboubacar the albino Negro is the devil like, the devil incarnate as they say on the advertising bill.'

'Oh.'

'Aye. And I found out they're into demonology, high magic as they call it, they're members of a secret society ...'

Billings. 'A society, back in London?'

'Aye. Aboubacar is the grandson of a slave,' Jasper checked his notes. 'Eliphas, his poor cobbler father trained for priest'ood but abandoned the church for occultism. Aboubacar followed in 'is father's footsteps. Occultism is a subject, I am told, that he is widely read but no scholar.'

'Jolly good,' I congratulated the young man. 'Where did you learn this?'

''e read it in the 'obart Town Gazette,' Billings cut in. 'Didn't ya Jasp?'

The rapping of knuckles on our office doorframe had us all in a twist. It was The Priest, one of the prison gatekeepers, leaning against the door and juggling his weight on his good leg.

'Mr Hunter.' He held out an envelope. 'For you sir.' As there was no room in the office for the man to join us, he passed the envelope to Jasper who passed it to Billings who passed it to me.

'Thank you,' I said. 'Who's it from?'

'Dunno sir, some young tyke on the street was out there bashin' on the gate and I told 'im if'n he didn't watch out I'd lock 'im up proper. That took the all importance off is grubby little face.' This seemed to amuse our gatekeeper.

'Is he still there?'

'Aye. The little bastard's waiting on a penny.'

I looked at the seal. It was a springing deer in red wax. I tore the envelope open and a card fell to the desk.

'What is it?' someone asked as I picked up what I now realised was a ticket.

'It's a ticket to the magic show, Phantasmagoria, at the Theatre Royal, dress circle, Saturday.' I looked in the envelope for a message. Nothing!

'Saturdee huh. That's tonight.'

'So it is.' I hurried to the gate. The boy was no older than eight; grubby, snotty nosed, barefoot and skinny. 'Who gave you this?' I asked him.

'Don't know the firker's name squire. Never seen 'im 'bout like neither.'

'What did 'e look like?'

''e was an ugly firker with curly 'air and a scar on 'is cheek. 'e give me a penny and says you would too.'

I fiddled in my purse. 'Here's threepence,' I said. 'And buy some soap to wash your filthy mouth out.'

'Don't know what's going on,' I said to the others back in the office, 'but the boy said whoever gave this envelope to him to deliver had a scar on his face.'

'Could be one of 'undreds in this town.'

'You may 'ave an admirer Caspy,' Fabian grinned looking at the ticket. 'But it's a ticket for one, weird huh?'

Something was familiar about the colour, the dark red wax of the seal. I sniffed it. The smell *and* the dark red wax were familiar, but I couldn't quite peg it.

'Right,' Fabian sat in his favourite spot, on the corner of his desk. 'Snake and me are joinin' you at the Theatre tonight, incognito like.' Fabian turned to Jasper. 'And you lad …'

'Sar.'

'Go to the theatre and buy two tickets in the stalls for tonight's show,' he ordered, unlocking the cash tin and fishing out a guinea.

'We can kill two birds with one stone,' I agreed.

'How's that?'

'Well we can take refreshments at the Shades Inn underneath the theatre before the performance and see if our friend who moved the barrels from the Bond Store is there.

Refreshments,' Fabian's face brightened. 'I like the idea. Snake, see we have pocket pistols, balls and powder. Small ones like, we need to conceal 'em.'

'Aye.'

'As soon as the curtains go down tonight we're goin' to arrest this Aboubacar.'

It was agreed I would turn up at the Shades before the other two. Fabian and Snake would be in evening attire; evening attire becoming of the theatre in Hobart Town and not the London's high society I might point out. I found the theatre in advancing dusk, its classical two-storey façade with Roman pillars lit by two tall street lamps at the main entrance. Built from local sandstone it is an imposing building strangely situated near an area of factories, an abattoir, brothels and pubs – namely Wapping. For this reason gentlepeople enter via Campbell Street main entrance and the local riffraff must enter the pit seating via an inn, called The Shades.

Outside the theatre a conjurer attracted a small crowd with his cups and balls trick and seemed to be doing a brisk trade. Aware of how they operate I watched a moment. The conjurer juggles a ball between three upturned cups on a small table and then invites someone in the crowd to pick which cup the ball resides under. A passer-by, in cahoots with the conjurer, repeatedly indicates the correct cup and takes money from the conjurer but when the mark tries his hand at the easy money the ball isn't where he thought it was.

I turned the corner from Campbell Street into Sackville Lane next to the Theatre Royal and the first thing I saw was Lynch Savage's sedan chair parked on the cobbles with one of his minders leaning against the wall and smoking a cheroot.

Then I remembered Savage telling us during dinner at the Sea o' Graves that he was paying a visit to the theatre this Saturday evening. With barely a nod the man acknowledged me and I descended the steep wooden stairs stepping into the stagnant fug of the Shades Inn under the theatre.

Immediately I was assaulted with smoke. It appeared every Jack Tar, whaler and theatre patron was crammed into this cosy space puffing on tobacco in one form or another. The smog fought for first place over stale spilt grog, sweaty bodies fermenting in the summer humidity and an ammoniacal miasma of urine where men had relieved themselves in dark corners rather than visit the latrine. I craved fresh air but I was here on business. With a push and a shove I managed to squeeze up to the bar.

'What'll it be 'andsome?' the petite saucy barmaid yelled over the din.

'Porter,' I yelled back and threw sixpence on the grog-soused counter. She held the tap handle running a salacious hand down its length with a suggestive smile, eventually pulling me a decent head of dark beer. She slid the tankard towards me and snatched up the coin. 'Anything else I can do for you sir, anything at all?' And she licked her lips. Titillating little tart!

I turned to face the taproom with elbows on the bar. The timber counter ran from wall to wall – all red brick – on the left as one descends the steps. The floor was packed earth, like most rural inns back in country England. The ceiling was low, extremely low, with huge beams supporting the theatre above. A dozen oil lanterns threw out sufficient light for me to peruse the packed noisy, smelly room and I couldn't help wonder what Mr Dickens, in London, would have made of the characters within.

Images of chaos if a fire broke out were plaguing my thoughts when I caught sight of Lynch Savage propped on a bench seat in a shadowy far corner. He hadn't seen me and I didn't make a point of attracting his attention. Three henchmen sat in the booth with him.

I was about to order another porter when I was shoved aside by a thirsty rival. I allowed the man space with a sideways glance. Suddenly it was the scar that grabbed my attention.

Yes.

I mentally searched back through my notebook. *Curly brown hair, pointy nose, bushy eyebrows, black patched coat, white shirt, thick bowed tie, he even had a clay pipe clenched between missing teeth lower right jaw.* And the young messenger boy's words … *ugly firker* rang like a church bell.

'Busy in here tonight,' I found myself making conversation with the man before I knew it. He looked sideways at me, more interested in attracting the barmaid's attention, and I just hoped he didn't recognise me, although I knew we hadn't bumped into each other before.

'Wha'?' he scowled at me. Some people are simply born with a sour face.

'Busy,' I reiterated. 'In here, the inn … busy huh?'

He answered with a grunt.

'Robert Pancras,' I introduced myself with a lie, shooting a hand out in greeting. He scowled even harder, ignoring the hand, but I wasn't giving up that easily. 'And you sir, you are … ?'

He turned to face me head on. 'You a turd burglar?' he said, finally managing a coherent sentence.

'A what … a … t-t … no sir! I most definitely am not.'

'Well go take ya chatter elsewhere.' And his lips moved muttering my name *Robert Pancras* as he shook his head.

'I'd be stayin' clear o' 'im sar.' The man who had squeezed in on my other side spoke so only I could hear. I tipped my head to him in greeting. He was a middle-aged, kindly looking man of middle stature, slender built and wiry but tolerably muscular, clearly a man of labour.

'Yes,' I smiled sideways, 'he isn't the friendly type, eh?'

'No sar, 'e ain't. 'e's a strong bugger an' all, and 'e loves a fight so ya best keep away.'

'Well thank you for your concern my friend … Caspian Hunter,'

I introduced myself with my back now turned on the sorrowful character.

'Nice ta make ya acquaintance young lad,' he said with a smile of healthy teeth, 'I'm a stage'and, a scene-shifter, from the theatre, me name's Fred.'

'You enjoy your work here Fred?' I said.

'Oh aye sar.'

'It would be interesting I should imagine, behind the scenes, especially on a show like tonight's performance.'

'Aye. I been 'ere for years sar. It opened in '37 and I been workin' 'ere since '45. I told management I ain't never leavin' sar ... never.'

Immediately a jolly rounded gentleman padded down the wooden stairs clanging a town crier's bell like the theatre was ablaze.

'Hear ye, hear ye!' he bawled in theatrical grandeur. 'Listen up all you'se what's partakin' o' tonight's theatre show, *Phantasmagoria*, get your persons up to ya seats quick like 'cos the show will start wiv or wiv out ya in precisely fifteen minutes.'

And with another flourish of the brass bell he climbed back to the street.

I left Fred to make his way to the stage door while half the taproom funnelled into an exit I hadn't noticed earlier that I discovered led to the pit seating – seating for the riffraff. As I turned the corner of the lane and towards the grand entrance, with my dress circle ticket held firmly in my hand, I caught a glimpse of Lynch Savage being manhandled into his sedan chair to be carried into the theatre.

My seat was two in on the left aisle of the dress circle. 'Wonderful,' I smiled inwardly. I watched with some interest as a barrel-shaped man with a tray walked the aisles shouting 'Grapes, oranges, walnuts,' and pondered whom my benefactor might be. Then from behind I heard a commotion and the grumblings of several patrons being forced this way and that. I turned to see Lynch Savage being manhandled by his minders down the tiers and towards me. He looked grand in a brass-buckled, double-breasted mauve coat with yellow britches, knee-high boots and his favourite tricorn hat festooned with ostrich feathers. He was clearly an enthusiast of piratical days gone by, a wealthy eccentric and patron of the arts. It was then that I realised the two seats to the aisle next to me were for Savage. A moment later one of his men removed the armrest between the seats, padded the area with cushions and Mr Savage himself was parked next to me.

'Mr Hunter,' he smiled broadly. 'What a pleasant surprise.' And he patted my knee.

'Mr Savage sir,' I returned the warm welcome. I was about to ask whether it was he who sent me the ticket when all at once the curtain was pulled back to a sombre tune from a quartet playing in the right wing. The oil lamps were extinguished by ushers and the limelights of the stage floor illuminated to present none other than he whom I recognised from the posters as Aboubacar.

Aboubacar was dressed as a Turkish Pasha complete with a scimitar large enough and bold enough to be used as an executioner's beheading weapon. A little tight matted white hair showed from under his turban and from where I sat I saw his eyes were red, heightened by his pale complexion, which gave him an eerie, if not spectral appearance. The white Negro held his arms up to the audience, already in awe, and the crowd grew silent.

'Ladies and gentlemen, one and all,' Aboubacar's heavily accented, yet powerful voice boomed about the theatre. 'The *Phantasmagoria* troupe, all the way from London's one and only West End, welcomes you all to the Theatre Royal of Hobart Town.'

Clapping was accompanied by shrill whistles and much armrest slapping, especially from the pit seating and the stalls.

Instantly the audience was treated to an acrobatic dance. The quartet silenced the crowd with a lively tune while nimble young lasses in colourful tight fitting blouses and stockings pirouetted, twirled and gambolled in a manner most gratifying to the male eye. It was during this alluring performance that I managed to pinpoint Fabian and Snake in the stalls below, four rows from the front and in a position to see me should they wish.

The dance was followed by Aboubacar himself, exhibiting an empty bag, displaying it inside and out, and then producing eggs from it, followed by silver coins and finally two wild fowl. Alive! The audience were in raptures, and as noisy as any I had shared a theatre with in Birmingham or London.

Whilst I am aware this is done by sleight of hand, I could understand the more ignorant amongst us labelling it as magic … or witchcraft.

Aboubacar followed his act with the 'beheading' of one of the young dancers. Her headless body was displayed to the audience before, miraculously, the head was reinstated to the body – under a sheet of course – to wild cheers and whistles as the *victim* walked free and off the stage.

After nearly an hour of entertaining magic, interval was announced, once more by the crier with the brass bell whom I noticed was more boisterous than ever after spending the first act in the taproom. Lynch Savage's men immediately brought us a salver of cheese, dried fruits, crusty bread and various sweetmeats like coconut ice and marzipan fruits. French Cognac was poured and all in all I was feeling quite special – but then I saw the ring.

The springing deer!

The gold ring was worn on Savage's little finger on his right hand and looked rather effeminate amongst the other solid gold and gemstone bijouterie adorning the man's plump knuckles.

'I must say I'm surprised to see you here lad,' he said, severing a crust of bread and cheese in two with his teeth as he spoke.

'Ah, as am I Mr Savage.'

'Lynch, please.'

'Lynch.' I was about to mention the complimentary ticket and the springing deer seal, but intuition forbade me. I had a distinct impression that the man knew nothing of it, so kept my silence. I slowly nibbled at a piece of coconut ice when I was acutely aware I was being watched. My eye line drifted to the private theatre box to my lower right when I saw Lord Philpot staring back. I automatically smiled. He simply continued staring. Maybe he thought I shouldn't be here. I restrained from waving, but felt obliged to nod. He returned a slight straight-faced bow and looked away.

'You know that cantankerous bastard?' Lynch had noticed my exchange with Lord Philpot.

'Yes. Business only,' I was quick to add.

'Well he's a cad and a rotten bastard and I don't care if he is a firkin' Lord or not.' Movement in the curtains caught both our attention. 'Ah, here she comes,' Lynch grew excited; the curtains were slowly drawing open once again for the final act.

'Mistress Ruby Blood,' he said with reverence and in a spray of Cognac spittle.

'Mistress Ruby Blood. Yes you spoke of her before.'

'Aye. She is Aboubacar's medium, a wondrous soul whom I desire to lay with me sometime. But,' and he lowered his voice as the chatter in the auditorium died away. 'I fear it will never happen, however a man can dream can he not?'

'Yes, dream you certainly can.'

'Who was this Mistress Ruby Blood?' I wondered, 'To agitate the loins of this rather large soul.'

Aboubacar swanned across the boards waving his arms and ranting his spiel about the magic powers of the 'Great, the magnificent, the one and only, Mistress Ruby Blood.' As could only be expected from the company present, there followed more feet stamping, armrest slapping, whistles and cheers. The lights went out. The quartet played a suitable introduction. Instantly we heard a clap of 'thunder' – compliments of gunpowder, drums and cymbals – and a flash of light instantaneously spot lit Mistress Ruby Blood before plunging the stage into darkness once more. There followed a drum roll while limelight spilt a soft light back over the stage.

She truly was a creature of beauty. I heard Lynch sigh. I found myself transfixed. The woman was in her early thirties, long red hair tied behind her head with as many feathers as Lynch had in his hat. She wore a tight bodice revealing large rounded white breasts with gold ringlets hanging from a body-hugging, emerald green, ankle high skirt. Ankle high red leather boots were exposed.

'You sir,' she said in a hushed but commanding voice, which I recognised as Southwark London. 'Yes you in the grey waistcoat with the long grey moustache.'

An older gentleman in the front row sheepishly pointed to himself.

'Yes sir, you recently had a death in your midst … someone close.'

The man was incredulous. 'My wife,' he whispered.

'Would you kindly speak up sir, so as all the theatre can hear you.'

'My wife,' he spoke louder. 'She died a month prior.'

'Yes, I know. She is here with us this evening. She died with problems of the blood did she not?'

'Flux … she died of the flux.'

'Yes, yes,' and Mistress Ruby Blood raised her eyes to the theatre ceiling as if the dear old soul was hovering there. 'And you made a visit to the seaside did you not, before she died. She liked the water she's saying. Liked to be near it or look at it, am I right so far?'

The elderly gentleman nodded. 'She liked the harbour ... here in Hobart Town she did.' Then he thought to add. 'We live at Kangaroo Bluff.'

'Ah yes, she told me. Yes. And her favourite colour was blue.'

'Green actually.'

'Yes blue green, same. Like water ... yes she now tells me it's green ... yes dear ... like the water. Wait ... she's telling me something, her birthday's in May, May or June or July ...'

'April actually.'

'What's that dear?' And Mistress Ruby Blood stared to the ceiling once more to consult the lady's spirit up there somewhere in the gods.

'April,' Ruby said clearly. 'Yes your husband just told me, April.'

By now I was filling in the gaps. Mistress Ruby Blood was no more than a conjurer of the mind. But she was as sweet as the marzipan fruits to the male eye and sharp as a tack dealing with the naïve.

The charade continued for half an hour and I must acknowledge her guesses were sixty per cent correct with artful adjustments of the truth to suit her 'readings' while convincing her mark that she was in contact with relatives or ancestral spirits. She was entertaining if nothing else and, as I said, pleasing to the eye.

Finally the moment the audience was waiting for: Mistress Ruby Blood's grand finale. She was to conjure up the spirit of the long dead. She would make the ghost of a long lost relative appear on stage and for all to see.

'Now this I have to see,' I whispered to Lynch as I leant forward in my seat. In preparation for the grand event, Mistress Ruby Blood requested the audience remain totally silent while she meditated in an armchair wheeled onto the stage. The quartet played a suitable moody melody while the curtains were closed momentarily and the medium meditated. However it was distinct to my trained ear that some preparation was going on out of the public eye.

The curtains pulled back on their rail, the plush red velvet sweeping dust into the wings as it went. I noticed the normally brightly burning limelights had been adjusted and the stage was suitably dark for a 'haunting'.

Mistress Ruby Blood looked comfortable in her high-backed armchair where a brazier was set up on a stand before her and I could now smell the smouldering paperbark scented with Oriental incense. Mistress Ruby Blood explained to the audience the complexity of materialising spirits from the other side. Eventually she began an incantation that included 'hocus pocus, tontus, talontus, vade celeriter iubeo' ...

And she threw a powder into the brazier. A multi-coloured flame danced from the fire.

Then it happened!

Slowly an apparition appeared before her, as she remained trance-like sitting in the armchair. At first it appeared as a faint mist, a vague shape. Then slowly, ever so slowly, a spectral figure of a man materialised.

The crowd gasped.

I heard sobs and whimpers, but mainly the theatre was deathly silent. The figure appeared to hover before the medium, arms out like a phantom in a graveyard. I must confess I was confounded by the spectacle. Mistress Ruby Blood remained in a trance. She then invoked, in a droning voice, while the manifestation drifted before her.

'Who-are-you-who-presents-themselves-before-us-this-night?'

'I am the spirit of Thomas Ryan,' the ghostly voice replied in a deep baritone voice.

'From-whence-you-come-good-sir?'

'I am the spirit of a merchant from Rye, in Kent.'

The theatregoers were entranced, beguiled by the supernatural spectacle before them. I saw a few leave the auditorium, so overcome by fear of the wraith before them.

'And-what-was-your-manner-of-death-Thomas   Ryan?'   the medium continued.

'I died of a disease of the heart.' The ghost levitated and floated before Mistress Ruby Blood and momentarily drifted in and out of vision, once or twice almost disappearing completely.

'For-what-reason-have-you-shown-yourself-tonight?'

The entity began to answer when without warning the most blood

curdling scream came from the stage ceiling high above the supernatural theatrics occurring below. Almost immediately the body of a
man dropped from above; falling with flaying arms and legs desperately clawing at space. He disappeared into the pits to the dreadful
sound of shattering glass.

The apparition was no more.

Total silence was finally met with the most awful racket of
screaming and shouting.

'Excuse me!' I vaulted over Lynch Savage and descended the stairs
four at a time. I crashed through the doors to the stalls and sprinted
to the stage. I climbed up and onto the stage and gaped down into
the pits.

And what I saw was devastation ...

'There 'e is!' Someone next to me stabbed a finger at a figure
sliding down curtain ropes like a monkey. He hit the floor running,
clearly the perpetrator. I pursued him, mounting the ill-lit stage and
ploughed into a traumatised Mistress Ruby who had jumped to her
feet. I had impelled her back into her chair.

'God I'm sorry!' I spluttered. She was beautiful. Our eyes met. I
felt a sparkle. I smartly lifted her back to her feet. 'Sorry, please excuse
me ...'

'Stop the mongrel!' someone screamed from amidst the pandemonium behind me. I raced across the stage, past the dressing rooms
in time to see the dark figure bolt out the stage door into the lane.
Without regard for my own safety, I propelled myself after him. The
dark shape shot down the lane and turned sharp right into an alley. I
rushed after him, took the corner ...

Slam!

An elbow to the face greeted me in the dark shadows. My feet
went from under me. Then the moment I fell I saw the curly hair,
pointy nose, bushy eyebrows, black-patched coat, white shirt, thick
bowed tie and the missing teeth snarl at me in utter contempt.

He truly was an ugly firker.

'The turd burglar!' he growled and then lashed out. The man was
armed with a cosh; a small club of elastic baleen with rope worked
lead balls at both ends.

Whack!

He caught me on my shoulder as I ducked. If he hit my head I would be dead. The pain shot through my body like a bolt from an electric generating machine. I was on my knees, desperate to jump to my feet and challenge the man when ...

'Stand to!'

A voice of authority thundered from the laneway. The assailant made to crush my skull with the cosh ...

Boom!

A loud report exploded in my ear and I was aware a shot had been fired. A brick in the wall of the alley detonated in a flurry of debris and dust. Outnumbered, the attacker turned and fled. Hal helped me to my feet. 'You alright sir?'

'Yes ... yes thank you.' I answered, noting he had called me sir for the first time.

We watched the murderer escape towards Wapping. There was nothing I could do now. He was fit and agile and I was groggy from the thump he gave me. 'What are you doing here?' I asked Hal.

'Fabian told me to keep an eye on ya.'

'Did he now?'

'Aye.'

By the time we made it back through the stage door and to the crime scene most of the patrons had been ushered out of the building. Some, believe it or not, were disgruntled that the show had finished early. Fabian was incensed.

'Ya saw a man die tonight,' he yelled at someone being herded out the stalls exit. 'What do ya want for a firkin' shillin'?'

He turned to Hal and me. 'He got away huh?'

'Aye.'

'Firk!'

I walked to the edge of the stage and peered down into the pits. Two figures lay dead while thick sticky blood still oozed from their badly lacerated bodies.

'What a week,' Snake said in his usual drawl. 'They're droppin' like flies sir.' I looked at the man a moment. His face was deadpan. I don't think he realised what he had said.

All about the bodies were shattered shards of glass. I took in a deep breath and exhaled, trying to calm myself from my ordeal outside, when Fabian saw the confusion on my face as I gazed upon the carnage. One body I now recognised as the man I met in the taproom of the Shades Inn, the stagehand Fred. He was the man who fell from the stage ceiling, but the other was a slender figure dressed in what could only be described as a white shroud.

'That's the ghost!' Fabian said and I sensed he wanted to laugh out loud at the irony of it all. 'Yes Caspian. The ghost is dead also.'

It took me a moment, with the help of the stage manager Mr Totten, to deduce what had happened. The glass was from one large sheet that had been placed on a forty-five degree angle on the stage between Mistress Ruby and the audience. Clever lighting and curtain use had rendered the glass invisible. Hidden below in the pits was a magic lantern and operator who shone a bright spot light onto the 'ghost'. The lantern reflected the 'apparition' onto the glass between medium and audience. It was an effect used all over Europe, Mr Totten told me. Fred the stagehand, who was operating the curtains from above, had been hit hard, with what we now know was the assailant's cosh. Fred fell from high above the stage crashing through the glass and landing on the actor; a dreadful, unnecessary and awful death.

'It was the man who we know helped remove the barrels from the Bond Store,' I said of the murderer. 'And the same man who sent the urchin to the Prisoners Barracks with my ticket.'

'You certain?'

'Positive.'

'What on earth's goin' on?' Snake muttered.

''e came to kill you Caspian, but some 'ow 'e got tangled up with the stagehand.'

'I spoke to them both this evening,' I told the gathering.

And went on to tell Fabian, Snake and Hal about my experience in the Shades Inn and how Fred the stagehand warned me about the other man. I suddenly remembered Lynch Savage has been present. I twisted about to look up into the dark dress circle. But of course he was gone.

'Lord Philpot was here this evening also,' I said.

'Yes, I saw the supercilious old buzzard up there in his box,' Fabian nodded.

'Now I'll be exposed as a fraud,' Mistress Ruby Blood said quietly, visibly shaken.

'Not at all,' I found myself consoling the performer. 'You are a showwoman, surely people don't really expect you to conjure up ghosts.'

'Oh but they do ... ah ... Mr ...'

'Hunter Madame ... Caspian Hunter,' I introduced myself and we shared a smile.

'Where is Aboubacar?' I asked.

'In his dressing room,' Mr Totten said. 'Shall I fetch him?' I was about to answer when Fabian said, 'Wait.' He turned to Hal.

'Hal.'

'Sar.'

'Go fetch the undertaker and see this is cleaned up. There's plenty of hands here, delegate.' Fabian ran an eye over the voluptuous entertainer. 'Maybe *we* can go to Aboubacar,' and Fabian shot me a knowing glance. 'Is there somewhere we can go to discuss this in private?'

Aboubacar was younger than he seemed on stage, maybe thirty. He was my height but marginally slimmer. Out of costume he was quite handsome, in an exotic way. His short wiry blonde hair I now saw was worn in thin dreadlocks, his forehead high and red eyes closer together than most, either side of a typical Negroid flat nose with flared nostrils. However his skin was as white as any Londoner.

Mr Totten, Mistress Ruby, Fabian, Snake and myself crammed into his small dressing room, wedging ourselves into corners as comfortably as was possible. Aboubacar's eyes were glazed and a little distant and I gathered he was a mistress to the demon laudanum.

'Right,' Fabian started. 'Why don't you tell me what's going on?'

'Cut straight to the chase,' I thought. 'What does Fabian suspect that I have missed?'

All was quiet. Fabian waited a brief moment.

'Mistress Ruby, will we start with you maybe?'

She looked at Aboubacar who was having difficulty concealing his anger, then she turned to Mr Totten. Mr Totten shrugged in submission.

'We've nothing to lose now Ruby,' Totten said. 'The show's over.'

Ruby took a deep breath and I stole a glimpse as her ample breasts heaved like they were bellow-driven. She noticed my brief observation.

'Since you represent Her Majesty's constabulary I guess we can tell you,' she finally said choosing to ignore my indiscretion, although privately I felt she was flattered. 'We were being extorted.'

'I knew it, I knew it!' Fabian slapped his thigh.

'That man you let escape ...' Aboubacar spoke at last, slowly. 'He is only the tip of the iceberg.'

'But he was the man threatening extortion, the man with the scar on his face,' I asked.

'Yes, he is the messenger boy,' Mistress Ruby said.

'They came to us after our first show last Saturday evening and threatened to ruin the entire production,' Mr Totten added.

'Who are *they*?' I questioned.

'There were two of them,' Totten said, 'the man with the scar on his face and another brute of a man ...'

'Like a gorilla he was,' Mistress Ruby cut in. 'Six foot six, bald head, large gold earring and he only had one ear ...'

'Cut off in a fight I should imagine,' Aboubacar shook his head.

'Do you have any idea who the gang leader is?' I asked.

Totten replied, 'Local thugs no doubt.'

Fabian's mood changed from detective to interrogator. 'Mr Aboubacar.'

'Just Aboubacar!'

'Aye. Aboubacar. Ya wearin' slippers I notice, for the stage.'

'Yes ... camel skin ... the real thing, from Persia.'

'Wha' do ya normally wear ... on the street like?'

'Boots, why?'

'Can I see 'em please?'

Although Aboubacar had removed his Pasha's turban he still wore what I would call exotic bed clothing or the clothes more suited to a harem; baggy trousers and open blouse exposing his white hairy chest; the theatrical attire of a sultan or pasha. He stood a little groggily and pushed past Fabian to a narrow wardrobe.

'Here,' he sighed, and passed them over. Fabian inspected the sole of each boot. They were clean and all hobnails intact. Fabian looked across at me and shook his head before throwing them back from where they came. 'Hmm ... so why did you require the use of a cart from Mr Cummings last Sunday?'

'Cart?' Aboubacar looked surprised. 'Why I engaged the services of Mr Cumming's cart to haul stage props from storage at Mr Wood's warehouse on New Wharf where they had been stored since we arrived on the island last Wednesday. Fred, God rest his soul, told me he had a friend who would loan me a cart for a small fee.'

'And where did you leave the cart before returnin' it to Mr Cummings?'

'In the stables at the rear of the theatre.'

Fabian. 'Didn't ya realise a steel hoop was missin' from the left wheel?'

'Yes I did … what's this all about?'

'Just answer the question.'

'Yes I did notice the hoop was missing and I assumed someone had stolen it, an urchin maybe, for scrap metal like.'

'Didn't you notice anything strange about it, besides the missing hoop, before returning it?' I asked. 'Like its condition?'

'Well now you mention it was a little muddy.'

'Didn't you ask the stable hand why?'

'Look, I've been distracted with getting this show together, a bit of mud was neither here nor there.'

Then I remembered the cylindrical brass chimney found at the murder site. I took out my notebook and flicked to a rough illustration I had sketched of the mystery article.

'Do you recognise this?' I asked Aboubacar.

He looked at it a moment. 'Well yes, that's my fog making apparatus.'

'Fog making?'

'Yes. It's a part of our theatre. Where is it?'

'It was found at the scene of a murder.'

'Oh God! And I thought it was stolen. It went missing the night I left the cart with the stables. It was hidden, like under a cloth. It's too heavy for me to lift on my own, see, so I thought it would be safe until I could get someone to help me carry it into the theatre.'

Mistress Ruby Blood turned from Aboubacar to face me. 'What is all this about Mr Hunter,' she said in a soft voice with the smallest flutter of eyelashes.

'We have proof that that cart was at the scene of a dastardly murder last Sunday,' I answered trying to ignore the eyelashes. 'And now this as well.' And I waved the drawing about.

'Miss Edith Philpot?' she gasped.

'Yes Madame, one and the same.'

'Ya know of the murder?' Fabian enquired.

'Why yes, who doesn't? Terrible business.'

With no reason now to arrest Aboubacar we made to leave when I had a thought. 'Tell me something,' I stared Aboubacar in the eye. 'Did you pay any money to these men, extortion money?'

'Absolutely not, I figure they were small time thugs and told them so.'

'One last question,' Fabian asked Aboubacar. 'You went to a séance did ya not, few nights ago, at a Mrs Celeste's residence?'

'Yes ... don't tell me that's against the law.'

'Nay. No mate. Not at all. Would ya mind tellin' me why?'

'As you must be well aware Mr Winter, I am interested in the occult, witchcraft, sorcery ...'

'And deception,' Snake said without thinking.

'Yes. And deception,' Aboubacar bemoaned. 'We all have to put bread and meat on the table one way or another.'

Aboubacar wiped makeup from his face with a damp cloth and studied his tired eyes in the mirror. 'But not everything is deception you must understand. Oh certainly there is much theatre, as you witnessed tonight with our ... spirit or ghostly image. But much of it is our spiritual connection also.'

'Oh,' Snake remained sceptical.

Aboubacar ignored Snake and singled out Fabian in the mirror. 'You seek a sea captain do you not ... Mr Winter?'

'Aye,' Fabian looked at me, but I could only shrug in ignorance.

'His spirit reaches out to me.'

Fabian. 'Spirit?'

'Yes. He has passed over.'

'No.'

'But I assure you Mr Winter, you will find the man's body soon enough.'

'Poppycock,' Snake couldn't hold back his thoughts any longer.

'And you sir,' Aboubacar turned to face Snake. 'You have desires for a young lady, her name is ... Shirley ... no no Shelley ... yes that's her ... Shelley Dove. She is an assistant at Mr Miller the chemist ... oh wait ... I see a tiny dog ... yes. She has a dog ... a Pekinese called

… Til … Tilly.'

Snake's mouth dropped open.

Aboubacar was on fire. 'Am I correct thus far?'

Snake was incredulous but the man was unerringly correct. Feeling uncomfortable, Snake left the room.

'We'll be needing to talk again, Mr Aboubacar,' Fabian said following Snake to the street.

'We won't be leaving any time too soon,' Mistress Ruby flashed me a smile. 'So if you need me, well you know where I'll be.'

'That bastard should be burnt at the stake for witchcraft,' Snake grumbled as we joined him on Campbell Street. He was clearly unsettled by Aboubacar's accuracy. 'Burnt alive I say!'

'Now now Snake,' I said. 'Can't be doing that these days, it is 1855 after all.'

'Argh!'

'What do you think?' I asked Fabian as Mr Totten secured the theatre with locks and the lamps were extinguished leaving us in moonlight. The sounds of revellers and a jolly fiddler carried to us from somewhere in Wapping and I noticed we were being observed by nymphs of the pavé across the street in the shadows.

'What do I think?' Fabian's head twisted towards the nymphs. 'It's rum o' clock, that's what I think.'

'No seriously.'

'Seriously. About the deaths? It's an extortion gone wrong. They didn't pay any money. Scarface has hidden in the theatre rigging to sabotage the show. Fred has caught the man. A fight broke out aloft and Fred fell to his death unfortunately killing the ghost as well.'

Such empathy from the man.

'Yes, I tend to agree,' I smiled inwardly.

'Wha' are your thoughts Snake?' Fabian asked the constable, who remained frowning. 'My thoughts? It's rum o'clock sir.'

Day Ten – Sunday

IAWOKE NAKED, LYING WITH A WHORE, AND MY FIRST thoughts went out to Miss Rosemary Atwater, my spinster land-lady at Red Rose Cottage.

What would she think?

Does it really matter?

My second thought went out to my throbbing brain. Mental note to self; try and drink less. But, if I am to be honest, after the events of last night a celebration was sort of in order.

We lay together, the whore and I, on top of her bed, the room warm and the window propped open with the help of an empty bottle. Outside on the dock, gulls fought over fish guts while nearby a ship prepared to sail; the bosun's commands clear on the morning breeze. From where I lay on the second floor of the Commercial Hotel, at Old Wharf, I could make out the masts of two vessels tied up at the stone wharves and another three of varying size anchored in the docks.

I had noted the night before, a man o' war and two whalers at moorings further out in Sullivan's Cove. Now the wherrymen were doing a brisk business rowing men back and forth as the single bell of the Anglican Mariner's Church reminded me it was Sunday.

It must be late morning I thought, but Sunday is a day of rest. I pondered what excuses I would spin to Miss Atwater when the young peach and cream at my side slowly woke. She sidled up against me, arousing my interest. The church bell wrestled with my conscience. But after a brief moment caressing and canoodling she teased me into a breakfast edition of last night's performance.

Somewhere a clock chimed the hour. We gambolled and rollicked until we were both quite spent.

Somewhere a clock chimed the quarter hour.

I half filled her chamber pot, splashed myself with water from a jug and basin, dressed, threw the whore a half sovereign as arranged and skipped, whistling, down the stairs to a fine breakfast.

This town is growing on me.

'Are you the new constable what's workin' with Fabian?' the waiting girl in the breakfast room asked. She was a buxom wench with generous but solid girth. Something to hang onto as Fabian would say.

'Well yes,' I smiled back. 'But I am what is becoming known as a detective, not a constable. You know Fabian then?'

'Who don't?' she giggled. She collected my empty plate and popped a strip of fat into her mouth that I had discarded from a chop. 'Best bit,' she laughed openly showing all her gums. The infectious giggle continued and she made a flirtatious route to the kitchen through a room of admirers.

Through the dining room window of the Commercial Hotel I noticed the harbour busying up. 'What to do?' I asked myself. 'Too early to visit the inns.' I left a crown on the table and stepped out into the sunlight.

'Caspian 'unter,' a voice put an end to my reverie.

'Who wants to know?' I answered warily, eyeing a grubby urchin no more than ten.

'Mr Savage squire. 'e would be much obliged if'n ya accompany me ta 'is sloop what's waitin' at Waterman's Dock.'

'Mr Savage? What does he want?'

'Well 'ow the firk would I know gov?' *Cheeky little buzzard!* 'All I knows is 'is skipper give me sixpence ta find ya an' another sixpence when I's deliver ya to 'is sloop.'

I held my eye on the boy a moment; a bare footed snotty nosed tyke with his gutter tongue.

'Well I suppose you can take me to the sloop then,' I finally conceded.

'How did you find me?' I asked as we walked at a pace across the docks.

'I just stuck me 'ead in a few taprooms, got talkin' to a few whores. You reckon you're the detective! Huh!'

The slender sloop *Samantha* was tied up at Waterman's Dock where two men waited, one sitting at the helm with his long bony fingers darting about in a small crock of jellied eel.

'Ah, Mr Hunter,' the other said in greeting. 'Nice o' ya to come sir.'

I recognised him from Savage's luncheon table days ago. He

flicked the lad a silver coin and the boy stood staring at me with big sad eyes. I foraged about and found a sixpence change from last evening's debauchery in my frock coat pocket. The lad snatched the proffered coin and scampered.

'Mr Savage wants to see me?' I asked, my boots firmly placed on the dock.

'Aye sir, if'n ya can spare the time like. Mr Savage thought ya would 'ave time ta be guest at 'is table 'cos it's Sundee like.' He saw me casting a guarded eye over the helmsman. 'That thar is Uncle Gus and ya remember me I'm certain. I'm Jack Bone. Climb aboard good sir, ya is in good 'ands.'

Much against my better judgement we soon rounded the Browns River headland in clear view of the Sea o' Graves Inn.

The man I had nicknamed Bilge Breath met us at the beach where I had to roll my britches up to the knees and wade ashore. He was friendly enough and although we were outdoors I still caught a hint of his miasmic breath. He rolled a toothpick from one side of his mouth to the other and grunted a greeting. We walked along an embankment path we had missed on our first trip having come ashore on the wrong side of Browns River.

The inn was empty of patrons, being Sunday I imagined, and the first thing I noticed was the taproom could do with a good airing. It stank of stale smoke, a lingering pong of unwashed bodies and spilt grog. Bilge Breath led me up the stairs to the stern cabin where Lynch Savage sat in his favourite chair, head of the table, looking out across the immense River Derwent. He wore his favourite costume except for his red frock coat that hung on a clothes hook along with his ostrich feather hat. I was pleased to notice a pleasant aroma teased my nostrils after the stink of last night's revelry on the deck below.

'Mr Hunter, Mr Hunter ... Caspian. Welcome to Sea o' Graves. Welcome ta me table.'

'Mr Savage,' I removed my hat and tipped my head.

'Call me Lynch remember ... please. Sit, sit up here with me lad.' He waved to Bilge Breath who was waiting to be dismissed. 'Get the man a towel to dry his legs.'

The door to the galley swung open and the French cook Jean Parton and the scrawny but wiry cove I met last time, with the chained mermaid tattoo who answered to the name Couta, struggled to the table with a platter holding a whole roasted suckling pig. Savage's attention was distracted while the men sat the feast at our end of the table. The animal had a golden crusty skin and was surrounded by tatties and half a dozen other vegetables. But the cook had done something I had never seen before; he had jammed a whole apple into the pig's mouth.

'Sunday dinner here, Caspian, is a bit of a tradition,' Lynch salivated talking to me whilst gazing upon the pig. 'Where are the others?' he looked up impatiently at Couta.

'I'll go shove a dirk up their arses sir!' Couta's face pinched like a fish head with a hook in its mouth.

'Please do,' Lynch was keen to start eating and drool dribbled down his chins. 'He's all class, is our Couta,' Lynch finally tore his eyes away from the roast. 'All class. But he's a good lad … when he wants to be.'

As the company arrived – four more of Lynch's men and six whores, two of whom I had met on my last visit, Fannie Peach and the Oriental Soo Yung – Jean Parton launched into carving up the pig. The wine flowed freely like the river below and I soon lost myself in the merriment. Although I had eaten a large breakfast two hours earlier I managed to do the feast justice.

I was on my fourth goblet of a fine French wine that Lynch told me was Shiraz, when I felt the distinct sensation of a toe tickling my fancies. Fannie Peach sat opposite crackling away at a piece of pigskin, when our eyes met and she wet her lips with a thespian flourish. 'She must have long legs,' I told myself. 'The slinky minx.'

'Last night at the theatre was a fiasco,' Lynch started. 'Poor little Mistress Ruby Blood. It must have been a terrible shock.'

'Traumatic I should imagine,' I answered.

'Any ideas, any leads who done it?'

'Extortion we're thinking,' not too certain whether I should be talking about the case. 'They were threatened only this week.'

'Threatened! My Ruby. Bastards!' Grease glistened on Lynch's angry chins and his eyes narrowed. 'Well ya can do me a favour Caspian,' and he pointed a piggy drumstick at me. 'Let me know who the suspects are and I'll sort it out my way, save you detectives the bother.'

The other rogues at the table agreed with vigorous nods and assorted grunts.

The wayward toe found its mark once more and I answered with a smile.

'So how is your other investigation going?' Lynch enquired.

'Aha,' I thought, 'this is why I'm here.'

'The *Ocean Maiden*?' I said forking a tattie.

'No Caspian,' Lynch actually stopped macerating a moment. 'The Miss Edith Philpot killing.'

'Oh, well, ah … it's ongoing. We are having problems in fact.'

'Really.'

'Yes. Actually I don't think I'm at liberty to discuss it.'

'Oh? We're all friends here Caspian,' he filled my glass. 'Aren't we?'

'Well yes, but you know how it is.'

Lynch continued eating and I noticed pig grease smeared his jowls. 'Ya know, I was partners for a while with His Firkin' Lordship,' he finally said.

'Philpot?'

'Aye. And a sad partnership that was I can tell ya.' I looked on not knowing what to say. 'The man's a tyrant,' Lynch spat. 'A user, a snake in the grass. Gold, Caspian, that alluring metal that won't tarnish, stays all shiny and leads men to an early grave.'

I could tell Lynch had a story to tell and tried to ignore the exploring toe.

'We was at Ballarat in '51, Philpot and me,' Savage went on. 'But we was never miners, not 'is royal highness and not me with me problem of excess baggage.' He chuckled with good humour. 'But we made a good team then. Me with me savvy and Philpot with 'is money. At my doin' we set up inns, hotels, providores, whorehouses and the like at Tent City in South Melbourne. It was all legit like, we made a killin', every miner needed the basics and we provided it on their way to the Ballarat and Bendigo digs. Two years I done this, then greed took 'old of the man. 'e hired thugs, got me thrown out o' Victoria. There was no document see, no contract. It was all done with the shake o' a hand. I didn't have a leg to stand on. But I had stashed away enough gold to start 'ere at Browns River, so 'elp me God. I've bounced back and I got a score to settle with that Lord Philpot.'

Not enough to kill his daughter, surely not?

'Ya know 'e's mates with Governor Henry Fox Young?'

'Yes, I knew that.'

'He knew 'im from Adelaide days. Although the guv's a good man I think 'e likes to keep Philpot in 'is grasp for political savvy.'

'You are possibly right.'

'Right! Damn right I'm right.'

We ate in silence a while. The wandering toe darted about my groin with not the slightest protest from me. She was after all a dark haired, olive skinned beauty in her early twenties exuding all the confidence of a global traveller at the Explorers Club of London.

'Ah, that was most scrumptious,' Lynch finally wiped the grease from his chin on his sleeve and belched. 'Now you lot,' he said loudly and slapped the table. 'Leave us a moment.' Eyes darted from Mr Savage to half eaten plates of food. '*Now* if ya please,' and he clapped his hands. 'Ya food ain't goin' nowhere.'

Seconds later Lynch and myself sat alone. 'Caspian. We are friends no?'

'Here it comes!' I thought. 'Ah, yes, I would like to consider myself your friend sir,' I said in all honesty.

'Good.' And he spotted a piece of pork crackle he had missed and snatched it off the plate faster than a starving gull. 'As I said Caspian, His Lordship and me have unfinished business, you understand?'

'Yes Lynch, but what's that got to do with me?'

'Well I need someone on the inside. Someone to keep me informed …'

'An informant? Are you trying to bribe me sir?'

'Nay lad,' and a loud crunch of crackle was followed by, 'o' course not.'

'Well what are you implying,' I said trying vainly to sound authoritative.

'Look, I'll be straight with ya. I'm not a man to beat about the bush. Not Lynch. What is your annual remuneration?'

I looked at him hard a long moment. 'Hundred guineas per annum.'

'I'll double it,' he said without blinking an eye.'

'Wha … double … and why would you want to do that Lynch? I told you I'll not be bribed.'

'I ain't wantin' to corrupt ya lad. All I want is to be kept up to speed with our friend Philpot.'

'His Lordship is an ungrateful swine, rude,' I told myself. 'What harm could come from the odd letter to Savage?'

'Do you know who killed his daughter?' I asked.

'Nay. I don't. And I'll be the first to say I wouldn't want any 'arm to befall 'er. But it's too late now, and that be the end of it.'

Lynch clapped his hands and the others spilt back in from the galley like boarders at St Giles at teatime.

'Couta,' Lynch ordered. 'Bring me a bottle o' that special Armagnac.'

'One more question,' I said.

'Aye?'

'That ring you wear on your finger, the one with the prancing deer, what is its significance?'

'Huh, I should melt it down and sell the gold,' he said with some annoyance holding his little finger out. 'But me and Philpot had the jumping deer as our business emblem like, when we was on 'appier terms. We 'ad the rings made from Ballarat gold. Like a lucky talisman, for all the good it done me.'

'Interesting. Do you wear your ring at all times?'

'What a funny question. As a matter of fact I take 'em off when I sleep, why? Ya not thinkin' of stealin' them are ya?'

'No. Good heavens no. Steal from Lynch Savage!' And I let out a nervous titter. 'I was just curious that's all.'

Couta returned with an Edam cheese wrapped in its dark red wax skin on a wooden board with crusty bread. *And how I love cheese.* He cut the giant ball in half and Lynch caught me staring. 'You like that Dutch cheese Caspian?'

'Oh yes,' I sighed in anticipation. 'Brings back memories of Christmas in Birmingham. My father would always spare no expenses at Christmas.'

'I don't know whether it's true or not,' Lynch mentioned. 'But I 'eard a story about an Englishman who was killed by an Edam cheese in 1784 during the Anglo-Dutch Wars.' I must have looked suitably curious. 'Aye. Apparently the Dutchies ran out of cannon shot and used stale cheese balls.'

We toasted the cheese story with several measures of a fine

Normandy Armagnac that Lynch told me fell off the stern of a ship. The toe returned with a vengeance and before I knew it I had Fannie Peach from behind, in a dark corner of the cock-fighting pit, closed because it was Sunday.

Perfect!

I walked up the path to Red Rose Cottage smelling of Armagnac and cheap perfume and saw her at the window – when I managed to focus. I don't know whether spinster Miss Atwater's wraith was piqued by the fact it was Sunday or the fact it was only five hours after midday and I was …

'Intoxicated!' her verbal anger attacked me before I had even tripped on the bottom step. 'This is not good enough Mr Hunter,' she launched into her rehearsed speech. 'Not good enough at all. I operate a respectable lodging house, not some … some … some back room in a waterfront inn. Some den of sin that you seem most partial to. No sir. What in heaven's name would your mother be thinking now?'

'She's dead!' *All right so I didn't mean those words to spill out quite so harshly.*

'Dear Lord.' She was appalled.

Is that my luggage stacked on the porch?

'I … I ah, admit Rose … Miss Hateater … I am partial to the odd little dwink. But ish the shtress mam … the shtress o' my work.'

I should have kept my mouth shut, all I was doing was digging a bigger hole for myself.

'There's your luggage Mr Hunter, I suggest you sleep off your inebriation in another lodging house, one that is more tolerant of your wicked, wicked ways.'

Day Eleven – Monday

'MY YOU DID SLEEP SOME MR 'UNTER.' I AWOKE TO the squealing of an unoiled prison door and the friendly voice of the gatekeeper at the Prisoners Barracks, the gatekeeper known as The Priest. ''ere ya go sir.' He waddled towards me with a tray of food and tea.

I sat bolt upright. 'My God I'm in prison!'

'Only for a kip sir, you was awful drunk when ya came 'ere bashin' on the gate last night.'

'So I'm not a prisoner then?'

'No sir,' and the man chuckled loudly. 'Prisoner! Goodness me no. Max stuck ya in 'ere for ya own safety. I wasn't 'ere, I started at six. No, Max said you was drunk as ten men.'

A vague memory of a ranting and raving Miss Atwater came to me. Then I saw my two pieces of luggage sitting neatly next to the bunk bed. Miraculously I had kept them with me.

'You drink ya tea sir, eat them vittles and you'll be right as rain.'

True to The Priest's word I felt a little more at ease an hour later. I cleaned up and changed in the gatekeeper's residence and after vowing to drink less grog I decided to start the new week with a visit to the hospital.

I found the dedicated Dr Bedford supervising the scrubbing of the mortuary slab in the vaults under the hospital. The forever-cheerless space was all gloom as expected.

'Good morning doctor,' I said, my eyes watering from a mixture of ammonia and bleach in a flickering lantern flame teased by the fumes and escaping methane from the dead.

'Mr Hunter,' Dr Bedford seemed happy to see me. 'Come to pay your respect to our latest cadavers have you?'

I nodded a grunt and looked at the two bodies from Saturday night's fiasco. It was particularly difficult to look at the man I only knew as Fred – lying stiff and waxy white on a stone slab. Next to him was the body of the *Phantasmagoria* ghost. 'What irony,' I told myself. My eyes adjusted to the poor lighting and I searched the shadows for Nathanial Rudder.

'Nathanial Rudder, his body's gone …'

'Certainly,' Dr Bedford said sending the cleaning nurse away. 'Couldn't keep that one above ground any longer I'm afraid. Stinking the place he was and so full of gases I was afraid he was going to explode.'

'He's been buried then?'

'Yes sir,' Dr Bedford emptied the leather bucket of blood down the drain and I made a note never to eat black pudding again. 'There was no one to claim the body so we wrapped him in a sail cloth and he was buried in a pauper's grave yesterday afternoon.'

'So much for the love of his life, Molly Mutton,' I mumbled.

'Who, what was that?'

'Oh, nothing really. Whereabouts is he buried?'

'Why, across the road in St David's.'

He turned to face me and the dancing light created macabre shadows amongst the man's many jowls and chins. 'Why, may I ask? Is there a problem?'

'Were his clothes removed?'

'Not in their condition Mr Hunter. They smelt rather bad. We buried him with his clothes and boots intact.'

'Then I need to exhume him sir.'

'Exhume him! Are you mad?'

'He may have been buried with vital evidence to do with this murder.'

'Well you will have to get a court order signed by the surgeon-general now, I'm afraid. Unless you want to do a Burke and Hare style midnight excavation,' he snorted at the thought. 'Now if you'll excuse me, I've been told I have another body coming in shortly.'

'Oh. Not a murder I hope.'

'No Mr Hunter, another drunkard who's fallen in the dock and drowned. We get three or four a week. Sailors mostly. But this one's a sea captain I've been told.'

'Sea captain!'

'Yes.'

'Do you know his name?'

'No, but I have been told he has been recognised as a local merchant.'

It came as no surprise when half an hour later I identified the latest contribution to the morgue as none other than Captain Durward Slade.

'I think this is a case of self-murder doctor,' I said, and went on to explain the circumstances.

Bonnie Nettles sat on a keg outside her Sailors' Rest Inn enjoying the early afternoon sun and a pipe of port-flavoured tobacco. She looked cheerful enough for a woman who had been stabbed in the chest by a madman and held hostage before a sniper's bullet assassinated her kidnapper.

'How's the wound?' I enquired.

'It was more a cut than a stab.' She forced a smile and revealed a bandage circumnavigating her voluptuous figure. 'I'll live. You've settled in then. How's ya room?'

'Couldn't be better,' I lied.

Bonnie had leased me a small room on the third floor at the back of her inn where a small window overlooked a quarry. But it was reasonably clean, I had *some* light and it was lice and rat free. But the tariff was fair and meals thrown in, so it would suffice until I found permanent lodgings elsewhere.

'What's ya poison?' she asked with sudden renewed vigour.

'Ah … it is a little early is it not,' I said, my head still foggy from last night's imbibing.

'Nonsense.'

We sat on a keg each and drank Bonnie's best gin – a Geneva – and made small talk about the inn business.

'To be a successful innkeeper round 'ere ya need a keen eye, a sharp hand, and a dirty pack of cards in the back parlour,' she said flashing me a wink.

I told her about Miss Rosemary Atwater of Red Rose Cottage evicting me.

'Huh! Rosemary Atwater. I know her. She's one o' them Temperance Movement women out to make inns and taverns less attractive to the lower classes. They want to put a ban on billiards, bagatelle tables, darts, dice, cards, or any games of chance. Prudes, the lot o' them. They even say no dancin'! How dare they. Damned virgins.'

As I had been merrily plugging away at the colony's less than virtuous, I could only but agree.

'There ya are sar.' Jasper stood before me with beads of sweat running down his cheeks. He must have run here. 'Fabian thought you'd be 'ere. Moved in 'ave ya?'

'For a while, yes. What's happening?'

'Well I was told to bring ya over to Old Wharf sar. Fabian wants ya. They found a body of a little girl.'

'Oh no!'

Fabian waited at the stone pier of Old Wharf across the cove a ways. He leant against a huge fluked iron anchor fresh from the foundry and destined to be ferried out to a merchant ship moored mid-cove.

'I got good news and bad,' he half smiled and smoke leaked from his nose as he tapped his pipe on the anchor.

'Bad news first,' I said.

'Little girl, seven to nine I'm guessin', found drowned.' As dreadful as this news was it was hardly detective work and I told Fabian so. 'But it's the Norwegian captain's daughter, he of the *Ocean Maiden*.'

'Oh!'

'Her name's written in this 'ere prayer book.'

Fabian opened the small damp book and, although the ink had run, her name was established as Serianna Brynjar.

'Where is she?'

'On that fishing boat.' Fabian tipped his head to a tired wooden craft nearby circled by a dozen gulls. We climbed aboard and the skipper, an old man who answered to the name Culver, showed us to the hold.

'Are you for earnest?' I was horrified. The small body lay covered in sailcloth and was lying in six inches of water amongst his morning's catch.

'What else could I do sar?' Culver loosened a macerated glob of chewing tobacco between gums and teeth with a gnarly finger. 'It seemed the best idea at the time Mr Hunter, I couldn't leave 'er up on the deck in the sun now, could I?'

I stepped through fish and pulled back the sail. The ghostly white face of an innocent child stared back. She had been dead some days now and showed signs of being eaten by crabs, but I thought it apparent she had drowned.

'Where did you find her?' I asked Culver.

'She were trapped amongst rocks, off the south o' Bruny.'

'And there's more.' We climbed back to the main deck where Fabian drew my attention to a yawl tethered off the stern of the fishing boat. 'That was found capsized washed up on the shore not far from the lass's body.'

'So this is what happened to the crew and passengers on the *Ocean Maiden*,' I said. 'For reasons we don't know they have abandoned the ship only to capsize at sea and all drown.' I returned to the fisherman. 'Any signs of anyone else?'

He raised an eyebrow. 'Nay sar. Fishes got 'em I'm thinkin' ... sharks more like.' And he hawked the glob of chewing tobacco over the side.

'Jasper,' I said.

'Sar.'

'Get the undertaker, see the body is taken to Dr Bedford, and please, some discretion.'

'Discretion sar?'

'Yes. Cover the body.' We stepped back onto the dock. 'So what's the good news then?' I asked Fabian. He now completed the smile he had reserved earlier and pointed to a sloop tied up near the fishing boat. 'Ya like it?'

'It's a boat. Nice. So?'

'It's official. It's ours for the service. Made from Huon pine. It sailed up this mornin' from the shipwrights at Port Arthur.'

The neat sloop sat low and sleek in the water. She looked fast and new. 'Aye. The governor promised us this months back. Now we can chase villains on the water too.' Fabian stood proud, his hands on his hips. 'And there's somethin' else.'

'Oh?'

'I have an order for two two-pounders.'

'Cannon?'

'Aye. We can collect them from the armoury when we're ready. Two Caspian! One for each side like. That'll firkin' scare the brigands eh?'

I stared blankly, wondering what to make of it when Fabian added,

'Don't look so worried, Snake, Billings and Hal are all experienced seamen.'

I noted the stern plate was blank. 'She hasn't been christened yet.'

'Ah ... I've thought about thart. Aye ... indeed ...'

'And?'

'Well ... I was thinkin' ... the ... ah ... *Fabian* would be a good name.'

'Oh did you now?'

Fabian swung his fob about on its chain and snapped it open. 'Will ya look at thart? It's drink o'clock,' he said with cheer. 'Let's debate the merits of her new name over a quart.' For me it was either take a nap or take hair of the dog.

'The Steam Packet's just across the wharf, I don't think ya been there yet.' And Fabian strode away.

The Steam Packet Inn stood out from the rest of the warehouses and inns along Hunter Street, as the only street on Old Wharf was called. It had a steep sloping attic roof and to me it was reminiscent of canal buildings in Amsterdam. Rowdy drinkers in the taproom could be heard as we crossed the dock, where an easterly breeze conveyed a fragrance redolent of the delights of Wapping in our direction.

'The whaler *Anaconda* from New Bedford docked this mornin',' Fabian said of the rabble. 'The boys are thirsty, been at sea a few months.'

Drinkers spilt out of the inn and onto the street and I was pushing my way through to enter when I was inadvertently shoved aside. I was about to protest when I noticed the perpetrator. He was six foot six, square jawed, bald and wearing a gold earring in his left earlobe. The other ear was missing and it appeared to have been chewed off as if the result of a fight. I clasped Fabian's arm.

'That's got to be him.'

'Who?'

'One of the extortionists that threatened Aboubacar and Mistress Ruby.' I nodded discreetly and we both watched as the man disappeared up an alleyway next to the inn. I sidled up to the corner of the cobbled lane and peered about. The alley led past an anchor smith and a slop seller to a coffin carpenter at the end who was working his trade out in the open. Our man spoke briefly to the carpenter who whistled into the workshop and another cove joined them.

'Mother Mary!' My jaw dropped. 'See who that is?'

'That scrawny beggar. Aye. Where 'ave I seen that cove before?'

'Sea o' Graves.'

'Aye.'

'He helps Lynch Savage's cook in the galley,' I reminded Fabian.

'Couta, yes ... Couta. That's his name.'

'And that big bald bastard is the one Aboubacar was talkin' about.'

'Has to be.' We waited as vigorous dialogue was exchanged by the three men. Finally Couta and the bald headed man turned back towards us. Fabian and I squeezed into the taproom where we watched the men through the inn window.

'Now what?' I asked. 'Will we arrest them?'

Fabian. 'On what charge?'

'Then we must follow them.'

'Aye.'

The two men were in a hurry. Rushing down the alleyway to the mouth of the rivulet they vaulted damaged barrels discarded by the slaughterhouse, clambering over upturned tenders. They slipped on slime-covered rocks exposed by the low tide and trudged in ankle deep filth up the creek bed. It was difficult to follow and harder still to remain unobserved. Once the men disappeared into the darkness, created by leaning ragtag hovels, we were able to shorten the distance between us.

'Shh!' Fabian waved me back in the shadows. 'Listen,' he barely whispered.

Besides the distant mournful cries of cattle in the slaughterhouse's holding pens, only the trickling of foul water along the squalid back-water could be heard. We stopped. Waited. Listened.

I looked down at my feet in the mulch and realised I was standing on a decayed dog. I made a suitable sound of disgust and stepped aside, noting we were surrounded by dwellings, the inhabitants of which must daily inhale these foul airs caused by the unbearable effluvia arising from this corruption.

Instantly we observed the light of a lantern lost amongst the gloom of the passage caused by overhanging structures. Fabian and I watched the two men climb up and into another passage or entrance above the high water mark of the passageway.

The light vanished. Taking that as a sign they had moved on we stealthily pushed forward. If it was not for the fact we had seen the men enter another passage, we would never known it was there.

'What the firk?' Fabian muttered softly, gaping bewildered at the rock wall. I ran my fingers along the irregular surface. After a moment I felt a horizontal ridge and I allowed my fingers to slowly work the anomaly.

'There is something here. Wait,' I found purchase with my fingers. I tugged and the hatch came free at one side. 'It's hinged,' I hissed at Fabian. I levered it open an inch and peered into the dark just in time to see the lantern light fading around the corner of what must be a decent length tunnel. Satisfied we were unobserved, I opened the door completely and climbed into the pitch dark space.

'Christ it stinks in 'ere worse 'n the firkin' rivulet,' Fabian's contorted face was then swallowed by darkness as we replaced the hatchway blocking all light. 'Now what? Can't see a firkin' thing.'

I led the way, stooped, as it was impossible to stand. Feeling our way in the blackness I felt the sides were brick and I mentioned it to Fabian. 'Aye,' he said. 'I reckon it's the old walls of the bridge foundations, before they built the new'on after the big flood a few years back. I'm thinkin' these coves 'ave turned it into a secret passage. Up to no good like.'

My eyes were adjusting to the darkness when I noticed a sliver of horizontal light emanating from what must be the bottom of a door further on. We forged ahead blindly. Either side of us I made out recesses in the brickwork. Then I heard voices, soft mumblings from beyond.

At that point we heard *kachink* … *kachink* … *kachink* followed by muffled voices once more.

Kachink … *kachink* … *kachink* … Now more animated mumblings. Sounds of approval. With my arms outstretched in front of me I ran deft fingers about what could only be a door. I felt a handle, a latch of some type.

'What are ya doin'?' Fabian whispered in my ear from somewhere in the gloom. I didn't answer, but lifted the hatch. The door opened slightly of its own accord. Thank god it didn't creak. Together we scanned what was clearly a small room. The large bald headed man with the chewed ear stood close to the door with his back to us; luckily he masked Couta who stood facing the door, his skeletal face hideous in the hard shadows. Between them they were operating some kind of mechanical device. *Kachink ... kachink ... kachink.*

Chewed Ear peeled something from the machine and held a sheet up into the waxen light from the overhead lantern. 'Now thart's a gooden,' he said pleased with himself. Fabian grabbed my arm, he too realised at the same moment. A Bank of England one-pound note!

The sheet, I noticed, was about the size of the page from a small book with the banknote printed cleanly in the middle. They would have to trim each note. In the dim light of the slightly ajar door I watched Couta lick his lips in exhilaration. He wiped his hands down the sides of his black-patched coat before pulling a folded piece of paper from his pocket. His eyes were wide. He unfolded the paper and I saw it was a one-pound note – an authentic note I assumed – for comparison. He held it next to the sheet Chewed Ear was holding.

'Firkin' lovely!' he sneered.

Suddenly.The unmistakable snick of a pistol hammer.

'Don't ya move a firkin' inch,' came a cold voice from the dark passageway behind us.

'Whoa!' Fabian sucked a breath between clenched teeth as cold steel pressed against his temple. 'Easy lad.'

Instantly the door flew open. 'What the firk!' Couta and the bald headed man with Chewed Ear stood gaping. 'Where the firk did they come from?' And more pistols were drawn and cocked.

'Seen 'em snoopin' round outside. Lucky I did huh?' It was Scar Face, the man wanted for the killing of Fred the stagehand and the ghost at the theatre.

Damn! There must be another way in here I surmised, maybe in one of the old bridge recesses; otherwise we would have seen light behind us when he entered.

'Well well,' Scar Face suddenly recognised me. 'If it ain't the turd burglar,' he said giving me a menacing, icy stare.

'Turd burglar?' Fabian asked and I caught his confused expression in the sallow light of the flickering lantern.

'Long story,' I said.

'Move it arseholes.' Scar Face motioned with his heavy navy issue pistol. We were herded into a small chamber, not much bigger than our office back at the Prisoners Barracks. Fabian immediately recognised the printing press as stolen from Mr Bent the printer in Elizabeth Street years earlier. An engraved copper plate of a perfect one-pound note sat on the printing panel of the press. I noticed a five-pound plate on the bench. Neatly pegged from wall to wall on a line to dry were hundreds of pounds in freshly printed five and one pound notes. Fabian whistled.

Whistled!

This was not the time for complacency I was thinking. Did he know something I didn't? At the far end of the room another door led out. I could only imagine it led up into the rabbit warren of shantytown Wapping overhead. Instantly something else caught my eye in the flickering flame.

Cheese!

'Dutch cheese,' I said without thinking. The remains of the waxed ball sat on the workbench with a plate of crusty bread and tankards of what I expect was ale.

'Dutch cheese!' Scar Face repeated disbelievingly, in a questioning tone. 'I got a gun at ya 'ead and ya 'ungry?' The three men laughed.

'It was you!' I blurted, suddenly realising Couta had managed to use Lynch Savage's ring to seal the letter sent to me containing the theatre ticket. I knew I recognised the smell of the wax on my letter, but I couldn't quite nail it.

'You used the wax off the cheese for the seal so that he would be accused of …'

Instantly the implication sent a chill down my spine.

'Accused of a murder,' Couta scowled. 'Aye … go on say it. Accused of your murder.'

'You knew he had a seat next to mine.'

'Smart bugger ain't ya?' Chewed Ear glowered.

'Why, why would you want to go to so much trouble?' I asked.

Couta pushed the muzzle of his pistol into my cheek. ''Cos ya was gonna get knifed that night. You first then ya mate 'ere. We don't need no Peeler investigators in this 'ere town.'

'But now,' Scar Face leered, 'ya just popped in all on ya lonesome like. Perfect.'

'Empty their pockets,' Chewed Ear stepped back oscillating his pistol between Fabian and me.

'Easy lads, easy,' Fabian tapped his pockets. 'I only got me pipe and baccy.'

He slipped his hand into his frock coat side pocket and took out a clay pipe and a leather pouch of pipe tobacco.

'Oh yeh,' he muttered nonchalantly. 'And there's me purse.'

And he fumbled a short while in the opposite pocket, finally lifting another small leather pouch free – to the chink of coins.

'Whoops!' Fabian dropped a half sovereign. All eyes looked fixedly at the gold coin.

'I'll 'ave that,' Couta bent down. Chewed Ear had the same idea. Heads cracked together. Fabian threw a punch at the lantern. The same instant the flame flared then extinguished, I saw Fabian duck. I ducked. We were instantly thrown into pitch darkness.

Boom!

A lightning flash of flame licked between us. The exploding pistol fired in the small room at such close range was deafening.

Blind punches followed.

Thump, oof, crack, thump, thump smack!

'Bastard!'

I tackled the body next to me, hoping it wasn't Fabian.

Slap!

The punch in the dark was to the side of my head. My feet shot out from under me and I fell. Instantly a soft light filled the room, barely enough to see what was happening. Then I realised the opposite door was open. Someone was escaping. I crawled across the floor on my hands and knees.

Crack! Slam!

I imagined the door to the passage was thrown open. I heard Fabian cursing in the blackness. 'Firker!' *Thump, slap, crack!*

I heard the chilling words, 'Shoot the bastard!' It was Scar Face. But in the darkness any target was impossible. More struggling sounds …

Boom!

Clumps of earth came crashing around us. The pistol had fired high. From my position, on all fours, I could make out the vaguest passage ahead leading to the hovels above. A figure cut across the faint light. Someone was escaping. I clambered to my feet and gave chase, groping at the walls for guidance. An instant later I crashed through rotten timbers, somersaulting into a dirt walkway between shanties. A cat screeched and dived off my back disappearing into the shadows.

Concerned yells from residents. 'Wha' the firk's goin' on 'ere?'

The walkway ended. It turned to an alley. I sprang forward and at that point saw who I was chasing. Chewed Ear!

He was like a rat down a privy. The place was a maze. If I didn't stay close I was certain I'd be lost. I passed rows and rows of hovels and shacks, stinking shanties leaning this way and that. I hit ground level and stopped at a T-junction. Looked left. Looked right.

'Shite!'

I lost him.

A noise to my left. The sound of breaking timber. Curses. Abuse. I dived down the alley towards the disturbance. Suddenly I hit a wall. Cornered. No escape but the way I had come. I twisted about; my heart thumping, gasping at the stale air …

And saw Chewed Ear!

He stepped out from hiding.

Somehow, in all my haste, I had passed him. Now in the narrow dead-end alleyway the man looked every bit of his six foot four. He pulled a knife from his belt; a ten-inch triple-blade, its steel reflecting what little sunlight filtered between the boards.

My heart sank.

I was trapped.

Savouring the moment, the killer took measured steps towards me with the intimidating grin of the ignoble victor.

'Think ya pretty clever Caspian firkin' Hunter,' he scowled weighing up his dagger, first in his left hand and then in his right. Enjoying the feel of the lethal blade.

'Smart 'n clever little detective all the ways from Birming'am.' I must have shown surprise. 'Oh yes, I know's all about ya.' He lurched forward swinging the dagger. Taking short stabs. I felt real fear. I backed hard against the wall. Desperate, not knowing what to do. He fed off the fear in my eyes, lurching once more, pulling back, jeering, teasing …

Without warning I saw a blur in the shadows behind him. Silent, stealthful, obscure movement.

Crack!

Wallop!

The huge thug fell towards me. I saw his eyes roll back in his head. I stepped aside and Chewed Ear smashed face first into the shanty behind me. Gobsmacked I looked up at my saviour.

'Hey bloke!' It was Nebena the native I had met at the wharf, standing proud and grinning at me with his handsome smile, his voice high-pitched but so welcome.

It took me a moment to comprehend the black man standing before me in his shabby military jacket with its brass buttons, the brass gorget worn proudly about his skinny neck displaying his family name, his tattered britches, bare feet with bicorn hat in one hand and a homemade club in the other.

'Him bad whitefella boss. You good whitefella. You give Nebena sixpence eh.'

I cannot describe the relief I felt. Nebena stepped forward and kicked the body. 'Him dead?' Then he rasped a smoker's cough and laughed. 'Nar. He sleep.'

'We need some rope Nebena; we need to tie this man up before he … wakes. Yes.'

I considered my good fortune. Nebena lived in one of the hovels I had passed. He whistled and his wives appeared from between planks conveniently swung as a door. They looked fifty although I guessed they were thirty – skin black as coal, cropped tight curly hair, flat noses, eyes dark as molasses and pear-shaped bodies from poor whitefella diet. But hearts of gold. Nebena rattled off something in his native tongue and they disappeared, only to return moments later with buoy ropes from fishing nets. We trussed Chewed Ear with tethers and lucky we did. He regained consciousness and started screaming vitriolic curses until I shoved a rag in his mouth, and together we dragged him into Nebena's shanty where the wives happily sat on the struggling bundle.

'I must find help,' I said promptly.

'Nebena 'elp,' Nebena grinned at me showing off his healthy but yellow teeth. I looked at Chewed Ear, he was secured well. I swung round to Nebena and thought to myself, 'I could certainly use some help.'

'Alright,' I said, against my better judgement, 'but there is no time to waste.' I rushed back down the alleyway and immediately I was lost. I turned to Nebena for guidance and cackling proudly he pushed past me to lead on. It was then I noticed he carried a piece of crescent shaped wood.

'What's that,' I asked hurrying after him, 'a club?'

'This boomerang.'

'Boomerang?'

'Come from blackfella in Port Phillip. You see.' Nebena turned left down a stinking laneway, then right rushing into a cul-de-sac. He stopped suddenly standing up to his bare ankles in slush. He wheeled on the spot looking about in the semi-darkness. He found what he was looking for and smartly disappeared behind vertical timbers. I followed thinking, 'No wonder I was lost.' Moments later we descended a muddy path into darkness and I realised Nebena was taking me to where I had lost Fabian.

'You know this place?' I asked.

'Whitefella cave. Nebena see bad whitefella here.' Immediately the faintest of light filtered from behind a shabby door, more a gate. There was no sound. Nebena soundlessly pushed it open. Sure enough it was the printing chamber. An abandoned lantern left in haste burnt a faint flame. The printing press had disappeared. The forged notes and copper plates were missing. There was no sign of Fabian, just the lingering smell of sweaty bodies.

'Fabian!' I whispered snatching up the lantern and swinging its light about the dingy chamber. Nothing. The bench was bare except for empty inkbottles, brushes and a few tools. It would have been a struggle, I surmised, for two men to carry the press away. I could only imagine they would have carried the press off down the passageway that led back to the rivulet. I squeezed back through the low doorway and stooped into the passage. Nebena followed, clicking his tongue and quietly cackling, clearly enjoying himself. With the lamp high, I chased the illuminated glow back along the foul smelling tunnel when …

Kathlut!

'Jesus Christ!' I cursed. My stubbed foot felt broken. I swung the light at my feet. 'What the … ?' Then realised the black shadowy object I had tripped on was the iron press. It had been abandoned, obviously too heavy.

'Hurry,' I said to Nebena, and pushed on towards the rivulet.

'Where the hell 'ave ya been?' Fabian stood beside the rivulet, panting profusely. Nebena and I jumped from the exit ledge to the creek.

'Fabian! You're alive!'

'O' course I'm alive. Where'd you go?'

'We caught one.'

'Really.'

'Yes, he's tied up.'

'Good work. I see ya met Nebena.' Fabian slapped the native on the back.

'Him good whitefella,' Nebena said to me smiling away cheerily.

'Aye.'

'You know each other?' I stammered.

'Everyone knows Nebena,' Fabian grinned. 'Blackfella King o' 'obart Town, ain't ya Nebena?'

'Aye boss.'

I looked down the rivulet winding its filth towards the Derwent.

'Where are the other two?'

'Got away. They gave me a bit o' a beltin',' Fabian finally admitted. It was then I saw the cuts and bruises on his neck. 'But they'll be worried now. We know who the bastards are.'

I had a sudden thought. 'I bet I know where they have gone first.'

'Where?'

'Hurry!' And I bolted back towards Old Wharf.

The whaler *Samson*, which moored in the middle of the cove earlier in the day, had finally ferried the last of her crew ashore. The men had been at sea for months, they were cashed up and in celebratory mood and the first port of call in Hobart Town was Old Wharf two hundred yards away.

'The whores'll be busy tonight,' Fabian said as we hurried back across the causeway heading to the Steam Packet Tavern. 'With the crew of two rival whalers and a navy ship in the one area,' Fabian said, 'it promises to be a lawless night of revelry.'

Fabian had warned me earlier that the constables rarely involved themselves in trouble on the wharves unless blood was spilt. Hobart Town's waterfront was a law unto itself and one of the roughest in the world.

We shoved through the drinkers spilling onto the cobbles and came to the lane running beside the tavern.

'Where's the carpenter?' I asked staring into a deserted alleyway. Fabian was about to answer when a hand-pushed cart trundled out of the workshop and headed towards us.

'There's ya man,' Fabian said. 'So what are ya thinkin'?'

I was about to reply that I was certain the two men would be seeking help from the carpenter, whom we knew was an accomplice, when I observed two coffins on the cart.

'I wonder?' I said aloud. At that moment the cart was upon us and pushed by no other than the carpenter.

'Hold it right there,' I ordered. The carpenter, a middle-aged man with an overhanging belly of the heavy ale drinker and exceptional ear hair, looked nervous. I smelt a rat.

'Where are you taking those?' I demanded, nodding to the coffins and a tool box with hammer and nails on the tray.

'Who wants to know?'

'The law!' Fabian stepped into view. The carpenter's eyes darted about. Now he was cornered. 'Well?'

'Gotta take 'em to the *Destiny* o'er at New Wharf, they was ordered this mornin' like, by the ship's mate. Couple coves died after she docked. Pleurisy I think it were.'

'Pleurisy ya say?'

'Aye.'

'Two at the same time?' I offered. 'Rather strange don't you think?'

'Don't ask me squire. I just like ta do me duty … now if'n ya don't mind.' And the man made to continue his journey. I stepped in front of the cart. 'Oh but I do mind.' Fabian was impressed and crossed his arms. I noticed the coffin lids were loose and pushed the one closest to me aside.

Boom!

A musket ball sizzled by my ear and plucked Nebena's bicorn hat from his head. I caught a glimpse of Couta and the smoking barrel the second Fabian slammed the lid back in place. The carpenter bolted off down the wharf. The crowds immediately went silent. 'Firk!' Fabian was incensed. He took the hammer and nails. 'Hold that firker closed!' Scowling Fabian thumped three inch nails into the coffin lid as Couta screamed blue murder within.

Nebena, offended, scooped up his hat and wiggled a finger through the bullet hole. He turned on his heels, watching the carpenter running like a blubbery whale, now fifty yards towards the causeway. Nebena was once again the native.

The hunter.

I watched in awe as he raised his boomerang with skill. He eyed his quarry, threw back his arm and launched the crescent-shaped weapon after the escaping carpenter. Silently the device spun in the air, chasing down its victim with lethal accuracy.

Thunk!

The boomerang knocked its prey off his feet. The carpenter tripped and fell heavily, his belly bouncing but his face slapping into the roadway. The crowd cheered. They roared. The boomerang continued its flight path. The swishing growing louder as it returned to Nebena who leapt up and caught the club with pride and prowess.

'Boomerang!' he beamed.

Meanwhile Fabian hammered the second coffin lid into position. 'They ain't goin' nowhere now,' he chuckled tensely.

The gatekeeper known as The Priest couldn't believe that the men who were only known as Couta and Scar Face had been apprehended.

'You done good lads, and in their very own wooden overcoats,' he laughed. I clawed the nails from the second coffin while Couta was extracted from his. They were immediately shackled in leg irons by the prison smithy.

'Oh and lookee 'ere, what's this?' The Priest lifted a worn red cloth carpetbag free from where it lay between Scar Face's legs. 'Got ya bag packed for prison an' all eh?'

'Thank you.' I took the bag from the jailer. 'I know exactly what is in that.'

'Oh?' The Priest pursed his lips and screwed up his nose in curiosity. I unclipped the latch and the bag yawned open, crammed with sheets of forged one and five pound notes, most still uncut. The gatekeeper, guards and smithy all whistled in unison.

'Gawd!' The Priest finally spoke. 'What did they do, rob a bank?'

'Counterfeit my friend,' I said snipping the bag shut. 'All forged and not worth the price of a halfpenny harlot.'

The message was clear. 'All is not what it seems. Meet me at six bells in the back parlour of the Lamb Inn. R.B.'

The letter smelt of perfume, French no doubt, and sat quietly awaiting me on my desk as I retired for the afternoon to write a report for the governor. I folded the letter and placed it in my pocket the moment Fabian walked into the office. He carried two mugs of stewed black coffee.

'Another message!' he smiled. 'My you are a popular one ain't ya?' He tipped a shot of rum into the coffees from a stoneware flask. 'Well,' he insisted. 'Who's it from then?'

'No one,' I held the coffee to my mouth but it was scalding.

'No one huh. Hmm … I can still smell perfume waftin' 'bout the office.'

'I didn't know the *Buckingham* was Lord Philpot's,' I thought smartly, keen to divert Fabian's attention.

'Aye. 'e 'ad 'er built in the Indiaman style by a shipyard in India about ten year ago. She's teak, real hard that wood is.' There followed a moment's silence while I set up paper, quill, ink and chalk.

'Three thousand four 'undred and five pounds,' Fabian finally broke the silence. 'Caspy!'

'Huh?'

'You are vague my friend. Three thousand four 'undred and five quid … o' forged notes.'

'Oh yes of course,' I made out I heard him the first time.

'That'll see the three o' 'em to the gallows,' he went on. 'They was planning to skedaddle quick smart. Hal found out they 'ad bought a berth on the *Sea Witch*. She's sailin' first thing in the mornin'. And they nearly made it. That was good deducing my friend. Coffins huh!' He nodded sagely. The cheeky grin returned. 'So who did ya say the letter from?'

Instantly Snake walked noisily into the office. 'All done sir,' Snake threw a bag into one corner. 'The *Fabian* is all kitted and ready for service.'

I looked up from my paperwork. Fabian turned slightly to face me. A second's silence. 'What?' he finally shrugged, a face of innocence.

'The *Fabian*?' I asked.

'Aye. Why not? Or would you prefer we name 'er the *Caspian*?'

'Anyway,' Snake intervened, 'the two swivels are bein' delivered from the armoury with powder and shot in the mornin'.

'Nice shiny brass ones they are,' Jasper put in, following Hal and Billings into our tight space.

'Aye,' Billings agreed. 'Old and shiny relics o' Waterloo I reckon.'

'As long as they shoot straight, eh men?' Fabian stood erect and brushed dandruff from his shoulder. 'You collected the forger's printing press without problem I take it,' he asked of the men he had sent to Wapping.

'Aye sir,' Billings was still trying to remove ink from his hands.

'And 'ere's the plates sar,' Hal handed Fabian the two engraved copper plates wrapped in chamois leather.

'Five quid 'n one quid,' Jasper said, proud to be involved. 'Bloody good 'n all they is sar.'

Fabian slipped the plates into his desk drawer. 'Well done. Now, I'm off to the Chop'ouse. Who's goin' ta join me?'

'I'll do the governor's report,' I said knowing I had an hour to fill before my rendezvous.

'O' course ya will,' and I caught Fabian shooting Snake a surreptitious wink.

'Oh Jasper,' I called out after the others filed out the door.

'Aye sar.'

'Where's The Lamb?'

'Brisbane Street sar.'

I slipped my fob watch from my waistcoat pocket. Forty-five minutes past the hour of five. I sealed the report for Governor Fox Young and delivered it to the gatekeeper's assistant who would see it was delivered to Government House. It was time to walk to The Lamb.

'Caspian ... oh Caspian!' Elizabeth's voice sang to me from her front gate. She looked arresting in her pink pleated crinoline hoop dress bustled at the rear. Her jacket bodice had an off shoulder neckline pointed front and behind, with her long blond hair cascading down her back. She was truly an alluring woman. And she was on her way to see me.

Damn!

'Are you all right?' she asked, concern etched on her pretty face. 'I heard you were in a kerfuffle ... that a villain fired a pistol at you ... how are you my darling?'

I looked about and swallowed hard. *My darling!* It appeared no one heard. She opened the gate and ran across the prison courtyard to me.

'Oh Caspian,' she swooned, 'why have you not come to me? It has been days since ... since our dalliance.'

'Ah ... oh ... I have been terribly busy Miss Mead, what with the ongoing investigations then this forgery business ... reports to the governor and all ...' Elizabeth threw her arms around my neck. 'Miss Mead!' I near squeaked.

'I'm Elizabeth my darling.'

'Elizabeth. Not here. Come.' I took her hand and we hurried back into the office where she was of the opinion I was seeking privacy. Well that was true, but for different reasons. Once out of sight of prying eyes, she threw her arms about me once more and stole a kiss.

'I don't care who knows my darling,' she said. 'I love you.'

Damn!

'But Elizabeth. Your father.'

'Daddy's going away, finally, to Oatlands,' she gave me a sly smile. 'Or is it Campbell Town?'

'I didn't mean that. I meant what would your father think of you and I?'

'Oh pooh to father. I am eighteen and will marry whoever I wish.'

'Marry?' Now my voice *was* high.

'You do love me do you not?'

'I ... ah ... I ... um ... Elizabeth ... I ...'

'Caspian!' Elizabeth's stunning almond-shaped hazel eyes welled with tears.

'Oh there you are sir,' The Priest walked in without knocking. 'Got a message from the gov'nor. Thought I better get it to ya real smart like.' The Priest looked at Elizabeth. 'Oh Miss Mead. A good evenin' to ya mam. I never seen ya there, please pardon me.'

Elizabeth hitched up her skirts and hurried out without a word. Priest looked over his shoulder and waited until she was clear of the storehouse.

'I thought ya needed rescuing sir,' he said half serious, half grinning. He passed me the correspondence.

'Thank you, yes ...'

'Women sir, can't live wiv 'em, can't live without 'em.' He watched me open the sealed letter a moment. 'If'n ya wantin' my advice Mr Hunter 'er old man can be a miserable ol' buzzard.'

'Thank you Priest, I'll remember that.'

'Aye.' He leant forward on his toes straining his neck to look at the document before me. 'Nuthin' too serious I 'ope sir.'

'No, I should hope not.' I placed the letter in my pocket and withdrew my fob watch once more; fifty-five minutes past five bells.

True to her word Mistress Ruby Blood was waiting for me in the back parlour of The Lamb Inn. She was alone and dressed to kill.

'Please close the door Caspian.' Her voice was soft, husky. 'You don't mind if I call you Caspian do you?'

'No. Not at all.' I closed the door behind me and instantly noted three things. We were alone, the curtains were drawn and the candle-lit room smelt of the same perfume on the letter she had sent me. I stood a moment before the door and she held my gaze with her emerald green eyes. Red ringlets escaped the updo that had been created on top of her head, falling softly around her face. She was older than me, maybe 10 or so years.

Mistress Ruby's chalk white breasts sought release from her tight grass green bodice, low cut at the front. But her matching green dress was hidden under the table at which she sat with a decanter of red wine and two goblets reflecting the warm light of a candle.

'Sit,' she purred, offering me the back of her hand in greeting. I took the soft white paw and kissed it gently before taking the chair opposite at what was a small table for two and it soon became clear the thespian was a glass or three ahead of me. In fact she had an incurable thirst.

'And how is it that I am honoured with the company of such a beautiful woman?'

Oh Caspian you Casanova you.

'Why Caspian, you flatter me.' She poured me a glass of wine. I offered her a salutation and drank more than I intended. This didn't go unnoticed.

'Thirsty?' She smiled.

'I've had a hectic day ma'am.'

'So I heard. You arrested three felons including Fred's murderer and our extortionists. That is the main reason I asked you here this evening. To say thank you.'

'Oh it was nothing really. It's all a part of my situation mistress ... '

'Ruby ... please.'

Mistress Ruby stood crossing the room to the door. Her steps were silent and it was then I realised she was shoe-less, in stockings only. I took the liberty of filling our glasses and distinctly heard the key turn in the lock behind me.

'I'm ruined here, in Hobart Town,' she said in a downcast tone. 'The whole town's calling me a fake.'

'All smoke and mirrors huh?' I uttered without thought, thinking of London's West End and some of the theatre trickery I had read about.

'But I'm a showwoman Caspian. A showwoman primarily. It's theatre.'

'But people don't see your psychic skills as showmanship ma'am.' *Easy mate or you will ruin the moment.*

'What I'm trying to say, Ruby, is that your stage persona ... your talent with clairvoyance is remarkable ... you are ...'

'I'm certain you're aware much of it is pure luck ... I mean to say, if an elderly gentleman, for instance, is in the audience alone there is a fair chance he is widowed.'

'Yes, I understand that, but most people do not.'

We drank in silence a moment when without warning the most profound invitation occurred. I felt her stockinged toes wiggle at my groin. I coughed. Ruby giggled. She leant forward and extinguished the candle with a single puff from practised lips. We savoured the peace and quiet a second longer in the dim light of the lone candle flickering with anticipation on the mantelpiece. There was no doubting her intentions.

'I leave in the morning Caspian,' she purred. 'And I just wanted to thank you in person ...'

Without further ado her chair shot backwards across the room as she jumped to her feet and pulled at a lace on her bodice. I was immediately greeted by the lushest pair of firm melon-shaped breasts I have ever encountered. They stared at me, wantonly, both nipples red, ridged and right for rogering. Ruby hitched up her skirt and tresses and straddled me where I sat. She clearly came prepared, as she was bloomer-less.

An hour later I slipped out the back door of The Lamb Inn, my mind filled with intoxicating, wonderful memories and wearing my crooked clothes with a broad smile. I believe I was even whistling as I promenaded down Elizabeth Street towards the Cove like a Versailles peacock – where I found the crew imbibing at The Derwent Chophouse.

Waiting wench Sally, big, buxom, blonde and beautiful, shoved patrons aside making a path for me from door to Fabian where he sat with the others enjoying after-meal drinks. I thought they looked rather pleased to see me. Fabian stubbed a cheroot out on the floor with his boot heel.

'Well now, explain ya self lad. Where ya been then?' The plate of chops and several porters had made his eyes lazy but he had the energy to muster a smug face.

'I had to write that report for Governor Fox Young remember?'

'Oh aye.' Fabian leant across and sniffed me as I sat next to him. 'Well 'ow come ya smell mighty strong o' perfume, like that thar letter sent to the office earlier?'

I immediately remembered the governor's correspondence.

'Letter!' I said aloud.

'Aye letter.'

I took the neatly folded and sealed dispatch from my pocket.

'What's thart?' But Fabian recognised the wax seal of Government House. 'Congratulations from the top dog are in order I'm sayin'.'

But my face relayed anything but a congratulatory message.

'What is it?' Fabian snatched the letter from me.

'The gov'nor's lettin' us know another dodgy pound note's been passed,' Fabian told the table. 'But it's no problem now,' he looked to me for assurance. 'We got the buggers *and* the press *and* the plates.' He gulped the remains of his tankard and waved it about for attention.

'Read on,' I said.

Fabian mumbled away, rapidly reading the letter to himself. '"'Ope an' Anchor",' he read aloud. '"It came to the notice of the cashier at the Bank of Van Diemen's Land when the note was passsed over by Mr Thomas the innkeeper to the teller for banking – last Friday." So?'

'Well,' I said. 'We were in the Hope and Anchor last Friday and if my memory serves me correctly, you paid with a pound note.'

'Oh shite! Are you suggesting ... ?'

'Where are the notes the governor gave you?'

Suddenly Fabian was uncharacteristically quiet. 'I thought I put them in me drawer but now you mention it ...' he said in a whisper.

'It was only an accident sir,' Hal muttered. 'Anyone could 'ave done that.'

'You was a bit pie-eyed sir,' Snake tried a smile.

Immediately Sally – good ol' Sal – stood before our sombre gathering. 'Cook's gone done roasted guinea pig tonight as a special treat like. Skin nice 'n crispy. Ya like it?'

Day Twelve – Tuesday

SEVERAL DAYS HAD PASSED AND I STILL HADN'T heard from the surgeon-general to obtain permission to exhume Nathanial Rudder's body.

'Damn the man!' I confided in Fabian. 'What I need to do will take minutes, then Mr Rudder can rest in peace.'

'Ya dealing with servants of the public lad,' Fabian clenched his unlit clay pipe in his teeth sucking at the dry tobacco, tasting its spices without igniting. I was impressed. I think he was doing it to oblige me. 'God only knows how slow the cogs turn within Her Majesty's services,' he finally added with a contemplative stare.

'Damn it!' I said impatiently. 'I feel like going in there tonight and just doing it. Christ, the ground's freshly dug, how hard could it be? I only need a minute. It's not as if I want to cart the body away.'

'Why don't ya then?'

'What?'

'Sneak in there tonight and dig the bugger up.'

'Are you serious?' I stared at Fabian a long moment. He just sat on the corner of his desk returning one of his naughty schoolboy grins.

'You *are* serious,' I said.

'Aye. As ya say. Easy diggin', only take a minute.'

'Damn right!' I walked to the door to see if anyone was within earshot. Snake, Billings, Hal and Jasper all stared back from the potbelly stove, all were holding their coffee, all raised their mugs in salutation. 'Hmm,' I sighed. 'It's settled then.'

In the end I thought it wise to keep the grave digging delegation down to three of us. Fabian insisted on coming and Jasper volunteered to dig. It was ten in the evening as we stood at the perimeter of the pauper's grave, where small wooden crosses had the names of the dead and buried scratched across them. We had the advantage of some hedging and newly planted oaks for cover but Fabian insisted on keeping watch, comforted by a flask of rum. I stood at the grave site holding a lantern masked with a black cloth so only necessary light spilt onto the dig.

The night was pleasantly tranquil and not cold as we were still enjoying the summer months. The sky was clear and the first quarter moon threw out only a little light. St David's Cemetery sits between the corners of Davey Street, Harrington Street and Salamanca quite near the New Wharf and several inns. At this late hour only the occasional carriage rolled by, or the odd horsemen, however the Anglesea Military Barracks were situated only three hundred yards up the Davey Street hill. We would have to be vigilant.

At only four feet down or thereabouts Jasper scraped the bagged corpse with his shovel.

'Brilliant,' I said nervously lowering the lantern well into the hole, keen to get the job done and leave. Jasper pulled his knife from its sheath on his hip and slashed the bag from head to toe. The smell wasn't as bad as I expected.

'Jesus Christ!' Jasper sprung from the hole.

'What is it?'

'It ain't 'im squire!'

'What?'

We all peered down upon the exposed corpse where plainly an old hag with her toothless gums sucked comically. 'Jesus,' I hissed. 'What have you done?'

'What 'ave I ... me? What 'ave *I* done? It was you what told me ta dig 'ere!'

I swung the lantern over the wooden cross. 'Nelly!' I read in a horrified whisper.

'Nelly firkin' Jenkins!' Fabian read aloud with a mix of surprise and respect. 'Christ! I didn't know ya carked it lovey.'

'Who's Nelly Jenkins?' Jasper stood gaping, scratching his head like he had lice.

'She's the baker's missus from Goulbourn Street, ya know the ...'

'Doesn't matter,' I said bluntly, desperately dangling the lantern over the crosses nearby. 'Here! Nathanial Rudder.' It was the grave directly next to Nelly's who must have been interred the same day as Nathanial. 'Quick Jasper, get to lad.'

'Are ya certain sir?'

'Yes, see for yourself.'

At that moment a carriage rolled along Harrington Street from the area known as Sandy Bay. 'Down!' I whispered. The two-horse four-wheel carriage rumbled over the gravel within five yards of the pauper's graveyard.

And stopped.

'Jesus, now what?' Fabian joined Jasper and myself lying flat on the dirt. Two men alighted from the carriage, laughing together while their driver sat keeping the horses steady. It soon became clear they were drunk and both men started to relieve themselves at the edge of the cemetery. 'Christ I needed that,' one said. The other murmured his approval and oscillated his piss left and right like he was hosing the garden.

'Ha!' the first one grinned. 'It's the cemetery,' he said drunkenly as if his eyes had only just focussed in the dark.

He appeared to look directly at us and it was then I realised some lantern light escaped from under the black cloth. Fabian and I looked at each other in dark silence. *Now what?*

It was when I was convinced that he had seen us when he suddenly went 'BOO!' and burst into laughter once more before climbing back into the carriage behind his friend.

'Jasper,' I sighed. 'Let us get this over with,' I whispered as the carriage continued on.

Ten minutes passed before we heard the now familiar sound of the shovel scraping on sailcloth. Once again Jasper slashed at the sacking. But it was tougher than the last. Eager to be free of our surroundings Jasper stabbed the bloated corpse at its midriff. There followed a farting sound and the repugnant stench of a rotten cadaver. He had punctured the body!

'Ah Jesus Lord!' Jasper fell back on the body, covered in worms and maggots while Fabian fell about laughing. Jasper spat. 'It's in me mouth … it's in me mouth!'

'Quiet!' I cried out, too loudly.

'Get me out!' Jasper had fallen across the putrescent remains. He flayed his arms about for assistance. Fabian and myself stood well back. Jasper crawled free and knelt on the grass vomiting. I had no choice. It was now or never. I slipped to the lower end of the body and holding the lantern with one hand I managed to pull one leg free then the other. Immediately we heard voices at the southern perimeter of the cemetery. Urgent voices. They had heard us.

'Firk! It's the night watchmen.' Fabian's laugh vanished. 'We gotta run lads.'

I climbed from the hole and frantically shovelled the dirt back onto Nathanial Rudder's rotting corpse, burying the lantern in the process. The nightwatchman's lamp danced amongst the headstones of the more wealthy occupants. He was searching for the source of the disturbance.

''urry fa firk's sake!'

With Nathanial re-buried, I was about to start on Nelly Jenkins when Fabian clamped onto my arm. 'Leave 'er. We gotta skedaddle lad.'

• • •

Jasper stood in the stables behind the Boar's Head in Murray Street feeling sorry for himself. Eddy Piggott the innkeeper relayed buckets of water from his well, which we used to drench the miserable constable.

'I 'ope ya got wha' ya wanted sir,' Jasper grumbled between mouth rinses and spits.

'I am sorry to say Jasper, but no. Now put these on,' And I threw him a pair of slops and a blouse Mr Piggott had lent us without question. 'And meet us in the taproom. You've earned a drink or two.'

'Aye Caspy,' Fabian's grin had returned. 'I think it's your buy tonight.'

The Boar's Head was but a mere cottage. Rectangular, two chimneys, shingle roof, two front windows with chunks of stucco missing from its façade. But a popular butcher worked from converted stables at the rear and the inn did a roaring trade with seafarers seeking Eddy Piggott's best ale.

Eddy Piggott was a tubby little man with brawny arms and a pleasant demeanour. He who wore a leather patch over one eye after losing it in a blacksmith shop. Fabian told me how a molten knob of iron flew off the anvil and took out his eye some ten years earlier. He had also lost the tip off his left thumb, lost in action while endeavouring to hack a pig carcass into pot size pieces with a meat cleaver. He admitted he had been drinking rum at the time. The man was a danger unto himself.

Jasper joined us in the taproom and I lobbed a crown onto the bar for our ale, which Fabian assured me was the best real ale in Hobart Town. House brewed. I just prayed it had no body parts like fingertips in its making.

'What will ya missus say when ya go 'ome in different clothes like, Jasp'?' Fabian scrutinised Jasper in his new three-quarter britches and a calico shirt, three sizes too big for him, with lace ties at the front.

'She's good to me sar. She trusts my judgement, knows I gotta work with whores and the like.'

'Amelia, her name is.' Fabian turned to me with his elbow bent in support of his quart tankard mere inches from his lips. 'Young Jasper 'ere met 'er the day she arrived in port like. Travellin' with 'er mother, but the mother died birthin', round Cape o' Good Hope.'

'Sorry to hear that,' I looked past Fabian to Jasper who was now busy explaining his attire to another drinker he appeared familiar with.

'Aye.' Fabian checked over his shoulder to make certain Jasper wasn't listening. 'She's only fifteen and already with bairn.'

'Oh!'

'Aye, she must o' got 'erself banged up on the voyage out, I'm thinkin'. There be plenty young bucks on board the ship an' all. But Jasper 'ere is certain it's 'is bairn, so good luck to 'im I say.'

'So he lives with her?'

'Aye. Jasper rents a tiny cottage up Collins Street that 'e shares with another family.'

A voice boomed across the taproom. 'Fabian firkin' Winter!'

I turned to look over a dozen heads for the source, only to watch a lump of a man shoving his way towards us.

'Didn't think you'd see me again, did ya now, Fabian firkin' Winter,' the man slurred, flushed red with drink and angry.

'Chase!' Fabian was clearly agitated. I had known him long enough to read he was thinking fast on his feet. 'Well well Chase … long time no see. What 'ave you been up to then?'

'What 'ave *I* been up to? *Me!*'

I shot the innkeeper a sideways glance and noticed him watching vigilantly with a nervous twitch beneath the patch.

'It's *you* ya firker, what 'ave *you* been up to more like.' The lump pushed past me spilling my ale. 'So me sister wasn't good enough eh

... first ya abuse me sister ...'

Aha, so that is what the man's been up to. Surprise surprise.

'Then, while I'm away fellin' trees, ya try ya luck on me wife.'

Felling trees! That will explain the arms of a gorilla.

The taproom was growing silent. I have always found it amazing how the news of trouble travels so fast.

'Your wife?' Fabian was floundering, and fast. His eyes darting about seeking an exit while maintaining pluck in the face of the enemy.

'Aye. Ya paid 'er a wee visit when Chase 'ere was down the Huon River. Police business ya said it were, just to get ya grubby boots in me door.'

'Oh yes,' Fabian was instantly animated. 'Now I remember. She had me by me truncheon!'

'She wha' ...'

The intended words never came. Fabian threw his ale in the man's eyes and pounded his fist into the lumberjack's stomach. Nothing. Naught. Not a sausage. He didn't feel a thing.

But I did.

Chase pulled back his arm to throw a punch, only to smack his elbow into my face. I did what came naturally. I smashed my tankard over the back of the man's head.

Now that hurt.

I know.

Because he roared in pain and spun about to face me.

Oh Christ! His massive left hand pinioned my throat while his right-balled fist came at me like a boulder. I managed to jerk my head sideways.

Crack!

His punch connected with the side of the face of the man behind me.

'Firk!'

Abruptly all hell broke loose. I drove my knee hard into the lump's soft genitals. Another loud groan. He released my neck. I ducked. The man behind me threw a punch. Chase cupped his hand over the flying fist. He twisted it and I heard wrist bones snap. I fell to the floor where Fabian was just picking himself up. All round us bedlam broke loose.

Splintering of furniture, shattering of windows, cracking of skulls. A dozen or more men now joined the fracas. Big men. Seafarers, whalers, shipbuilders, blacksmiths …

I followed Fabian crawling on hands and knees towards the door.

'Where's Jasper?' I hissed at Fabian as a body somersaulted over us smashing onto a table. More upset drinkers. More lads into the fight!

'Jasper … oh Christ! There he is!'

Jasper was skipping along the bar, dancing around broken glass and throwing wild blows with his pewter quart mug as a weapon.

Crack! Firk!

I saw loose teeth fly.

'Where are you goin'?' Chase roared. He caught Fabian on all fours near the door. He lifted Fabian effortlessly to his feet.

Crack!

Fabian staggered backwards from a punch to the head. He tripped over a limp body. I bounced to my feet and leapt on his attacker's back, my arm about his throat in a stranglehold. But Chase bucked like a wild bull. He threw me clear. I landed awkwardly on my side and took two others with me. Bodies bounced off the wall. I snapped my head about to face the man once more. He snatched a bottle, crushed its neck over a table and came at me with the jagged, wicked weapon. To my right a blurred vision. An adrenalin fuelled scream …

Karthud!

Fragments of broken chair rained about me. *Jasper!* He had walloped Chase over the head with a bar stool. The man fell, crashing to the floor like a fallen eucalypt. Two men fell on top of me, wrestling to the floor. I was kicked in the head. Fell sideways and fighting to regain some dignity when I saw it!

The hobnail boot missing the nail, left foot, heel! It was unmistakable. It was without a doubt the murderer's shoe. I lunged for the leg. The man turned with a scowl. He was big, damned big, no neck, arms like hams. He swung a punch, missed. Kicked with the strength of a mule. I lost my grip and the man bolted.

At the same instant the innkeeper discharged a shotgun.

Kaboom!

The shot tore an uneven hole in the ceiling. Rats' nests and debris rained about as Piggott cranked back the hammer on the second barrel.

'Right you meatheads!' he bawled through a mist of dust whilst waving the menacing barrels. 'Who wants some?'

There was no time to lose. I careered onto the street. Somewhere towards the darkened harbour on my left I heard the police rattle of a night guard. They had heard the shot and commotion at the Boar's Head. Another disturbance to my right grabbed my attention. A dog barking. Twisting about I caught sight of my man turning into an alleyway a hundred yards distant. I bolted after him. Hemmed between M. Denison Ironmonger and a Haberdashery I found that the laneway led to a blacksmith's workshop.

Without waiting for help, I hastened down the narrow corridor. A wooden gate screeched open and then slammed shut. I heard crashing in the darkness as if someone had stumbled over chains. I shouldered my way through the gate and into the smithy where the light of the remaining coals glowed enough to throw a vague luminescence about the workshop. The forge was made of sandstone; one and a half yards square, two feet deep and full of glowing coals. An anvil stood bolted to the top of a tree stump next to the fire pit with bellows at one end to feed air into the fire.

A shadow shot between the smouldering red coke and myself.

'Avast!' I yelled, praying I had authority in my tone. 'I want to talk with you. Naught else sir.'

I squinted, trying to adjust my eyesight to the blackness. But I saw nothing. No movement. I took small steps forward and now felt the heat radiating from the fire pit.

'Sir. I mean you no harm. I merely need to ask you some questions.'

I was unarmed. I peered into the dark recesses hoping to find a weapon of some sort or at least something to defend myself when suddenly I was thrown to the ground. The man had circled me.

'Wanna talk does ya? Firkin' lawman!' The man had bestial strength. He was clearly the blacksmith. I was lifted bodily off my feet and dragged like a rag doll to the fire. He took a fistful of my hair and forced my head towards the forge. I fought panic; I felt bile rise into my throat. I threw wild punches into the man's kidneys, but he was a brute force to be reckoned with.

'Sir, I beseech you, don't do this.'

'Huh! I'm sick of being victimised by you lot. I done me time. Ten years fa stealin' a firkin' sheep to feed me starvin' family! Ten years fa tryin' to feed me ravenous bairns. Ten firkin' years!'

He pushed me closer to the red-hot coals. The heat was fierce.
I felt my strength draining away. My strength to fight back was no
match for this Herculean monster. Like a drowning man snatching at
straws my arms flayed about. I caught hold of sacking cloth about the
bellows. It fell into the coals instantly exploding in flames. The conflagration momentarily filled the shop with the light from the blaze and
I caught the demonic look in the man's eyes. The look of a desperate
man who knew he had gone too far and there was no turning back.
The look of a killer. Sucking air through gritted teeth he forced my
face within inches of the inferno.

My brain screamed.

This is it!

When unexpectedly ... *Thwack!*

I will never forget the look in Jasper's eyes ... *Thwack! ... Thwack!*

The lad still held onto his tankard and was beating the ogre of a
man repeatedly until Fabian stepped up behind him, clasping a fist
around Jasper's raised wrist.

'Easy lad, ya don't wanna go and kill the firker!'

With the aid of the night soil man and a length of rope we managed to
transport our trussed felon to the Prisoners Barracks. There his head
was bandaged and he was kept in a lockup cell – the same one I had
slept in only days earlier – until he composed himself. Now shoeless,
he sat on the bed and wept silently. I turned the boots over and had
no doubt I was holding the boot from the crime scene.

''e ain't a bad man Mr Winter, Mr Hunter sir,' the night guard gatekeeper Bartley Barrow said of the blacksmith away from the cells. He
knew him well apparently. He looked at me with his pasty face – in
contrast to my left cheek, which was still red from the fire. ''e's had it
tough, has our Beowulf.'

'Beowulf!' I asked, incredulous.

'Aye, thart's wha' his mates calls 'im, Beowulf like in the Anglo-
Saxon poem sar.'

'Yes I know who Beowulf is Bartley,' I said. 'But what else do you
know about him?'

''is real name is Edmund Clay. 'e wouldn't 'urt a wee ant sar.'

'Well 'e near firkin' killed Caspy 'ere Bartley,' Fabian said, 'if'n it weren't for Jasper lad givin' the smithy a walloping with 'is tankard.'

'Well I'm just sayin', thart's all,' he insisted, and jammed his little finger in his ear and gave it a good scratch. 'It's most unlikely for 'im to be'ave like this.'

'Mr Edmund Clay,' I started with confidence, back in the lockup and feeling safe on the outside of the cell bars. 'Why did you run from me?'

The giant of a man looked up from where he sat on his cell bench. His eyes, red from drink or his employment I wasn't certain, had mellowed.

'I done me ten years sar, I panicked. I don't want to go to prison no more.'

'Well you damn near killed me.'

'Aye. And for that I apologise ...'

'See, I told ya sir, 'e's not a bad man,' Bartley Barrow was determined to put in a good word.'

'Please Mr Barrow,' I said. 'Leave us a moment.' He walked off head bowed and scuffing his feet.

'You're 'ere, Mr Clay, on a charge o' murder,' Fabian said, his right eye purple as an eggplant from Chase's punch at the Boar's Head.

'Murder!' The blacksmith jumped to his feet and grabbed the bars. 'I never murdered no one ...'

'Your boot prints were at the scene of a murder,' I said, stepping back out of reach from the bars.

'Aye,' Fabian snapped. 'The murder o' Miss Edith Philpot, the daughter o' Lord Philpot.'

'Christ's blood no! That's not possible. I would never kill anyone ...' He looked at me with pleading eyes. I returned a look of no confidence.

'I was just trying to save me own skin sir, when I fought ya like ... just tried to scare ya sir.'

'Oh,' Fabian nodded. 'Ya did thart alright.'

'Honest ... ya gotta believe me.'

I took a deep breath, sighed. 'Your boots match prints we found,' I held up the boots and shuddered at the thought of the boot print on Edith's young face. 'Boot marks we found on the deceased's body.'

'Oh! But they ain't my boots sar.'

'Eh?' Fabian grew angry. 'They was on ya feet.'

'I only 'ad them boots a day sar. I exchanged them from a nurse what's employed at the 'ospital. I fixed new handles on 'er pot like. She don't 'ave money – who does these days? So I barter with 'er. Them boots for two pot handles.'

'Name?'

'Penny Dove sar.'

Day Thirteen – Wednesday

Government House

'YOUR EXCELLENCY,' I SAID, HARD ON THE HEELS OF Samuel Wheaton the secretary. 'Thank you for the audience at such short notice ...'

''e's figured it out sir,' Fabian intervened. pushing the office door so hard it thumped the wall. He was like an excited schoolboy and proud as Punch. 'It's so simple when ya know 'ow. And some folks was talkin' of a ghost ship, sea monster, pirates ...'

'You are here about the *Ocean Maiden* I take it gentleman,' the governor was an understanding and patient man, sitting in his gentleman's office chair directly under the newly completed Knud Bull portrait of himself. In fact it was so recently completed I could smell the fresh oils.

Governor Fox Young clearly noticed Fabian's black eye.

'Goodness me Mr Winter! You have been in the wars.'

'Aye sir.' He was about to elaborate when we noticed the governor was reading a copy of the Hobart Town Gazette. The man caught me reading the headline.

Bodies exhumed at St David's cemetery.

'What kind of sick person would dig up the dead I ask you? I thought that sort of business only happened in London twenty or more years ago.' The governor shook his head.

I nodded in agreement. 'Yes indeed sir.'

Fabian flashed me a sly grin. 'Sick Your Excellency,' he feigned disgust. 'Damned sick to be sure.'

'Now,' Governor Fox Young sat the paper aside. 'The *Ocean Maiden*.'

'Aye!' Fabian near shouted. 'The *Ocean Maiden*.'

'Well let Mr Hunter explain Mr Winter, as it appears it is his theory.'

Fabian's eyes bulged. 'Oh it ain't no theory gov ... ah Your Excellency it's ...'

Henry Fox Young held his forefinger erect, decreeing silence. Fabian bit his tongue and I had the floor.

'The entire mystery sir,' I started, 'is a string of rare events and coincidences worthy of a Herman Melville novel.'

His Excellency leant back in his chair, elbows on the armrests and tapped his fingertips together in front of his face.

'The key element in the whole sad kerfuffle is the nine barrels of grain alcohol stored with the other cargo,' I said. 'Six were breached, rolling from the pile of rum kegs where they smashed open on the cargo deck. I might add here that they were poorly situated ...'

'They should 'ave been stored separately,' Fabian cut in. 'And secured individually to the lower deck proper like and ...'

'Yes Mr Winter, kindly allow Mr Hunter the floor.'

'Oh aye.'

'That's correct sir,' I went on. 'However they were not secured properly and that will be highlighted in my report. Now for the interesting part ...' And once again Fabian fidgeted impatiently until the governor shot him a look.

'I made enquiries,' I continued, 'with whalers along the coast of Storm Bay and then did much reading in the Prisoners Barracks library where they have a complete set of Encyclopaedia Britannica. You see sir, the whalers spoke of feeling a minor earth tremor...'

'Seaquake!'

'Aye, seaquake, early of the evening the day before the *Ocean Maiden* was found abandoned. My reading led me to believe the ship sailed over the epicentre of the earth tremor ... seaquake ... somewhere well out at sea. This seabed tremor has sent violent shock waves to the surface. It is a rare phenomenon but it is documented. This would have frightened the crew and all those on board the *Ocean Maiden*; the more superstitious would have thought it a monster or something supernatural ...'

'We know's they was superstitious 'cos o' the horseshoe nailed to the mast,' Fabian said eagerly, pacing the room to expel energy.

'Exactly,' I said. 'It was the tremor also that knocked the galley stove off its chocks. But, when the ship shook for a time the grain alcohol barrels would have fallen from the pile and smashed open. The highly inflammable spirit drained into the bilge where eventually it would have evaporated ...'

'And that's why we found the sounding rod up on deck,' Fabian interrupted once more. 'They had tested the depth of the bilge with it, then abandoned it.'

I agreed. 'But the vapour had risen to the upper decks where the crew and captain, his mates and family were about to have their evening meal. You see Your Excellency, one naked flame in the wrong place would have blown the ship sky high. So the good captain, Captain Brynjar Evjen has ordered all hands into the yawl where a rope was connected to the stern of the ship and they have drifted along well behind her in relative safety ...'

'And they left everythin' behind ... everythin'. Food on the table ... everythin',' Fabian intervened.

'Except the navigational aids. The compass was taken from the binnacle and there was no sign of a chronometer, sextant or navigation book left on board ...'

Fabian interjected once more. 'Except the ship's manifest was found in the first mate's cabin.'

'That set me to thinking Your Excellency. My theory is that some time in the night the rope, that's the tow rope, has come loose from the ship; probably not tied properly in the panic to get off the ship. Then, to everyone's horror, the ship has sailed away from them under minimal sail ...'

'A sudden fresh wind maybe!' Fabian said. And almost like an omen, a fresh breeze blew across Sullivan's Cove where we could see craft bobbing and sails flapping as shore crews made all secure.

'Exactly,' I agreed. 'Or maybe even a small squall.'

'Without anyone at the helm!' Fabian muscled in again.

'Mr Winter!' His Excellency tapped his fingertips together. 'Please.'

Fabian sighed.

But the governor was impressed. 'How amazing,' he said. 'And totally believable.'

'Told ya! Sir.' Fabian was flushed with success, albeit *my* success.

Henry Fox Young stroked his chin in contemplation. 'So where is the ship's yawl and its passengers?'

Fabian crossed to the window as the increasing wind kicked up a dust cloud in the garden. 'Tell 'im about the young'un!' he shot over his shoulder.

I started. 'A young girl's body was found …'

'Washed up on South Bruny!' Fabian spun about and leant on the governor's desk, his fists balled, and now *I* shot him a look. To his credit he kept quiet a brief moment.

'The body has been identified as Serianna Evjen, the Norwegian captain's daughter. My way of thinking sir, is that the yawl has capsized by a rogue wave and all hands were drowned. Only the young girl's body was caught on rocks.'

'Well what about the only survivor who was senselessly murdered through greed?' The governor asked.

'I believe, for some reason, he was accidentally left on board …'

''e had long orange-red 'air sir,' Fabian chimed. 'Bad luck on board any ship …'

The governor's mouth was wide with interest. 'Are you saying he was abandoned?'

'Possibly,' I said. 'But it's more likely that in all the panic to get into the yawl he has slipped, cracked his head on the ship, and lay senseless …'

Fabian champing at the bit. 'It was night remember … dark like.'

'Yes,' I agreed. 'And he regained consciousness shortly after. The ship was deserted. He had lost all memory. He panicked, saw fires on the shore and swam for it.'

'Good heavens Mr Hunter,' the governor nodded in contemplation. 'I think you've solved the mystery.'

'And then sir,' I went on, 'several hours later at five o'clock of the morning, the *Georgette* with myself as passenger came across the drifting ship that was now becalmed on a flat sea in a thick fog.'

A gentle tapping sound snapped us from our conjecture. It was Samuel Wheaton, the governor's secretary, standing in the open doorway.

'Samuel!' The governor looked up, all smiles.

'Lord Philpot is here to see you sir.'

'Marmaduke!'

'Yes sir, he said you requested to see him.'

'I did?' The governor looked troubled. 'I … ah …'

The sound of me clearing my throat grabbed the governor's attention. 'It was me sir. I sent a message to say you required seeing him urgently. I hope you don't mind.'

For once Fabian kept his mouth shut.

'Mind? On my behalf ... what on earth's going on?'

'Your Excellency, may we speak in private a moment? This is of the utmost importance.'

The governor looked at me long and hard. He could see I was deadly serious.

'Leave us a moment Samuel ... please. Tell Marmaduke, ah His Lordship, that I'm at a meeting and if he wouldn't mind waiting ...' Henry Fox Young shot me a stern eye. 'Five minutes ... that's all.'

'Certainly Sir.'

'Oh, and Samuel ... see he is offered tea.'

'Well Mr Hunter,' and the governor held a humourless gaze, 'making appointments on the governor's behalf is no laughing matter. Please explain yourself.'

Five minutes turned into fifteen. To his credit the governor sat and listened, totally astonished. Finally he pulled the sash behind his desk to summon his secretary, and in a sombre and sobering atmosphere Lord Philpot was shown into the office. The man walked in with a nervous smile and a confident swagger, but the moment he saw Fabian and myself the wealthy entrepreneur knew the walls of Jericho were about to come crashing down around him.

'Why, why Marmaduke?' the governor was clearly in shock. 'You, of all people, a murderer ...'

The room was suddenly oppressive. It felt like demons were lingering in corners in a feeding frenzy of dark energy. Lord Philpot treated Fabian and myself to glares of pure unadulterated hatred. His face reddened, his eyes wide and he physically shook. He knew he was trapped, cornered like the rat he had become. Finally he composed himself and he remained standing at the end of the governor's desk. He was not invited to sit.

After a moment's awkward silence Philpot spoke.

'The vile creature was blackmailing me Henry. First he seduced my baby girl ... my darling Edith. He seduced her and made certain he got her with child. He wanted so desperately to become part of the family. Part of the Philpot dynasty! Can you imagine it?' Philpot now shouted. 'The filthy miscreant wanted to marry into the family ... he would have inherited my wealth Henry. Imagine.'

Governor Fox Young kept his eyes on his friend, incredulous that the man had taken another's life. Yet hints of sympathy crept across his face.

Philpot read his friend's emotions.

'He worked at the Commissariat and Bond Store you see Henry … he was a lowly clerk. Somehow he found out about the Hartog Marbles.'

I noticed the governor flinch. He looked at me, acknowledging that what I had told him a little earlier, about smuggled rare stolen classical marbles, was all true.

'God knows how he knew,' Philpot was talking freely, not holding back. There was no point. 'I suspected he was intercepting my mail. I had suspicions some of the wax seals on my correspondence from London and Greece had been resealed. He must have searched the barrels, discovered the marbles hidden in barrels of tea …'

'So was Captain Brynjar Evgen of the *Ocean Maiden* aware of the smuggled cargo?' the governor asked Philpot.

'Of course not,' the lord proceeded. 'I have a shipping agent in London who deals with that side of the business.'

'Business?' I asked. 'There have been other smugglings?'

Philpot completely ignored me, but answered as if His Excellency had asked the question.

'There were two others. The statue of the goddess Hebe in my garden is actually a Greek classic. 310BC Henry.'

The governor clenched his teeth and shook his head. 'And you told me it was an Italian copy you had commissioned.'

'I couldn't tell you the truth, now could I?'

'I must say, I thought it was masterly crafted.'

'And I have a bronze of Poseidon hidden in my cellar. It is 460BC, a magnificent example of classical Greek craftsmanship. It was taken from a museum in Athens in the '40s. I paid a black marketeer the equivalent of twelve hundred guineas for it and it was smuggled here with furniture I had ordered for my residence.'

Governor Fox Young. 'But the Hartog marbles?'

'They were looted from the Acropolis in 1815. Once again I purchased them from black marketeers.'

'And the Greeks have been trying to find them ever since,' I said.

'So,' the governor asked, 'Mr Rudder knew of the Hartog Marbles and blackmailed you?'

'Exactly.' Lord Marmaduke Philpot's eyes clouded over with hatred. 'He had to go Henry. I couldn't stand for it.'

His Lordship lifted his eyes from the floor to his friend as the hatred turned to tears.

'My sweet sweet angel,' Lord Philpot cried. 'My little Edith Verity. He took advantage of her. He planted his vile seed in her, violated her, impregnated her with his lower class filth.' And Philpot bawled in racked sobs.

'So you decided to dress as a woman,' I said without sympathy. 'You dressed as a poverty stricken woman of the street, an old rag lady you thought no one would take note of?' Philpot looked at me with contempt. 'You used one of your wife's wigs and you worked on your deceased wife's clothing to make it look torn and soiled?'

Fabian stepped in again. 'One o' ya big mistakes that was sir, ya smelt sweet o' soap. Ya didn't stink like an unwashed rag lady. A witness what seen ya at Mr Rudder's cottage in the laneway noticed that.'

'Then you bashed Mr Rudder over the head with a blunt weapon,' I said. 'So hard you crushed his skull above the right ear …'

'But 'e survived the initial blow,' Fabian said. 'And some'ow escaped to the rivulet down the lane fifty yards away where you shot 'im in the 'ead with a gentleman's pocket pistol what I'm certain we will find when we search your residence.'

Lord Marmaduke Philpot hung his head in shame.

'So it is all true Marmaduke,' the Governor asked, now lacking pity, 'just as these detectives have stated?'

Philpot's answer came in the form of uncontrollable sobs.

'And,' I finished up without mercy, 'that is why you didn't want to post a reward for your daughter's murderer. You didn't want to attract attention to yourself.'

His Excellency must have been feeling the tension in the room also. He stood and opened the French doors onto the veranda. The sea breeze cleansed the room, shuffling papers on the governor's desk until he weighted them with a pewter pounce shaker and inkwell. From where I stood there was a panoramic view of Sullivan's Cove with ships docked or moored in the bay; from our sloop, *Fabian*, at Old Wharf to the east, across the cove to Philpot's *Buckingham* tied up at New Wharf amongst half a dozen whalers.

'Mr Winter,' the governor's voice was breaking. He cleared his throat.

'Sir.'

'I think we could all use a brandy. If you wouldn't mind.' And he tipped his head to a cedar sideboard dressed with decanters and crystal. Hardly protocol, I could read Fabian's thoughts; but what the hell.

'So what happened to Miss Edith Philpot?' the governor desperately wanted to know. 'I'm certain your proven skills have solved this mystery also, Mr Hunter.'

But I had the impression the governor was almost afraid to ask.

'Aye,' Fabian said over his shoulder as he poured the brandy into crystal goblets with more verve than the moment dictated. 'That's the irony of it ya see.'

'Irony?' the governor asked as Lord Philpot stiffened.

'Yes,' I cut in with tact before Fabian blundered on with his usual lack of discretion. 'I do not think you realised Your Lordship that the man you murdered was the man who killed your daughter only hours before!'

Philpot spun on his heels to face me. 'What!'

The governor took a gulp of his brandy.

'Well,' I started on the sad saga. 'I remembered something Elizabeth Mead told me. Elizabeth is the prisoners Barrack's superintendent's daughter ...'

Philpot. 'I know who Elizabeth Mead is.'

'She said Nathanial Rudder and Edith's relationship had been floundering for the past week or so before Edith was murdered because Edith realised she was being used ...'

Philpot harrumphed.

'You see Miss Philpot was easily impressionable and naïve, falling for what she thought was true romance ...'

'Yes yes we know all this,' Philpot spat.

I ignored him. 'From the time she met Nathanial Rudder at the theatre, which we now know was contrived, she was a victim of class distinction. Nathanial, she knew, was well below her station in life. He was a clerk in the Bond Store. He seduced Edith, made her pregnant ...'

Philpot's voice was high pitched. 'We know all this Hunter ...'

'If you will allow me Lord Philpot,' I said curtly. 'His Excellency doesn't know all the facts.'

Philpot wheeled about to Henry, who put a hand up to silence the man.

'Now was the time to tell her father,' I continued, speaking to the governor. 'Nathanial Rudder wanted desperately to marry into the Philpot dynasty. But he worked at the Bond Store and somehow, maybe by accident, he discovered Lord Philpot wasn't the honest philanthropist he made out to be.' Philpot shook his head at me in silence. 'His Lordship was excessively wealthy and had an expensive passion, collecting ancient antiquities.' And I looked to Philpot who decided now was the time to look out the French doors to the harbour and quaff half his brandy in one gulp.

'Unfortunately most of the pieces that took his fancy were extremely rare and therefore stolen from museums. He was smuggling these black market pieces into Van Diemen's Land ...'

Philpot snapped. 'We know this Hunter!' The governor shot him another fierce, black glance.

'That was what was in the barrels marked with the springing deer,' I continued. 'That was the face I saw hidden in the barrel of tea leaves, the face of an ancient Greek marble bust. So then Nathanial Rudder decides to blackmail His Lordship. He wants Edith's hand in marriage. He wants to inherit Edith's fortune. This incensed Lord Philpot ... true?'

Philpot nodded begrudgingly.

'It totally consumed him,' I stabbed a finger at Lord Philpot. 'Consumed him enough to murder the would-be son-in-law. Meanwhile Edith had found out about Molly Mutton ...'

Henry Fox Young had his brandy half way to his mouth. He stopped dead. 'Well who is Molly Mutton?'

'A bar wench in the taproom of the St John's Tavern in Murray Street sir.'

'Aye, and a good looker,' Fabian muttered, then realised his lack of tact and drank from his goblet.

'Yes well,' I went on. 'Molly Mutton was Nathanial Rudder's true lover ...'

'Swine ... mongrel ...' Philpot squeezed his crystal goblet so firmly I feared it would break.

'Now, Edith had had her suspicions for a few days at this stage. Someone had informed her. Someone with a grudge against Nathanial I'm guessing, as it is unlikely Edith would have attracted much sympathy from the poorer classes. Anyhow Edith arranges to meet Nathanial after the service on Sunday at the Catholic St Peter's Hall in Wapping ...'

'Catholic! Catholic!' Philpot spat vitriol as if I had said she had a date with Beelzebub himself. 'Edith was Anglican ...'

'Maybe sir, but all the same,' I said, 'she had met him here before, and in secret.'

Lord Philpot drained his brandy and stormed over to the decanter to fill his glass.

'At some stage when they are alone she confronts him about Molly Mutton. She tells him she never wants to see him again. He is enraged; just think, he is so close to becoming a rich heir, or so he believes, and now it's all out the window. He loses his temper, strikes the pregnant Edith who falls and smashes her head on the flagstones ...'

'You have no proof of this,' Philpot groaned.

'No. But I know I'm close,' the brandy was warming in my hand. I smelt the vapour and supped the spirit, enjoying the fire in my belly at this awkward moment. 'I must say Governor, Lord Philpot, that I really do not believe Nathanial Rudder meant to kill Miss Edith Philpot.'

'Huh!' Lord Philpot looked at me through teary red eyes.

I continued certain with the knowledge I had nailed the truth.

'But now she is ...' I tactfully searched for the suitable words. 'Now that she has passed on, Nathanial panics. Only an hour earlier he had seen Aboubacar unload a cart of stage props in through the stage door of the Theatre Royal near the church. Being Sunday there are few people about. I interviewed the stablehand at the stables behind the theatre. He said although he knew he was doing the wrong thing he rented Savage's cart, the one Aboubacar had used, to another man for two hours. Just to make a quick crown. He told me he rented it to Nathanial Rudder whom he knew and who told him he wanted to move some barrels from the Bond Store where he worked. He didn't ask any questions.'

'Of course he didn't.'

'He takes the cart, disguises Miss Edith's body under a tarp and transports her to the Cascades in the foothills of Mount Wellington, an area he is familiar with, with the help of his friend's horse, which we also know he borrowed that very afternoon. Once there he found a lonely opening in the bushland at the end of a deserted track and proceeded to make the scene look like a black magic murder sacrifice ritual, including the pitchfork through Edith's chest. The boot mark on Edith's cheek was particularly incriminating.'

'My God man, some discretion please,' Governor Fox Young glanced at Lord Philpot who had not said another word but simply wept.

'With the permission of the surgeon general,' I lied, 'I managed to have Nathanial Rudder's body exhumed and found he was buried barefoot. His boots had been removed. However later that evening, by sheer good fortune, I discovered those boots being worn by a certain blacksmith named Edmund Clay. He had repaired an iron pot for a nurse named Miss Penny Dove who removed Mr Rudder's incriminating boots before his body was sewn into a sailcloth.'

'Bravo!' Fabian called out enthusiastically without thinking. I looked to Lord Philpot who was now weeping uncontrollably.

'Oh God!' he managed between sobs. 'They'll hang me ... Henry ... they will hang me.' His Excellency stared into his brandy then looked up at Fabian and myself with suddenly tired eyes.

'Gentlemen,' His Excellency said. 'Would you leave us for a moment ... if you please?'

Fabian was keen to make the arrest. 'We'll 'ave to ...'

'For just a moment Mr Winter, ten minutes is all I ask.'

Fabian paced the antechamber with an ear tuned to the closed and locked office door. The long clock's chime echoed within the wood-panelled room, while outside the wind picked up and the sky darkened. A summer storm was approaching.

'He wants time alone! What's that all about?' Fabian grumbled.

'They have been close friends for many years I believe,' I said.

'Aye, too long.' Fabian was unforgiving. 'Lord or no lord ya can't go 'round shootin' people in the 'ead. And the man's a firkin' thief any'ow, buyin' all them stolen statues.' Fabian flipped open his pocket watch. 'It's been more like fifteen minutes ... what's the governor up to?'

At that moment Samuel Wheaton entered the antechamber from the main passageway. 'Gentlemen, I have a … ah … a concern.'

'Oh,' I said, all ears.

'His Lordship Marmaduke Philpot is in a spot of bother is he not?'

'Aye,' Fabian stopped pacing. 'You'll be hearing of it sooner than later.'

'Well,' the secretary said, 'Hobart Town's a small place is it not Mr Winter, and word is already out that Lord Philpot has been involved with smuggling antiquities from Greece.'

'That was quick,' I said.

'Yes,' Wheaton looked poker-faced. 'Word came from the Prisoners Barracks.'

I made a note to reprimand the constables.

'Smugglin,' Fabian verified. 'And 'e's guilty of murder too no less.'

Wheaton's eyes bulged unnaturally. 'Murder!'

'Yes.'

I was about to suggest to Fabian that we keep the information quiet for the moment when the secretary grew agitated. 'But the *Buckingham* is preparing to sail!'

'*Buckingham*?' my mouth dropped open.

'Lord Philpot's *Buckingham*?' Fabian stopped dead in his tracks.

'One and the same,' Wheaton said. 'She was victualled early this morning and I know for a fact his crew were recalled from the Rodney also this morning.'

'Damn! Damn his eyes!' Fabian rushed to the office door and rapped his knuckles on the panels.

No answer.

'This way gentlemen,' and Wheaton led us out a side door and around Government House where we mounted the flagstones of the veranda and entered the office through the French doors.

'Shite! Firk!' Fabian slapped a fist onto the desk. 'They've gone.'

I hurried down the garden path to the gazebo, jumped up onto a barrel and climbed onto the roof.

'There!' I yelled, pointing to New Wharf nearly half a mile away. I could just make out Philpot manhandling Governor Fox Young towards his ship, the *Buckingham*.

'He's holding the governor hostage,' I called out shading my eyes against the afternoon glare. 'I'm certain of it.'

'Firk, damn and shite!'
'I think he's holding a gun to his head.'
'Bastard!'

● ● ●

Fabian and I raced to the waterfront where the fresh wind had all ship owners busying themselves preparing for a storm. The sky had turned ashen with heavy northerly rain clouds rolling down river from off the central midlands. And hundreds of gulls, which knew better, flew screeching inland towards the mountain foothills.

We shoved our way through the activity and across the busy wharf, but it was immediately clear to us the *Buckingham* sails were unfurling and her mooring lines had been cut with axes. They were in a hurry to leave. Almost immediately the *Buckingham* helmsman had manoeuvred around the docked whalers and was mid-harbour.

'Lord Philpot knew he was in trouble,' I bawled at Fabian. 'There are too many leaks from our constabulary damn it.'

Fabian spun about. Red-coated Government House guards had followed us. 'You, you know who I am?' Fabian yelled at the nearest.

'Aye sir, you're …'

'Never mind. The governor's been kidnapped. Hurry to the Prisoners Barracks, to the constabulary, and get help. At the double man. It's a matter o' life and death for the governor.'

By now another guard joined us, a horse from the stables in tow. The horse whinnied at the distant thunder, the whites of its eyes wide, and pawed the wharf. The guard mounted the horse. The animal turned, whinnying and snorting, feeding off the excitement.

'Ask for Snake,' Fabian ordered the guard. 'Tell him all hands on deck. NOW!'

'Ye-ha!' And the guard slapped the horse's arse and the beast took off at a gallop towards Campbell Street.

'Caspian.'

'Sir!'

'To the *Fabian*!'

I must concede the man is excellent under pressure.

The sloop *Fabian* was sleek and fast as we manoeuvred our way out of the port. But the *Buckingham*, which was now under full square-rigged sail, forged down the expanse River Derwent and towards the open sea before a full northerly gale.

Snake shouted to Fabian over the sloop's snapping canvas and the stinging rain, 'What's the plan cap'n?'

Cap'n!

Fabian's chest pushed out with self-importance. Was it pride or ego? Either way I felt the man had found his vocation. *Pirate!*

'Cap'n?'

'Plan?' Fabian scratched his head. 'Plan? Catch that villain Lord firkin' Marmaduke firkin' Philpot. That's the plan.'

Fabian yelled from the bow to Hal at the helm, 'Steer true Hal, I want to run that bastard down.'

'In this sir?'

'Aye … Jasper!'

'Aye cap'n.'

'Go to the arms lockers aft, fetch a brace o' pistols and a cutlass for each one of us.'

I stood at the bow, my knee braced on the gunwale to steady my hand and my eye fixed to the lens of a spyglass as we dipped and rose on the ever-increasing chop.

'What d'ya see?' Fabian swung one-handed on a ratline next to me as we dived into another trough.

'I see his Lordship …'

'The murderer!'

'Yes well … His Lordship the murderer is at the stern of her as we speak. I'd say we've put the fear o' Christ into him.'

'Any sign o' the governor?'

'No,' I said. 'I reckon he's locked below.'

'Bastard! Now he will definitely hang.'

'What on earth is he thinking anyway, kidnapping the governor?'

'Maybe he plans to leave him down the coast.'

Snake stumbled towards us trying vainly to find his footings in the increasing swell. 'We're gainin' on 'em sar.'

'Aye, that we are.' Overhead gathering storm clouds kept pace with the sloop. I watched a spark of lightning flash out of the sky and briefly illuminate the *Buckingham* moments before the roll of thunder.

'Tell the others to get ready to board 'er. Tell Hal to remain at the 'elm and you, Billings and Jasper get the grapple 'ooks ready.'

Without warning.

Kaboom!

I saw the spew of flame and smoke before I heard the cannon. The ball flew harmlessly across our bow. A warning. Stay away!

'The cheek o' the bastard.' Fabian shook a fist in the air. 'That was a four pounder I'm thinkin'. 'e's a merchant and most merchants carry two four pounders. Four at the most. Bastard. Doesn't that captain know 'e'll hang with His firkin' Lordship for shootin' at a government vessel?'

'Some men will do anything for gold.'

'Aye.'

Kaboom!

Another cannonball whistled by. This one closer and over the stern.

'Jesus!' I stepped backwards. 'I've never been shot at by cannon before.'

'Well ya better keep ya 'ead down, it looks to me like they're wantin' a fight.'

Kaboom!

Another ball sizzled by. Too close. I looked at Fabian who seemed to be enjoying himself.

'Snake!' he roared over the din of tempest and battle.

'Aye sar.'

'Get them two pounders on the rails. Hasty like now.'

I kept my head down while Snake and Billings hefted the brass swivel guns into their brackets on the bow gunwale. Jasper fetched powder and balls. The lads soon had the two guns loaded under the shelter of canvas. I looked to the land for bearings. We were about abeam of a farming bay on our western shore that I was told was Taroona.

'Hal,' Fabian shouted to the helm. 'Hold tight to their stern, their guns are mounted port n' starboard so they won't be able to use 'em.'

Hal managed a thumbs up and I felt a sharp turn to starboard. Moments later we gained once more and crept up behind the merchantman. Fabian swivelled the first gun aiming at the stern cabin windows. We were now less than a hundred yards distant. Fabian waited for the sloop's bow to rise.

'Fire!' he screamed.

Boom!

Instantly the two-pound ball shattered the stern windows splintering the wooden framework.

'Huh!' Fabian screeched. 'Take that ya firker! Jasper, re-load. Snake. Fire at will.'

Boom!

More glass and timber shattered at the rear of the *Buckingham*.

'Right lads,' Fabian drew his cutlass and swung it about his head like he was reliving a past life as a buccaneer. 'Now they know we're serious. Another two shots and we'll board 'er.'

But horror of horrors! The men of the *Buckingham* had managed to wheel a four-pounder to the stern cabin and now its muzzle poked through the missing window and tilted down at our sloop only thirty yards away.

'Down!' Fabian screamed as we all saw the flash of powder explode over the touchhole.

Kaboom!

The sloop shuddered as the iron ball slammed into the deck. Slivers of needle sharp wood and shredded decking flew about the craft. Miraculously no one was wounded.

'Firk!'

'Jasper!'

'Sar.'

'Loaded?'

'Aye.'

'Fire at will, but watch the swell mind.'

Boom! Boom!

Karshatter!

More of the merchantman's stern tore apart. I heard screams.

Snake bawled over the racket, 'Someone's hit!'

The sloop dived into a trough and a wave exploded over the bow drenching our two pounders and I saw the open keg of gunpowder float along the swamped deck.

'Jesus! There goes the powder.' Billings chased the keg, but it was too late.

'Down!' someone yelled.

Kaboom!

Flisst!

I heard the four-pounder hiss by me.

'We'll have to back off or they'll sink us.' I bawled to Fabian.

'Aye. Hal. Hard to port.'

Hal spun the wheel. The heavy boom swept across the deck and Billings ducked just in time. The sloop listed and a strong gust hit us at the same moment. Our starboard side lifted from the depths exposing timbers.

Kaboom!

Smoking hot iron pummelled the Huon pine. The sloop settled back on an even keel but now we had been holed below the waterline.

'She's takin' water!' Jasper rushed up the companionway, his ears ringing from the hit in the confines of below deck.

'Christ!'

'They're gettin' away!'

'Shite!'

Immediately the sloop slowed. 'She's takin' on water at a devil o' pace.'

'It can't be that bigger 'ole, jam somethin' in it.'

'Like what sar?'

'I don't know,' Fabian was beyond anger. 'Jam ya firkin' head in it!'

Then a surreal moment washed over me. We were sinking and I wasn't a great swimmer. The only comfort I felt was that the shore was only half a mile away.

'They've beaten us!' I muttered to Fabian, vanquished but defiantly standing with one leg up on the bow rail with his hands on his hips seething with anger at the escaping murderer.

'We'll have to beach her or she'll sink and we'll all surely drown,' I said.

'Aye,' Fabian agreed with undisguised disappointment in his voice, the wind knocked from his own sails. 'Give the order will ya?'

The nearest place to beach the sloop was the cove next to Browns River. I gave Hal the order and he turned the wheel hard to starboard when we were immediately greeted with a most magnificent sight appearing from behind the headland.

'The *Revenge!*' I yelled.

With every square inch of canvas catching the northerly, Lynch Savage's two-masted schooner *Revenge* sailed out from the safe haven of Browns River. He had heard the gunfire and his lookout surmised immediately what had happened.

'Huzzar huzzar!' we all roared. All was not lost. While Hal did a masterly job of beaching the *Fabian* onto safe sands, we watched the *Revenge* close in on the *Buckingham*. I could only imagine what Lord Philpot was thinking at this moment.

Built for speed the *Revenge* was within firing range within minutes.

Kaboom! Kaboom!

'Six pounders!' Fabian cheered. ''e's got six pounders!'

Kaboom! Kaboom!

'Aye, and four o' 'em.'

I fastened a keen eye to the eyeglass and gave the crew a running commentary as the damage mounted. Lynch Savage, I saw, was propped on the quarterdeck dressed like Henry Morgan himself.

God bless his knee-high boots!

Red frock coat, plumed hat feathers blustering in the wind, the man was in his element, barking orders like he was about to invade Panama all over again.

'The man's a hero!' I shouted, one eyed glued to the action.

I watched as the reloaded six pounders were trundled through the gunports. I saw the touchhole powder explode, I heard the thunder of cannon fire when …

KABOOM!

A stray cannonball had hit gunpowder. Whether it was loose powder in a keg on *Buckingham's* deck or the magazine below deck I don't know, but the explosion was significant to lift the stern from the water several feet. Immediately tongues of fire, fuelled by storm winds, licked up the mast igniting sails. Pandemonium broke out. Even at a mile or more distant I could tell the ship was doomed.

Instantly craft pushed off from shore, anything available. A small sloop appeared from Browns River.

A voice cried out, 'You lot, climb aboard!' I spun about to see Bilge Breath and two others I recognised manning the sloop. Moments later we skipped across the choppy swell to join the crew of the *Revenge* now plucking people from the water.

Our sloop sailed up behind the *Buckingham*, but she was foundering fast. She listed to port dangerously and would sink within minutes.

'There!' I yelled as a fresh wind whipped us about under full sail. Governor Fox Young was climbing from the stern windows; the same shattered windows we had smashed with our swivel guns only moments earlier.

'He'll have to jump!' someone bawled over the shouting babble and tumultuous uproar of panic and confusion. 'JUMP!' Governor Fox Young's eyes were wide. He scoured the dark uninviting waters below. Then another serious of explosions lit the stern cabin behind him.

Brilliant flashes of red, yellow, blue … and the man was thrown clear of the cabin, somersaulting with a scream into the deep.

Bilge Breath, at our sloop's helm, skilfully manoeuvred over the area. Nothing!

'Where is he?'

'Christ knows!'

'There!'

We rushed to starboard. The governor's arms were flapping helplessly below the surface. Fully dressed he was sinking fast.

'His coat's draggin' him under!'

I didn't hesitate. I ripped off my coat and kicked away my boots, diving off the gunwale. I landed awkwardly in the freezing water immediately thinking it was not the most sensible thing I had done in my short life. The sloop sailed on past, caught a gust of wind and made a masterly turn about twenty yards distant. I took another deep breath and dived below the surface. The governor clamped a hand on my shoulder. He was desperate, but kept his composure. The man held me tight and I kicked off for the surface. With lungs bursting, we gulped air, but the weight of the governor's heavy clothes threatened to drag him down once more. Fighting panic myself, I trod water until the sloop made another pass and half a dozen arms reached down for us, wrenching us unceremoniously back onto the deck.

Now for the first time I felt the heat of the inferno. The *Buckingham* was ablaze. To the lee side of the conflagration I watched the *Revenge*, under instruction from Lynch Savage, pulling the wounded and the drowning from the six-foot swell.

Bilge Breath skilfully pulled alongside the *Revenge*. At close proximity, the schooner looked more like a privateer or a blockade-runner with her cannon wheeled out. The deck was packed with survivors and her crew attended to the wounded.

'That stopped the thievin' mongrel,' Lynch screamed out from the quarterdeck with a raffish grin.

'Where's Lord Philpot?' one of the *Buckingham's* crew hollered.

'Philpot be damned!' Lynch answered.

'There he is!' another shouted.

Lord Philpot appeared at the stern cabin window. His figure was the centre of a swirl of acrid smoke with a cloudy gaze of total capitulation chiselled across his face. He had accepted his fate. Be rescued and certainly hang for murder, or go down into the Fiddler's Green with his ship.

If he had any last doubts they were dashed as a final explosion ripped through the lower aft deck and the *Buckingham* plunged to the sandy bottom of the Derwent Estuary.

I looked over at the Governor of Tasmania, himself a shambling figure, wringing wet and exhausted lying on the deck with total disbelief etched on his face. He dragged himself up with the support of the mast and beckoned me over.

'Thank you Caspian Hunter, I owe you my life.'

Day Fifteen – Friday

Two days later

IT TOOK TWO DAYS TO SECURE A BARGE SUITABLE for our salvage operation. We sat anchored over the *Buckingham's* wreck site, eating a late lunch of cold pork pie and washing it down with warm ale. A bittersweet victory celebration of sorts. The detective team was together, Fabian, me, Snake, Hal, Billings and Jasper. But although we had been successful in solving three major crimes, our efforts out on the water were in vain.

Lord Philpot's body had washed up on the beach at Browns River the morning after the sinking, not far from where we beached the *Fabian*. The *Buckingham* lay on a sandy bottom in eight fathoms of water, her cremated mastheads protruding from the depths as a warning to other ships.

By all reports the Hartog Marbles were still on board the ship, stowed in the hold along with many other treasures His Lordship had planned to escape Van Diemen's Land with. But the native women divers we recruited to search the wreck site had returned with the news that the ship was empty. There was no cargo.

'No cargo. No firkin' marbles?' Fabian's purple bruised eye twitched.

'Aye. No cargo. 'ow does that work?' Billings spat flecks of pastry in my direction while a persistent fly circled his head.

'We searched Philpot's mansion,' Snake said. 'And they ain't there.'

'Is there anywhere else at his estate he could have hidden them?' I proposed. 'I mean we found the bronze Poseidon in his cellar, but I'm thinking, did he bury them maybe, out in the garden? After all, his estate is some area.'

'Aye,' Hal agreed. 'Maybe 'e was planning to come back for them one day?'

'I doubt it,' Fabian said. 'Any'ow we was told at least half a dozen cartloads o' possessions was delivered to the wharf Wednesday mornin'.'

Fabian swallowed his ale and pulled the cork from another bottle with his teeth. He held the bottle high in offering.

'Don't mind if I do sar,' Jasper reached out with his empty mug. Ever since saving Fabian's and my skin the night of the Boar's Head debacle, he had gained my respect, not to mention confidence.

'The marbles must be down in the lower deck,' Snake said. 'With the ballast like.'

'Aye,' Hal concurred. 'Them marbles'd be heavy as rocks eh?'

'Then they are beyond recovery,' I groaned. How I disliked unsolved mysteries. But something niggled at my subconscious. My eyes wandered from my debating colleagues to surreptitious activity ashore. Here I noticed much comings and goings over at the Sea o' Graves Inn a mile distant and nestled on the lee side of the hill, now guarded by the embracing shadows of late afternoon.

I could just make out a trail of small figures reminiscent of Cornish moonlighters I had seen in an old oil painting back home. Men struggling with all manner of crates from the beach and up into the bowels of the inn. While my colleagues drank to our success, I took up the spyglass and levelled it at the stern window of the Sea o' Graves. And there was the man himself, Lynch Savage, propped up on a barrel in all his Henry Morgan regalia. He watched the progress below and sipped what I could only imagine was his favourite wine from Burgundy. Immediately I sensed he saw me and he held up his glass in tribute.

'The crafty bugger,' I thought, 'he's beaten us to it …'

And I returned the toast.

Writer's Note

Van Diemen's Land was a tough place to live, as tough if not tougher and more dangerous than America's Wild West. From early settlement years many ex-convicts became constables and in 1810 Governor Macquarie ordered a police force be established. By 1840 Governor Sir John Franklin introduced what he considered a less expensive problem to law and order in the fledgling colony.

Convicts of 'very good conduct' were given a 'conditional pardon'. Convicts sentenced to seven years would be admitted to the police after three years in custody and could receive a conditional pardon after one year in the police. Convicts sentenced to fourteen years in the colony could join the police after four years and receive a conditional pardon after two years in the police.

It was thought these incentives would 'purify' the force and induce good conduct. As an idea of payment, a labourer could expect to earn one shilling per day in the country or three shillings per day in Hobart Town. Police were paid less so it is understandable why free men did not sign up for the 'force.'

In 1855, the year of this fictional story, Chief Police Magistrate Francis Burgess appointed detectives to deal with serious crime, leaving a force of constables to keep law and order.

The Police Detecting Agency stationed at Campbell Street Prisoners Barracks in *Shadow Hunter* is fictional.

www.ingramcontent.com/pod-product-compliance
Lightning Source LLC
Chambersburg PA
CBHW051340020726
47501CB00007B/2192

* 9 7 8 0 9 8 0 5 6 7 8 2 3 *